William Tooke, Charles Churchill

The Poetical Works of Charles, Churchill

Vol. I

William Tooke, Charles Churchill

The Poetical Works of Charles, Churchill
Vol. I

ISBN/EAN: 9783337003180

Printed in Europe, USA, Canada, Australia, Japan

Cover: Foto ©Andreas Hilbeck / pixelio.de

More available books at **www.hansebooks.com**

Charles Churchill.

THE POETICAL WORKS OF
CHARLES CHURCHILL

WITH A MEMOIR BY JAMES HANNAY
AND COPIOUS NOTES BY
W. TOOKE, F.R.S.

REVISED EDITION IN TWO VOLUMES

VOL. I

LONDON:

GEORGE BELL & SONS, YORK ST., COVENT GARDEN,

AND NEW YORK

1892

CHISWICK PRESS:—C. WHITTINGHAM AND CO., TOOKS COURT
CHANCERY LANE.

ADVERTISEMENT.

THE present edition of Churchill's Poems is founded on the late Mr. Tooke's Second Edition; but in preparing the book for the Aldine Series (in 1866) the Publishers availed themselves freely of a marked copy kindly lent to them by the late Mr. John Forster, by the aid of which they were enabled to correct various inaccuracies and to bring the notes within reasonable compass.

At the same time the text was carefully collated by Mr. Howard Spalding, and a memoir by Mr. James L. Hannay, was prefixed.

1892.

CONTENTS OF VOL. I.

	Page
THE ROSCIAD	1
THE APOLOGY	63
NIGHT	80
THE PROPHECY OF FAMINE	97
AN EPISTLE TO WILLIAM HOGARTH	123
THE DUELLIST. Book I.	154
Book II.	163
Book III.	174
GOTHAM. Book I.	194
Book II.	213
Book III.	236

MEMOIR OF CHURCHILL.

CHARLES CHURCHILL, the most popular English satirist between the ages of Pope and Byron, was the eldest son of the Reverend Charles Churchill, rector of Rainham in Essex, and curate and lecturer of St. John's, Westminster. He was born in Vine Street, Westminster, in February, 1731; and at eight years old was sent to Westminster School, where he received his education at a remarkable period of its history. Vincent Bourne and Dr. Pierson Lloyd were among the masters; while among the boys were Warren Hastings, Cowper, George Colman, Robert Lloyd, and Bonnell Thornton. The talents of Churchill showed themselves in his boyhood; when a candidate for admission to the foundation, he went in head of the election at fifteen. His father designed him for the church, and wished him to graduate at one of the universities. But he missed a scholarship at Merton

College, Oxford; and though he was entered at Trinity, Cambridge, he never resided there. The details of his life, especially of this part of it, are obscure; but Mr. Forster's conjecture appears probable that Churchill's prospects were thus early blighted by an imprudent marriage, into which he entered at eighteen years of age. He was married within the rules of the Fleet prison; and the match turned out a bad one from the beginning. His father, the clergyman, however, showed him great kindness. He took the couple into his house; and partly there, and partly in the North of England, Churchill prepared himself for orders. Ordained a deacon, his first curacy was South Cadbury in Somersetshire, where he officiated till 1756, in which year he took priest's orders and moved to Rainham as curate. In 1758 his father died, and Churchill succeeded him in his charges at St. John's. He had already been obliged to open a school, and in his new position he was compelled to eke out his small income by teaching of more than one kind. His family was increasing; his wife, so far from being a good manager, was herself extravagant; and he was soon harassed by duns, and chased by bailiffs. In this darkest hour of his life, the excellent Dr. Lloyd, then undermaster of Westminster, gained his reverence and gratitude for ever, by stepping forward to save him. The doctor saw the creditors, and prevailed on them to accept a compromise, which he aided Churchill to carry out. This vital and timely aid enabled the unlucky curate to exert himself in a walk towards which he felt impelled as he had never felt impelled to the church. Robert Lloyd, his old schoolfellow and his protector's son, had recently taken to literature, and the example of the younger Lloyd came in aid of the kindness of the elder one. Churchill began to offer poetry to the booksellers. His first work, a poem called the *Bard*, was peremptorily declined. His second, the *Conclave*, a satire on the Dean and Chapter of Westminster, would have been brought out if the publisher had not feared that it was a libel. This was so far encouraging, to a man suited for satire by his genius, and ripened for it by his circumstances. He looked round for a subject into which to put his whole force; chose the stage, which he had always relished as an amusement; and after two months' special attendance at the theatres for the purpose, published the *Rosciad* in March, 1761.

The choice of subject was excellent. The English stage had not yet sunk to relying on mechanical spectacle, and imported farce; but was what the ancients thought the stage ought to be, an image of life, and a school of manners. The leading actors were not only excellent in their art,

but were many of them men of good general parts
and education; fit companions for gentlemen,
and the habitual associates of scholars. What
was done by and written about them, therefore,
naturally interested all cultivated and fashionable
London; and the advantage of this fact to the
Rosciad can hardly be overrated. But there
were other circumstances of the period which
told in Churchill's favour. The sweet mechanism
of Pope's verse was beginning to pall upon the
English taste. Gray was not fully appreciated.
Goldsmith was still in obscurity. Cowper and
Burns had not arisen. The most effective writing
of the time was in prose; and to all the vigorous
sense of good prose writers, Churchill added the
charm of a freer music, and a heartier enthusi-
asm than that of the fashionable poets. The
Rosciad accordingly made an immediate and
striking impression. The noise in the theatrical
world was like that caused by the report of a
gun in a rookery. The actors ran about the
town spreading their own grievances and the
satirist's fame at the same time. It was soon
known that the satirist was Churchill; and those
whose vanity he had hurt took the usual sordid
revenge of their kind by bringing against him
some charges that were lies, and some that, if
true, were only disgraceful to him in the eyes of
the basest upstarts. They declared that he had

let two corpses wait hours in the churchyard, because he had been in the orchestra of Drury Lane when he ought to have been reading the Burial Service. And they attributed his severity in handling actors to the fact that "they had the impudence to dine on fish and fowls in a superb apartment, while he was forced to duck into a cellar in St. Giles's, where the knives and forks were chained to the table for fear the company should steal them, and there dine sumptuously upon ox-cheek."* Every man who uses satire for moral, political, or literary purposes, must expect to be assailed with trashy calumny of this kind. Churchill took the wisest course. He picked out the most formidable of his assailants, the *Critical Review*, and bestowed on it in his *Apology* a chastisement such as that bestowed by Byron, afterwards, upon the *Edinburgh Review*. How formidable he had now become was proved by the effect which a passage in the *Apology* had upon Garrick. The favourite actor of the day had affected to hold cheap the honours which had been lavished upon him in the *Rosciad*. But no sooner did the vigorous lines beginning,—

* The *Churchiliad*. Goldsmith, who was then writing the *Citizen of the World*, and had not yet made his mark on the age, has a contemptuous allusion to the last charge in Letter cxiii.

" Let the vain tyrant sit amidst his guards,
His puny green-room wits and venal bards,
Who meanly tremble at the puppet's frown,
And for a playhouse freedom lose their own;" -

make their appearance, than Garrick suddenly
became first frightened and then servile. He
eagerly sought Churchill's friendship through
Lloyd, and they were on intimate terms till the
close of the satirist's life.

Churchill had thus suddenly sprung from the
position of an obscure and struggling curate into
that of a famous writer whose pen could command
money. The *Rosciad* and the *Apology* had
brought him in more than a thousand pounds.
He heartily enjoyed his success, and freely aired
his enjoyment of it. He exchanged his clerical
dress for a " blue coat with metal buttons, a
gold-laced waistcoat, a gold-laced hat, and
ruffles ;" and went about town with a cudgel, in
ostentatious defiance of the men whom he had
satirised. A separation from his wife, and the
resignation of his equally uncongenial lectureship, took place within a short time of each other.
But if sudden prosperity somewhat turned his
head, it did not spoil his naturally good heart.
He made a proper provision for his wife ; assisted
his brother and sisters ; and paid in full the creditors with whom Dr. Lloyd had arranged a composition. His indulgence, however, in all the

freedoms of his new position as a quasi-bachelor and quasi-layman, was a constant theme of public remark; and in October of the same year, 1761, he brought out *Night, an Epistle to Robert Lloyd*, by way of vindicating his course of life. The philosophy of this poem is of a kind sufficiently familiar, in the eighteenth century, to readers of *Tom Jones, The School for Scandal*, and some of the least valuable but not least brilliant poems of Burns. It is the philosophy of what we now call Bohemianism, and rests on the principle that the vices of a generous man are better than those of a hypocrite,—as if no *third* alternative were possible, and mankind were divided into good fellows who were profligate, and prudent decorous men without wit or heart. There is little in *Night*, accordingly, that is worth remembering; except some indications that Churchill's philosophy failed to make him happy; and a passage which heralded his career as a political satirist. "What honest man," asks Churchill,—

> " What honest man but would with joy submit
> To bleed with Cato, and retire with PITT?"

Pitt had retired on the 3rd October, 1761, because his colleagues would not join him in declaring war against Spain, which they were forced to do themselves before three months were over.

The reign of Lord Bute was beginning, with its shameful peace, and its furious domestic agitations; a period when neither the assailed nor the assailants command our sympathy; when imbecile or corrupt statesmen on the one hand were opposed by corrupt and wicked demagogues on the other. During this period the king of the demagogues was Wilkes; and he had a greater and better man than himself, Churchill, for poet-laureate. If the private life of Churchill was reprehensible, his political life was honest. He sincerely believed that Pitt's successors were rascals; would have made no personal terms with them; and wanted nothing from them. But Wilkes was without morals of any kind; and only fought for "liberty," when there was nothing to be made by jobbing. To him, more than to most of the many evil demagogues who have lived since, the words of Aristophanes might have been applied:—

'" As country fellows fishing eels, that in the quiet river,
Or the clear lake, have fail'd to take, begin to poke and
     muddle,
And rouse and rout it all about and work it to a puddle,
To catch their game—*you* do the same in the hubbub and
     confusion."*

The acquaintance of Wilkes and Churchill began in 1762, and soon became a close friend-

* I quote from the excellent translation of the *Knights*, by Mr. Frere.

ship. Churchill worked with him in the *North Briton;* and the happiest of all his satires, the most ingenious, fanciful, and stinging, was wrought out of materials which he had at first intended to work up into a *North Briton* article. This was the *Prophecy of Famine,* to which Wilkes justly predicted a great success, as being at once "personal, poetical, and political." "If the vulgar are ever right,"—said Lord Chester-field in those times—"they are right for the wrong reason. What they selected to attack in Lord Bute was his being a Scotchman, which was precisely what he could not help." There was, in fact, such a rage against the Scotch, just then, as had not been felt even in the days when Scotch adventurers rushed up to London after the accession of James the First. Scotland had not yet become what it now is, a province from which the ablest Scotchmen make haste to escape; and many a good Scot took the part of John, third Earl of Bute, in this time of his trouble, not from mere sympathy with his application of Jacobite views of monarchy to the support of the new young King of the House of Hanover; but because he was one of the nobles of their race, and sprung from an ancient though illegitimate cadet of their fallen royal house. The war thus became a war of nationalities; and Wilkes, some of whose earliest and favourite friends had been

Scotsmen,* and Churchill, whose own blood was
partly Scotch,† stormed against the northern
part of the United Kingdom with a ferocity such
as Englishmen had ordinarily reserved for the
Spaniards or the French. The time for Englishmen to share Churchill's anger, or Scotsmen to
be pained by it, is past; and both may unite
in admiring his brilliance and his point. He
sustains through many lines a keenness of
satire which Cleveland in the previous century had only reached in one or two couplets.
Such lines as—

"They've sense to get what we want sense to keep;"

and,–

> "Become discreetly all things to all men,
> That all men may become all things to them;"

such pictures as—

> "The Highland lass forgot her want of food,
> And, whilst she scratch'd her lover into rest,
> Sank pleased, though hungry, on her Sawney's breast;"

and,—

> "No flowers embalm'd the air but one white rose,
> Which, on the tenth of June, by instinct blows;"

have, the first, more condensation, and the
second more colour, than are common in the

* See *Autobiography of Dr. Carlyle, of Inveresk*, pp 169, 70.
† *Prophecy of Famine*, ll. 145 and 222

satires of Churchill, who was often a diffuse, and seldom an imaginative writer. The *Prophecy of Famine*, appearing early in 1763, answered all the expectations of Wilkes and himself. The year was an eventful one in their history. In April, the notorious No. 45 of the *North Briton* was published; and warrants were issued against them both. Thanks to the presence of mind of Wilkes, who addressed him before the officers, to whom he was unknown, as "Mr. Thompson," Churchill escaped, and passed the summer out of town, part of it in Oxford, and part in Wales. He was accompanied by a Miss Carr, the daughter of a Mr. Carr of Westminster, variously represented as sculptor, or stone-cutter, whom he had seduced from her father's house. Southey has made for this worst incident of Churchill's life the only plea of which the circumstances admit. "His moral sense," says that good man and excellent writer, "had not been thoroughly depraved; a fortnight had not elapsed before both parties were struck with sincere compunction, and . . the unhappy penitent was received by her father. It is said she would have proved worthy of this parental forgiveness, if an elder sister had not, by continued taunts and reproaches, rendered her life so miserable that in absolute despair she threw herself upon Churchill for protection." They lived together till his death, and he left her an annuity somewhat smaller than that which he bequeathed to his wife. There is an affecting allusion to his consciousness of wrong-doing in this matter, in his poem *The Conference*. At first, when approaching the subject, he exclaims—

> " Ah! what, my Lord, hath private life to do
> With things of public nature?"

A most inconsistent doctrine for *him* to broach, who never spared the private life of Sandwich or of Holland. But he soon proceeds honestly to own his offence, and his remorse; and only claims for himself the credit of political sincerity and of loving England, which cannot be denied him. The *Conference* came out in November 1763. It had been preceded by the *Epistle to Hogarth*, a satire in which the great painter— a higher satirist than Churchill—was punished for his incomparable caricature of Wilkes. So unsatisfactory were the causes in which this vigorous fighter was doomed to fight! So much was wasted, in his instance, of a satirical talent as genuine as Ulric von Hutten brought to the cause of the Reformation, or Andrew Marvell to that of the old English liberty and the old English domestic character!

When Churchill returned to town in the

autumn of 1763, he found Lloyd a prisoner in the Fleet, and hastened to console and assist him in his own hearty way. In November his *Duellist* appeared—another result of his zeal for Wilkes. Like the *Ghost*, the *Duellist* is in octosyllabics, a metre which Churchill always handled less successfully than heroics. Neither poem ranks with his best works; but the attack in the *Duellist* on Bishop Warburton—

> " Who was so proud, that should he meet
> The Twelve Apostles in the street,
> He'd turn his nose up at them all,
> And shove his Saviour from the wall"—

has a vigorous freedom, and a keenness of edge, almost worthy of our greatest English satirist, Swift. The *Duellist* was followed before the end of the year by the *Author*, where he speaks of himself as—

> " Bred to the Church, and for the gown decreed,
> Ere it was known that I should learn to read;
>
> * * * * *
>
> Condemned (whilst proud and pamper'd sons of lawn,
> Cramm'd to the throat, in lazy plenty yawn)
> In pomp of reverend beggary to appear,
> To pray and starve on forty pounds a year."

But the *Author*, however much esteemed by some contemporary critics, is below the mark of the *Prophecy of Famine* or the *Epistle to Hogarth*. Churchill was writing too much;

and though there are admirable passages in the
poems which flowed from his energetic nature
in 1764—the last year of his life,—none of them
as a whole reaches the level which he might
have been expected to attain.

His activity, however, was extraordinary.
" He has shown more fertility than I expected,"
said Dr. Johnson, whom he had ridiculed, not
in his best vein, in the *Ghost*.   " To be sure, he
is a tree that cannot produce good fruit: he
only bears crabs.   But, sir, a tree that produces
a great many crabs is better than a tree which
produces only a few."   The first of the crop for
1764 of the fruit that the good Doctor thought
so sour was *Gotham*.   In this, the least exclu-
sively satirical of his works, Churchill draws
the picture of an ideal kingdom, of which he is
the ideal monarch; and often catches the spirit
of the best didactic poetry with an ease of execution worthy of his favourite Dryden.   There
are touches, too, of a softer beauty than we
meet anywhere else in his writings; and streaks
of poetic colour which would probably strike a
reader of our time, knowing Churchill only by
hearsay, with surprise.   " *Gotham*," said Cowper, "is a noble and beautiful poem . . . a
masterly performance."   Nevertheless, the world
received it with less cordiality than usual.   The
satirist had spoiled the palates of his admirers

for anything less stimulating than burnt brandy;
and an opportunity arose immediately of giving
them their favourite beverage. Lord Sandwich
came forward to contest with Lord Hardwicke
the High Stewardship of the University of
Cambridge; and Churchill assailed him in the
Candidate. Sandwich had been foremost in
the recent proceedings against Wilkes for his
blasphemous and obscene *Essay on Woman;*
but his own character was such, that he could
not attack the blackest scoundrel without doing
him more good than harm; and Wilkes, though
he had been driven by the ministerial prosecution to France, was stronger in popularity than
ever. The *Candidate* contains some good satire,
but much that is sadly prosaic, and not a little
merely ponderous abuse, which cannot be ranked
as satire at all. The most interesting passage to
a modern reader is that in which we find the
celebrated line, still to be read over the author's
grave in the old churchyard of St. Martin's at
Dover;

"Life to the last enjoy'd, here Churchill lies."

And his life was now drawing to a close.
Since his return from Wales, he had resided for
some months at Richmond, and then at Acton
Common, the last place in which we know him
to have been settled. The *Candidate* was fol-

lowed by the *Farewell,* and the *Farewell* by the
Times—a satire, some touches of which recall
Juvenal more vividly than almost any satire in
our literature. After these came *Independence,*
where we have a remarkable portrait of his own
person, drawn by his own hand, with all its
massive ugliness, in its half careless, half showy
garb :—

> " Vast were his bones, his muscles twisted strong;
> His face was short, but broader than 'twas long;
> His features, though by nature they were large,
> Contentment had contrived to overcharge,
> And bury meaning, save that we might spy
> Sense lowering on the pent-house of his eye;
> His arms were two twin-oaks; his legs so stout
> That they might bear a Mansion-house about;
> Nor were they, look but at his body there,
> Design'd by fate a much less weight to bear.
>   *   *   *   *   *
> Just at that time of life, when man by rule,
> The fop laid down, takes up the graver fool:
> He started up a fop, and fond of show,
> Look'd like another Hercules turn'd beau."

Independence came out about the end of September, 1764, and was the last work published
in his life-time. An unfinished *Dedication to
Warburton* was found among his papers; but
the unfinished *Journey* was the latest thing he
ever wrote, and passages in it have a mournful
significance when read in connection with the
event which so soon followed. He speaks of the

growing impression that he was, so to speak,
"scourging" his brain instead of letting it lie
fallow; that,—

> " He might have flourish'd twenty years, or more,
> Though now, alas! poor man! worn out in four."

and there is a half-tone of melancholy, a smile
of sadness, about him as he says it, which seems
to show that he felt its truth. And the concluding line of all—

> " I on my journey all alone proceed,"

proved prophetic. Friendship for Wilkes had
been one of the strongest passions of his life, and
was now, indirectly, a cause of his death. He took
a sudden desire to visit Wilkes in France, and
writing hastily to his brother, " *Dear Jack,
adieu, C.C.*," started for Boulogne on the 27th
October. On the 29th he was seized with a
miliary fever of great severity. When he found
himself in danger he induced his friends to make
an effort to remove him, that he might die in
England, but the attempt only accelerated the
end, and he died at Boulogne on the 4th November, in his thirty-third year; meeting his
fate with great fortitude. His body was brought
to Dover, and interred in the old churchyard—
now closed—of St. Martin's, where the following

inscription is still to be read on a gravestone placed over the spot :—

HERE LIE THE REMAINS
OF THE CELEBRATED
C. CHURCHILL.

Life to the last enjoy'd, *here* Churchill lies.
The Candidate.

Byron visited this humble resting-place in 1816, just before leaving England for the last time, and celebrated it in the fine poem, *Churchill's Grave,* which has done much to keep the satirist's name alive.

Among Churchill's papers was found the commencement of a satire on Colman and Thornton, whom he believed to have deserted their common friend Lloyd in his distress. This fragment Wilkes destroyed. His personal relics sold at high prices. He had made a will on his death-bed, of an equitable character; and had committed the charge of his literary reputation to his " dear friend, John Wilkes, Esquire," expressly desiring him " to collect and publish " his works, with " the remarks and explanations he has prepared and any others he thinks proper to make." This was a task peculiarly necessary in the case of a writer who had written so much on the politics of the hour. It was a task for which Wilkes could with the greatest ease have procured all the necessary materials; and to which he was called not by the sacred duties of friendship only, but by the plainest considerations of even the commonest gratitude. Few of the greatest profligates in history would have neglected such a request made under such circumstances, but Wilkes did, and left Churchill's reputation to shift for itself. His satires after a few years were neglected; the details of his life and conversation perished with his contemporaries; and at this moment we know him less familiarly than almost any man of equal celebrity in his whole century. Nor was the fate of his family more fortunate. His sons turned out badly, and in 1825 his grand-daughter is known to have been an inmate of St. George's Hospital.

"I rate Churchill much lower than you," wrote Thackeray in 1854. It is, indeed, easy to rate him too high. Let it be said, at once, that he cannot be placed by any sober admirer in the first rank of satirists;—with Aristophanes, Horace, or Juvenal; with Rabelais, Dryden, or Pope. Neither in imagination nor humour, nor in that fine subtle wit of which Pope especially is so great a master, can Churchill be compared with these men. He had a poorer field to work in, for one thing, not because there was any lack of villains or fools in his time, but because they were small villains and unimportant

fools; and he was deficient in that artistic feeling which prompts to finished elaboration of
material, whether the best material be accessible
or not.   But he had distinct genius, notwithstanding; was of the blood of the Juvenals and
Drydens, though a poor relation as it were;
and with all his carelessness, roughness, and
even commonplace, has those brilliant flashes of
insight, and spontaneous felicities of expression,
by which every true critic at once distinguishes
the man of natural power from the man of mere
cultivation.   He rarely gives perfect satisfaction
to the student, and never long-continued satisfaction; but the kind of pleasure he gives in his
best moments is akin to that given by the greatest writers of his kind.   There are some who,
with less dross, turn out worse metal. Churchill
is frequently dull, but never mediocre; and if
he is wearisome in one paragraph, is as likely
as not to make up for it by being wonderful
in the next.   All satirists, it has been said, take
with more or less directness either after Horace
or Juvenal.*   Churchill is a Juvenalian; a
suckling of the Roman wolf; fierce but jolly;
savage yet not unkindly. Of course, too, he
has points in common with all the great satirists, for they have the distant likenesses of
a clan as well as the nearer likenesses of a
family.   He has the Aristophanic heartiness,

* *Satire and Satirists*, Six Lectures, 1854.

though not the Aristophanic poetry; the good-
fellowship of Horace, with far less subtlety and
familiar grace; a good deal of Dryden's vigour
and eye for the points of a satirical portrait, but
inferior penetration of glance, and far less comprehensive sweep, whether of reasoning power,
poetic humour, or fancy.

But if Churchill falls below the first rank, it
would be absurd to exclude him from any complete collection of the English poets.   He is
entitled to a place there, not only by his power,
but by his influence. He helped to form Cowper.
He helped to form Crabbe. It is not likely that
Burns was ignorant of his writings. And, generally, he showed a love of reality and of nature
which heralded at the distance of a whole gene-
ration the great revival of our literature under
Scott and Wordsworth. No heartier man, writing
from spontaneous impulse, caught the world's
ear between the Queen Anne men and that
revival. Churchill is thus always sure of a place
in our literary history; and will be read (or at
least occasionally looked at) and remembered,
long after many a critic that has depreciated him
is forgotten.

His sketch of his powerful and ungainly figure
has been already quoted; and we need only say
that his person had the rough vigour of his mind.
There were incidents in his life which cannot·be
defended, and which he did not attempt to de-

fend. His passions were strong, and his morals too often loose. But if there was much to blame in Churchill, there was also a great deal to admire and respect. He was an honest man, a brave man, and a generous man; and many far inferior characters, with less excuse from circumstances, have gone through life in the enjoyment of perfectly respectable reputations. We always hear the worst of satirists, from the nature of the case. Many of them have been among the warmest hearted of mankind, and have lashed knaves and fools so heartily because they had an intense love of worth and sense. But, as David Hume said long ago, the blockheads of the world are a large and powerful body; and they resent satire very naturally. Feared and hated during life, the satirist is too often calumniated in his grave. Some critics seek credit for morality by inveighing against his faults, and some for fine sentiment by deprecating his severity. When the excitement of his immediate effect is over, his reputation appeals hopefully only to the few. Those few will, in the case before us, refrain from overrating Churchill's importance, or denying his faults; but not the less will they emphatically admire him for his strong old English wit, and his stout old English heart.

JAMES HANNAY.

THE ROSCIAD.

Unknowing and unknown, the hardy muse
Boldly defies all mean and partial views;
With honest freedom plays the critic's part,
And praises, as she censures, from the heart.

ROSCIUS deceased, each high aspiring player
    Push'd all his interest for the vacant chair.
    The buskin'd heroes of the mimic stage
No longer whine in love, and rant in rage;
The monarch quits his throne, and condescends
Humbly to court the favour of his friends;
For pity's sake tells undeserved mishaps,
And, their applause to gain, recounts his claps.
Thus the victorious chiefs of ancient Rome,
To win the mob, a suppliant's form assume,   10
In pompous strain fight o'er the extinguish'd war,
And show where honour bled in every scar.
    But though bare merit might in Rome appear
The strongest plea for favour, 'tis not here;

We form our judgment in another way,
And they will best succeed, who best can pay :
Those, who would gain the votes of British tribes,
Must add to force of merit, force of bribes.
   What can an actor give? in every age
Cash hath been rudely banish'd from the stage ; 20
Monarchs themselves, to grief of every player,
Appear as often as their image there ;
They can't, like candidate for other seat,
Pour seas of wine, and mountains raise of meat.
Wine! they could bribe you with the world as soon,
And of Roast Beef, they only know the tune :
But what they have they give ; could Clive do more,
Though for each million he had brought home four?
   Shuter keeps open house at Southwark fair,
And hopes the friends of humour will be there ; 30
In Smithfield, Yates prepares the rival treat
For those who laughter love, instead of meat.
Foote, at Old House, for even Foote will be,

---

[27] Robert Lord Clive, the restorer, if not the founder of the
British Empire in India. He died in 1774.
   [29] Edward Shuter, a comic actor, who, after various theatrical vicissitudes, died a zealous Methodist and disciple of
George Whitfield in 1776.
   [31] Richard Yates, from filling the most insignificant characters, gradually rose to eminence in the comic line.
   [33] Samuel Foote the well-known author of several of the
best farces in the English language, received his education
in the university of Oxford, from whence he moved to the
Temple ; but the law not suiting his inclination, he, in 1747,
hired the old Playhouse in the Haymarket, which had been
built in 1720, and opened it, in the double capacity of author
and performer, with a dramatic piece of his own writing,
called " The Diversions of the Morning," in which he introduced several well-known characters in real life, whom he
very amusingly represented.

In self-conceit, an actor, bribes with tea;
Which Wilkinson at second-hand receives,
And, at the New, pours water on the leaves.
  The town divided, each runs several ways,
As passion, humour, interest, party sways.
Things of no moment, colour of the hair,
Shape of a leg, complexion brown or fair,   40
A dress well chosen, or a patch misplaced,
Conciliate favour, or create distaste.
  From galleries loud peals of laughter roll,
And thunder Shuter's praises ;—he's so droll.
Embox'd, the ladies must have something smart,
Palmer! oh! Palmer tops the janty part.
Seated in pit, the dwarf with aching eyes
Looks up, and vows that Barry's out of size;
Whilst to six feet the vigorous stripling grown,
Declares that Garrick is another Coan.   50
  When place of judgment is by whim supplied,
And our opinions have their rise in pride;
When, in discoursing on each mimic elf,

³⁵ Tate Wilkinson, a comic actor, whom our author in a
subsequent part of this poem characterizes as the mere
shadow of Foote, was, at the publication of the Rosciad,
principal proprietor and one of the managers of Sadler's
Wells; he died in the summer of 1803.

⁴⁶ John Palmer, a favourite actor in genteel comedy. He
married Miss Pritchard, daughter of the celebrated actress of
that name, and died about the year 1780.

⁴⁸ Spranger Barry, an actor of first rate eminence, was in
his person above five feet eleven inches high, finely formed,
and possessing a countenance in which manliness and sweetness of feature were so happily blended, as to form one of the
best representatives of the Belvedere Apollo.

⁵⁰ John Coan, an uncommonly diminutive dwarf, was a
native of Norfolk, and died in March 1764. He, during
some years before his death, gratified the curiosity of his
countrymen at the small charge of sixpence per head.

We praise and censure with an eye to self;
All must meet friends, and Ackman bids as fair
In such a court, as Garrick, for the chair.
At length agreed, all squabbles to decide,
By some one judge the cause was to be tried;
But this their squabbles did afresh renew,
Who should be judge in such a trial:—who? 60
For Johnson some; but Johnson, it was fear'd,
Would be too grave; and Sterne too gay appear'd;
Others for Franklin voted: but 'twas known,
He sicken'd at all triumphs but his own;
For Colman many, but the peevish tongue
Of prudent Age found out that he was young:
For Murphy some few pilfering wits declared,

55 A small comic actor of the time.
62 Sterne's Tristram Shandy, published in 1760, was now at the zenith of its popularity.
63 Dr. Thomas Franklin, the translator of Sophocles, Phalaris, and Lucian, and the author of a volume of Sermons.
65 George Colman, the translator of Terence, and of the Art of Poetry, and the intimate friend and favourite of our author, was the son of Francis Colman, Esq. resident at the court of the Grand Duke of Tuscany. He was educated with Churchill at Westminster School, and thence proceeded to Christ Church, Oxford, where he engaged with Bonnel Thornton, in writing the Connoisseur, a periodical paper of merit. He was called to the bar, but never practised. His first dramatic work, Polly Honeycomb, was performed at Drury Lane theatre in 1760, with success; and the next year his comedy of the Jealous Wife met with unbounded applause. In 1764 Lord Bath died, and left him a liberal annuity, which was enlarged by General Pulteney. In 1767 he became a Patentee of Covent Garden theatre, but in 1770 sold his share, and purchased Foote's theatre in the Haymarket. Mr. Colman died on the 14th of August 1794, at the age of 62.
67 Arthur Murphy, the translator of Tacitus, and editor of Fielding, and a friend of Dr. Johnson's. He died at Knightsbridge, 18 June, 1805, in the seventy-fifth year of his age.

Whilst Folly clapp'd her hands, and Wisdom stared.'

To mischief train'd, e'en from his mother's womb,
Grown old in fraud, though yet in manhood's
    bloom,   70
Adopting arts by which gay villains rise,
And reach the heights which honest men despise;
Mute at the bar, and in the senate loud,
Dull 'mongst the dullest, proudest of the proud,
A pert, prim, prater of the northern race,
Guilt in his heart, and famine in his face,
Stood forth; and thrice he waved his lily hand,
And thrice he twirl'd his tye, thrice stroked his
    band;
    " At Friendship's call" (thus oft, with traitorous
    aim,
Men void of faith usurp faith's sacred name)   80
" At Friendship's call I come, by Murphy sent,
Who thus by me developes his intent:
But lest, transfused, the spirit should be lost,
That spirit which in storms of rhetoric toss'd,
Bounces about, and flies like bottled beer,

[75] The person thus alluded to was Alexander Wedderburn, then an aspiring barrister, afterwards made Chief Justice of the Common Pleas, on which occasion [in 1780] he was raised to the peerage by the title of Lord Loughborough; and lastly Lord Chancellor, on his retirement from which office in 1801 he was created Earl of Rosslyn. In parliament, to a seat in which he was first introduced by Lord Bute, Mr. Wedderburn was an eloquent defender of ministerial measures, and a warm promoter of the persecution against Wilkes, as he was at a later period of that against Dr. Franklin. When Lord Chancellor he gave Murphy, to whom he had been through life a steady patron, the appointment of a Commissioner in Bankruptcy. Junius says of him, " The wary Wedderburn never threw away the scabbard, nor ever went upon a forlorn hope." He died 3rd Jan. 1805.

In his own words his own intentions hear.

"Thanks to my friends, but, to vile fortunes born,
No robes of fur these shoulders must adorn.
Vain your applause, no aid from thence I draw ;
Vain all my wit, for what is wit in law ? 90
Twice (cursed remembrance!) twice I strove to gain
Admittance 'mongst the law-instructed train,
Who, in the Temple and Gray's Inn, prepare
For client's wretched feet the legal snare ;
Dead to those arts which polish and refine,
Deaf to all worth, because that worth was mine,
Twice did those blockheads startle at my name,
And foul rejection gave me up to shame.
To laws and lawyers then I bade adieu,
And plans of far more liberal note pursue. 100
Who will may be a Judge—my kindling breast
Burns for that chair which Roscius once possess'd.
Here give your votes, your interest here exert,
And let success for once attend desert."

With sleek appearance, and with ambling pace,
And type of vacant head with vacant face,
The Proteus Hill put in his modest plea,—

[107] Sir John Hill, son of the Rev. Theophilus Hill, born
about the year 1716, was originally an apothecary and a
student in botany, in which latter pursuit he was encouraged
by the patronage of the Duke of Richmond and the Lord
Petre; but being unsuccessful in it, he made two or three
attempts as an actor and dramatic author; a failure in both
drove him back to his former trade of an apothecary and to
his botanical studies, in which he had more experience if not
more talent. He engaged in a variety of works, mostly
compilations, which he published with incredible expedition ;
and though his character was never in such estimation with
his booksellers as to entitle him to an extraordinary price for
his writings, he was known by such works, by novels,

" Let Favour speak for others, Worth for me."—
For who, like him, his various powers could call
Into so many shapes, and shine in all?   110
Who could so nobly grace the motley list,
Actor, Inspector, Doctor, Botanist?
Knows any one so well—sure no one knows—
At once to play, prescribe, compound, compose?
Who can—But Woodward came,—Hill slipp'd
   away,

pamphlets, and a daily paper called the Inspector, the
labour of his own head and hand, to have earned in one
year the sum £1500. In the midst of all his employment,
he found time and means to drive about the town in his
chariot, and to appear at all public places, and most
private parties, at Batson's coffee house, at masquerades,
and at the opera and play houses, splendidly dressed, and,
as often as possible, in the front of the boxes. Towards the
end of his life his reputation as an author was so sunk by
the slovenliness of his compilations, and his disregard to
truth in what he related, that he was forced to betake himself to the vending a few simple medicines: namely, essence
of waterdock, tincture of valerian, pectoral balsam of honey,
Canada balsam, tincture of sage, and Bardana drops; and, by
pamphlets ascribing to them extraordinary virtues and as
extraordinary cures, imposed on the credulity of the public,
and thereby got, though not an honest, a competent liveli-
hood. In 1773, he received from the King of Sweden the
investiture of the Order of Vasa, or the Polar Star, in return
for a present to that monarch of his Vegetable System, in
twenty-six folio volumes, a magnificent work, which he
completed at the expense and under the patronage of the
Earl of Bute, who warmly interested himself for a time in
favour of the author, and obtained for him the management
of the royal gardens; but the grant was never confirmed.
He died about the year 1775.

[115] This alludes to a paper war in which Hill was engaged with Woodward the comedian, in consequence of an
insult the latter had received in the exercise of his profession.
Woodward represented him on the stage in the character of
a quack doctor.

Melting like ghosts before the rising day.

With that low cunning, which in fools supplies,
And amply too, the place of being wise,
Which Nature, kind, indulgent parent! gave
To qualify the blockhead for a knave;   120
With that smooth falsehood, whose appearance
          charms,
And reason of each wholesome doubt disarms;
Which to the lowest depths of guilt descends,
By vilest means pursues the vilest ends,
Wears Friendship's mask for purposes of spite,
Fawns in the day, and butchers in the night;
With that malignant envy which turns pale
And sickens, even if a friend prevail,
Which merit and success pursues with hate,
And damns the worth it cannot imitate;   130
With the cold caution of a coward's spleen,
Which fears not guilt, but always seeks a screen,
Which keeps this maxim ever in her view—
What's basely done, should be done safely too;
With that dull, rooted, callous impudence
Which, dead to shame and every nicer sense,

---

[117] This severe invective was directed against a Mr. Fitzpatrick, who was the ring-leader of the riots at the theatres
in the year 1763. Mr. Garrick, on the revival of Shakespeare's Two Gentlemen of Verona, made an order that
nothing should be taken under the full price. In consequence
of this regulation, the disturbance began at Drury Lane.
Mr. Fitzpatrick and his party insisted that half price should
be taken at every theatrical exhibition, except the first
season of a pantomime. Mr. Garrick not complying with
their demand, they proceeded to the grossest outrages. At
length not only Mr. Garrick, but Mr. Beard, the manager of
Covent Garden, found it necessary to acquiesce.

[123] The ninth ed. of the Rosciad reads "guile," for "guilt."

Ne'er blush'd, unless, in spreading vice's snares,
She blunder'd on some virtue unawares;
With all these blessings, which we seldom find
Lavish'd by Nature on one happy mind,   140
A motley figure, of the Fribble tribe,
Which heart can scarce conceive or pen describe,
Came simpering on; to ascertain whose sex
Twelve sage, impannell'd matrons would perplex;
Nor male, nor female; neither, and yet both;
Of neuter gender, though of Irish growth;
A six-foot suckling, mincing in Its gait,
Affected, peevish, prim and delicate;
Fearful it seem'd, though of athletic make,
Lest brutal breezes should too roughly shake   150
Its tender form, and savage motion spread
O'er Its pale cheeks the horrid, manly red.
Much did It talk, in Its own pretty phrase,
Of genius and of taste, of players and plays;
Much too of writings, which Itself had wrote,
Of special merit, though of little note;
For Fate, in a strange humour, had decreed
That what It wrote, none but Itself should read.
Much, too, It chatter'd of dramatic laws,
Misjudging critics, and misplaced applause;   160
Then, with a self-complacent jutting air,
It smiled, It smirk'd, It wriggled to the chair,
And, with an awkward briskness not Its own,
Looking around, and perking on the throne,
Triumphant seem'd; when that strange, savage
          dame,
Known but to few or only known by name,
Plain Common Sense appear'd, by Nature there
Appointed, with Plain Truth, to guard the chair;

The pageant saw, and, blasted with her frown,
To Its first state of nothing melted down.　　170
　Nor shall the Muse, (for even there the pride
Of this vain Nothing shall be mortified)
Nor shall the Muse (should fate ordain her rhymes,
Fond, pleasing thought! to live in after-times),
With such a trifler's name her pages blot;
Known be the character, the thing forgot:
Let It, to disappoint each future aim,
Live without sex, and die without a name!
　Cold-blooded critics, by enervate sires
Scarce hammer'd out when Nature's feeble fires 180
Glimmer'd their last; whose sluggish blood, half
　　froze,
Creeps labouring through the veins; whose heart
　　ne'er glows
With fancy-kindled heat;—a servile race,
Who, in mere want of fault all merit place;
Who blind obedience pay to ancient schools,
Bigots to Greece, and slaves to musty rules;
With solemn consequence declared that none
Could judge that cause but Sophocles alone:
Dupes to their fancied excellence, the crowd,
Obsequious to the sacred dictate, bow'd.　　190
　When, from amidst the throng, a youth stood
　　forth,
Unknown his person, not unknown his worth;
His look bespoke applause; alone he stood,
Alone he stemm'd the mighty critic flood:
He talk'd of ancients, as the man became
Who prized our own, but envied not their fame;
With noble reverence spoke of Greece and Rome,
And scorn'd to tear the laurel from the tomb.

" But more than just to other countries grown,
Must we turn base apostates to our own ?　　200
Where do these words of Greece and Rome excel,
That England may not please the ear as well ?
What mighty magic's in the place or air,
That all perfection needs must centre there ?
In states, let strangers blindly be preferr'd ;
In state of letters, merit should be heard.
Genius is of no country ; her pure ray
Spreads all abroad, as general as the day ;
Foe to restraint, from place to place she flies,
And may hereafter e'en in Holland rise.　　210
May not, (to give a pleasing fancy scope,
And cheer a patriot heart with patriot hope)
May not some great, extensive genius raise
The name of Britain 'bove Athenian praise ;
And, whilst brave thirst of fame his bosom warms,
Make England great in letters as in arms ?
There may—there hath—and Shakspeare's muse
　　aspires

[201] A favourite accusation against our author and his
literary associates, was what the reviewers termed an affected
contempt of the ancients, apparent, as they alleged, in all
the productions of this set of writers. It is remarkable, however, that Colman, Thornton, and our author, were all good
classical scholars; and Lloyd, in whose mouth Churchill
puts this vindication of the moderns, was thoroughly versed
in ancient literature. His Latin verses and his imitations of
the Greek and Roman poets place him in the first rank of
modern latinists, and he had not the least tincture of pedantry
in his composition.

[205] This line affords the first specimen of our author's
political views, which, though in him honourably directed to
sound constitutional objects, were, owing to his unfortunate
connection with Wilkes, made subservient to the purposes of
an interested faction.

Beyond the reach of Greece; with native fires,
Mounting aloft he wings his daring flight,
Whilst Sophocles below stands trembling at his
    height.   220
   Why should we then abroad for judges roam,
When abler judges we may find at home?
Happy in tragic and in comic powers,
Have we not Shakspeare?—is not Jonson ours?
For them, your natural judges, Britons, vote;
They'll judge like Britons, who like Britons wrote."
   He said, and conquer'd.—Sense resumed her
    sway,
And disappointed pedants stalk'd away.
Shakspeare and Jonson, with deserved applause,
Joint judges were ordain'd to try the cause.   230
Mean-time the stranger every voice employ'd,
To ask or tell his name.—Who is it?—Lloyd.
   Thus, when the aged friends of Job stood mute,
And, tamely prudent, gave up the dispute,
Elihu, with the decent warmth of youth,

[232] Robert Lloyd, the bosom friend of Churchill, had at
this time acquired considerable reputation by his poem
entitled the Actor, which not only gave proof of great
judgment, but had also the merit of smooth versification and
strength of poetry.   Intoxicated with his literary success,
he quitted his situation of usher at Westminster school, and
relied entirely on his pen for subsistence; but being of a
thoughtless and extravagant disposition, he soon made
himself liable for debts which he was unable to discharge.
In consequence of this improvidence he was confined in the
Fleet Prison, where he depended for support almost wholly
on the bounty of his friend Churchill, whose kindness to him
continued undiminished during all his necessities.   On the
death of his liberal benefactor, Mr. Lloyd sunk into a state
of despondence, which terminated his existence on the 15th
of December 1764, less than one month after he was informed
of the death of Churchill.

Boldly stood forth the advocate of Truth,
Confuted Falsehood, and disabled Pride,
Whilst baffled Age stood snarling at his side.
    The day of trial's fix'd, nor any fear
Lest day of trial should be put off here.   240
Causes but seldom for delay can call
In courts where forms are few, fees none at all.
    The morning came, nor find I that the sun,
As he on other great events hath done,
Put on a brighter robe than what he wore
To go his journey in the day before.
    Full in the centre of a spacious plain,
On plan entirely new, where nothing vain,
Nothing magnificent appear'd, but Art
With decent modesty perform'd her part,   256
Rose a tribunal; from no other court
It borrow'd ornament, or sought support;
No juries here were pack'd to kill or clear,
No bribes were taken, nor oaths broken here;
No gownsmen, partial to a client's cause,
To their own purpose turned the pliant laws;
Each judge was true and steady to his trust,
As Mansfield wise, and as old Foster just.
    In the first seat, in robe of various dyes,
A noble wildness flashing from his eyes,   260
Sat Shakspeare.—In one hand a wand he bore,
For mighty wonders famed in days of yore;

---

[256] Nearly all the ed. of Churchill's Poems (including the fourth and ninth 4to. of the Rosciad) read "tuned," for "turned." The seventh ed. 4to, however, which was issued during the lifetime of the author, has "turned."

[258] Sir Michael Foster, one of the puisne judges of the Court of King's Bench, and author of an excellent treatise on Crown Law. He died the 7th of November 1763.

The other held a globe, which to his will
Obedient turn'd, and own'd the master's skill:
Things of the noblest kind his genius drew,
And look'd through Nature at a single view:
A loose he gave to his unbounded soul,
And taught new lands to rise, new seas to roll;
Call'd into being scenes unknown before,   269
And passing Nature's bounds, was something more.

Next Jonson sat; in ancient learning train'd,
His rigid judgment Fancy's flights restrain'd;
Correctly pruned each wild luxuriant thought,
Mark'd out her course, nor spared a glorious fault:
The book of man he read with nicest art,
And ransack'd all the secrets of the heart;
Exerted penetration's utmost force,
And traced each passion to its proper source;
Then, strongly mark'd, in liveliest colours drew,
And brought each foible forth to public view: 280
The coxcomb felt a lash in every word,
And fools, hung out, their brother fools deterr'd.
His comic humour kept the world in awe,
And laughter frighten'd folly more than law.

But, hark!—the trumpet sounds, the crowd
        gives way,
And the procession comes in just array.

Now should I, in some sweet, poetic line
Offer up incense at Apollo's shrine,
Invoke the muse to quit her calm abode,
And waken memory with a sleeping ode: 290
For how should mortal man, in mortal verse

---

290 The allusion here is to Mason's Ode to Memory, which
was also ridiculed by Lloyd in an Ode to Oblivion. as Gray's
were by Colmau in an Ode to Obscurity.

Their titles, merits, or their names, rehearse?
But give, kind Dulness! memory and rhyme,
We'll put off Genius till another time.

First Order came,—with solemn step and slow,
In measured time his feet were taught to go.
Behind, from time to time, he cast his eye,
Lest this should quit his place, that step awry;
Appearances to save his only care;
So things seem right, no matter what they are: 300
In him his parents saw themselves renew'd,
Begotten by Sir Critic on Saint Prude.

Then came Drum, Trumpet, Hautboy, Fiddle,
    Flute;
Next, Snuffer, Sweeper, Shifter, Soldier, Mute:
Legions of angels all in white advance;
Furies, all fire, come forward in a dance;
Pantomime figures then are brought to view,
Fools hand in hand with fools go two by two.
Next came the Treasurer of either House,
One with full purse, t'other with not a sous: 310
Behind, a group of figures awe create,
Set off with all the impertinence of state;
By lace and feather consecrate to fame,
Expletive kings, and queens without a name.

Here Havard, all serene, in the same strains

---

³¹⁰ Covent Garden theatre became rich under the management of Beard, who, with Miss Brent in the Beggar's Opera and Artaxerxes, turned the tide of public favour for several seasons to the advantage of that house.

³¹⁵ William Havard was the son of a vintner at Dublin, and was originally intended for the practice of surgery. His first engagement as a player was at the theatre in Goodman's Fields; he then entered into the service of Rich, at Covent Garden; but moved to Drury Lane upon his friend Garrick becoming the patentee of that theatre. As an actor he was

Loves, hates, and rages, triumphs, and complains;
His easy vacant face proclaim'd a heart
Which could not feel emotions, nor impart.
With him came mighty Davies. On my life,
That Davies hath a very pretty wife:—   320
Statesman all over!—in plots famous grown!—
He mouths a sentence as curs mouth a bone.
    Next Holland came,—with truly tragic stalk

pleasing though not powerful.   Havard retired from the
stage in May 1769, and died in 1778, at the age of sixty-
eight years.   The amiable qualities of Havard are better
conveyed than expressed in his epitaph:—

> " The clay cold tenant underneath this stone
> Had once those virtues which a prince might own."

319 Thomas Davies, a bookseller, actor, and author. He
failed in the two former avocations, but has deservedly established a reputation for amusing biography, by his dramatic
miscellanies and a gossiping life of Garrick. He died in
1785. Mrs. Davies was sometimes called upon to perform
Mrs. Cibber's parts, particularly Cordelia in Lear; and her
figure, look, and deportment corresponded so well with the
idea of this amiable character, that she was received with no
inconsiderable share of approbation. At their house, Johnson
first met Boswell.

323 Holland, a pupil of Mr. Garrick, under whose tuition
he made some proficiency, though he seldom merited more
praise than that of being a tolerable copy of a fine original,
first appeared on the stage in 1755. He was a good-looking
man, but had an affectation of carrying his head either stiffly
erect, or leaning towards one shoulder, which gave an awk-
wardness to his person, which was not otherwise ungraceful.
Holland's ear was perfectly good, and he had great good
sense, industry, and application, with a moderate share of
sensibility. He had also a fine and a powerful, melodious, and
articulate voice, and by a constant attention to the tone,
manner, and action of Mr. Garrick, did not displease when
he represented some of his most favourite characters; particularly Hamlet, Chamont, Hastings, and Tancred; in the
last he manifested an uncommon degree of spirit. He was,
however, always most correct when acting under the eye and

He creeps, he flies,—a hero should not walk.
As if with Heaven he warr'd, his eager eyes
Planted their batteries against the skies;
Attitude, action, air, pause, start, sigh, groan
He borrow'd, and made use of as his own.
By fortune thrown on any other stage,
He might, perhaps, have pleased an easy age; 330
But now appears a copy, and no more,
Of something better we have seen before.
The actor who would build a solid fame,
Must imitation's servile arts disclaim;
Act from himself, on his own bottom stand;
I hate e'en Garrick thus at second-hand.
Behind came King.—Bred up in modest lore,
Bashful and young he sought Hibernia's shore;
Hibernia, famed, 'bove every other grace
For matchless intrepidity of face. 340
From her his features caught the generous flame,
And bid defiance to all sense of shame:
Tutor'd by her all rivals to surpass,
'Mongst Drury's sons he comes, and shines in Brass.
　　Lo, Yates!—Without the least finesse of art

immediate direction of his master; he was then scrupulously
exact; and if he never rose to excellence, his endeavours to
attain it merited and obtained the approbation of the public.
　　337 Thomas King, though much displeased, expressed no
resentment against the author for his notice of him. His
most admired characters were Brass in the Confederacy, Sir
Peter Teazle in the School for Scandal, the Grave-digger in
Hamlet, &c; but his *chef-d'œuvre* was Lord Ogleby, in the
Clandestine Marriage, which he performed with peculiar
chasteness and discrimination. For dry humour and articulate volubility Mr. King was unequalled. He was born in
1730 and died in 1805.
　　345 A defect of memory or a vicious habit on the part of
Yates occasioned his frequently repeating a sentence two or

He gets applause; I wish he'd get his part.
When hot impatience is in full career,
How vilely "Hark'e! Hark'e!" grates the ear!
When active fancy from the brain is sent,
And stands on tip-toe for some wish'd event,   350
I hate those careless blunders which recall
Suspended sense, and prove it fiction all.

In characters of low and vulgar mould,
Where Nature's coarsest features we behold;
Where, destitute of every decent grace,
Unmanner'd jests are blurted in your face,
There, Yates with justice strict attention draws,
Acts truly from himself, and gains applause;
But when, to please himself or charm his wife,
He aims at something in politer life,   360
When, blindly thwarting Nature's stubborn plan,
He treads the stage by way of gentleman,
The clown, who no one touch of breeding knows,
Looks like Tom Errand dress'd in Clincher's clothes.
Fond of his dress, fond of his person grown,
Laugh'd at by all, and to himself unknown,
From side to side he struts, he smiles, he prates,
And seems to wonder what's become of Yates.

Woodward, endow'd with various tricks of face,

three times over, as "Hark you, Hark you, Polly Honycomb."
He died suddenly in 1796.
    353 The fitter word clown was substituted by Churchill for
that of fop, which appears in the earlier editions of this
poem.
    364 A humorous character in Farquhar's comedy of the
Constant Couple, in the principal character of which, Sir
Harry Wildair, the author is supposed to have intended his
own portrait.
    369 Henry Woodward was born in London in 1717, had a
liberal education at Merchant Taylors' School. and was at

Great master in the science of grimace,   370
From Ireland ventures, favourite of the town,
Lured by the pleasing prospect of renown ;
A speaking Harlequin, made up of whim,
He twists, he twines, he tortures every limb,
Plays to the eye with a mere monkey's art,
And leaves to sense the conquest of the heart.
We laugh indeed, but, on reflection's birth,
We wonder at ourselves, and curse our mirth.
His walk of parts he fatally misplaced,
And inclination fondly took for taste ;   380
Hence hath the town so often seen display'd
Beau in burlesque, high life in masquerade.
    But when bold wits, not such as patch up plays,
Cold and correct, in these insipid days,
Some comic character, strong featured, urge,
To probability's extremest verge ;
Where modest Judgment her decree suspends,
And, for a time, nor censures nor commends ;
Where critics can't determine on the spot
Whether it is in nature found or not,   390
There Woodward safely shall his powers exert,
Nor fail of favour where he shews desert ;
Hence he in Bobadil such praises bore,
Such worthy praises ; Kitely scarce had more.
    By turns transform'd into all kind of shapes,

first engaged in the business of a tallow chandler. He was
then bound apprentice to Mr. Rich, the manager of Covent
Garden Theatre, under whose tuition he became qualified for
a harlequin. He afterwards engaged at Drury Lane in 1738,
where his comic powers acquired great applause. Bobadil,
Bessus, Parolles, and Cacafogo, were esteemed his master
pieces. He died in 1777.

394 Kitely, in Jonson's Every Man in his Humour, was a
favourite character of Garrick's.

Constant to none, Foote laughs, cries, struts, and
    scrapes :
Now in the centre, now in van or rear
The Proteus shifts, bawd, parson, auctioneer.
His strokes of humour, and his bursts of sport
Are all contain'd in this one word, *Distort.*   400

    Doth a man stutter, look a-squint, or halt ;—
Mimics draw humour out of Nature's fault ;
With personal defects their mirth adorn,
And hang misfortunes out to public scorn.
E'en I, whom Nature cast in hideous mould,
Whom, having made, she trembled to behold,
Beneath the load of mimicry may groan,
And find that Nature's errors are my own.

    Shadows behind of Foote and Woodward came;
Wilkinson this, Obrien was that name.   410

₃₉₆ Foote was outrageously offended at this attack, and
was most violent in his anger. He wrote a prose dialogue,
wherein he lampooned Churchill and Lloyd, but was too wise
to publish it. With his usual fondness for alliteration, and
with as little wit as truth, he called Churchill the *clumsy
curate of Clapham.* Foote died in October 1777.

  ₃₉₈ In several of his farces, particularly the Minor and
the Orators, Foote personated three or four of the principal
characters himself. In the former farce the author in the
characters of Mrs. Cole and Mr. Smirk, represented those of
the celebrated Mother Douglas and Mr. Langford the auctioneer, and in the conclusion, or rather epilogue to the piece,
spoken by Shift (which Foote performed together with the
two other characters) he took off to a great degree of exact-
ness the manner and even person of George Whitefield.

  ₄₀₅ In his poem of Independence, our author has given no
very flattering portrait of his own person.

  ₄₁₀ William Obrien was originally a fencing master, and
made his first appearance as an actor at Drury Lane Theatre
in 1758, in the part of Captain Brazen. After continuing
on the stage six years, he married Lady Susan Strangeways,
daughter to the Earl of Ilchester, and soon after went over to

Strange to relate, but wonderfully true,
That even shadows have their shadows too!
With not a single comic power endued,
The first a mere mere mimic's mimic stood;
The last, by Nature form'd to please, who shews,
In Jonson's Stephen, which way genius grows,
Self quite put off, affects with too much art
To put on Woodward in each mangled part;
Adopts his shrug, his wink, his stare; nay, more,
His voice, and croaks; for Woodward croak'd
    before.   420
When a dull copier simple grace neglects,
And rests his imitation in defects,
We readily forgive; but such vile arts
Are double guilt in men of real parts.
   By Nature form'd in her perversest mood;

America, where he enjoyed a profitable post under government. He wrote an unsuccessful comedy called the Duel, a
farce still on the acting list, called Cross Purposes, and another
intitled, A Friend in Need is a Friend Indeed.

[414] Wilkinson appears to have made a more favourable
impression on the poet, if we are to give credit to the following
anecdote in that Actor's diary: " On 20th August, 1763, I
acted Bayes in the Rehearsal, my imitation of Holland in the
following lines, —

   ' How strange a captive am I grown of late!
   Shall I accuse my love or blame my hate?
   My love I cannot, that is too divine,
   And against fate what mortal dares repine;'

had such an effect, that Mr. Churchill, who sat in a balcony
with Lucy Cooper, after laughing to a very violent degree,
most vociferously encored the speech, which was echoed by
the whole voice of the theatre, and complied with by me of
course with great pleasure. Mr. Churchill said, that he was
convinced I was not a mimic's mimic, for the imitations were
palpably my own. He also encored my mock hornpipe, which
was a resemblance of the manner of stage dancing."

With no one requisite of art endued,
Next Jackson came.—Observe that settled glare,
Which better speaks a puppet than a player;
List to that voice—did ever Discord hear
Sounds so well fitted to her untuned ear?   430
When to enforce some very tender part,
The right hand sleeps by instinct on the heart,
His soul, of every other thought bereft,
Is anxious only where to place the left;
He sobs and pants to soothe his weeping spouse,
To soothe his weeping mother, turns and bows:
Awkward, embarrass'd, stiff, without the skill
Of moving gracefully or standing still,
One leg, as if suspicious of his brother,
Desirous seems to run away from t'other.   440

　Some errors, handed down from age to age,
Plead custom's force, and still possess the stage.
That's vile—should we a parent's faults adore,
And err, because our fathers err'd before?
If, inattentive to the author's mind,
Some actors made the jest they could not find,
If by low tricks they marr'd fair Nature's mien,
And blurr'd the graces of the simple scene,
Shall we, if reason rightly is employ'd,
Not see their faults, or seeing, not avoid?   450
When Falstaff stands detected in a lie,
Why, without meaning, rolls Love's glassy eye?

---

[427] Jackson afterwards had the chief management of the
Theatre Royal at Edinburgh; he was a native of Westmore-
land, and though possessed of a good person and some judgment, was a very indifferent performer, owing to the disadvantages of a harsh voice and provincial accent. He was
the author of three tragedies.
[452] James Love, an actor and dramatic writer. He was

Why?—There's no cause—at least no cause we
  know—
It was the fashion twenty years ago.
Fashion—a word which knaves and fools may use,
Their knavery and folly to excuse.
To copy beauties, forfeits all pretence
To fame—to copy faults, is want of sense.
  Yet (though in some particulars he fails,
Some few particulars, where mode prevails)   460
If in these hallow'd times, when sober, sad,
All gentlemen are melancholy mad;
When 'tis not deem'd so great a crime by half
To violate a vestal as to laugh,
Rude mirth may hope presumptuous to engage
An Act of Toleration for the stage;
And courtiers will, like reasonable creatures;
Suspend vain fashion, and unscrew their features;
Old Falstaff, play'd by Love, shall please once more,
And humour set the audience in a roar.   470
  Actors I've seen, and of no vulgar name,
Who, being from one part possess'd of fame,
Whether they are to laugh, cry, whine, or bawl,
Still introduce that favourite part in all.
Here, Love, be cautious—ne'er be thou betray'd

educated at Westminster, from thence went to Cambridge,
and while there wrote a Pamphlet called " Yes, they are, what
then?" in answer to one called "Are these things so?" Sir
Robert Walpole sent Love £100 as a gratuity for this sea-
sonable reply. His real name was Dance, and the memory
of his father, the surveyor to the city of London, will be co-
eval with the ponderous edifice which he erected for the residence of the chief magistrate of the metropolis. He was a
performer on Drury Lane stage, and excelled in the character
of Falstaff. He wrote Pamela, a comedy, and some other
pieces. He died in 1774.

To call in that wag Falstaff's dangerous aid;
Like Goths of old, howe'er he seems a friend,
He'll seize that throne you wish him to defend.
In a peculiar mould by Humour cast,
For Falstaff framed—himself the first and last—
He stands aloof from all, maintains his state,   481
And scorns, like Scotsmen, to assimilate.
Vain all disguise! too plain we see the trick,
Though the knight wears the weeds of Dominic;
And Boniface disgraced, betrays the smack,
In *anno Domini*, of Falstaff's sack.
   Arms cross'd, brows bent, eyes fix'd, feet march-
     ing slow,
A band of malcontents with spleen o'erflow;
Wrapt in conceit's impenetrable fog,
Which Pride, like Phœbus, draws from every bog,
They curse the managers, and curse the town   491
Whose partial favour keeps such merit down.
   But if some man, more hardy than the rest,
Should dare attack these gnatlings in their nest,
At once they rise with impotence of rage,
Whet their small stings, and buzz about the stage.
" 'Tis breach of privilege!—Shall any dare
To arm satiric truth against a player?
Prescriptive rights we plead, time out of mind;
Actors, unlash'd themselves, may lash mankind."

434 Dryden's Spanish Friar.
445 The jovial landlord in Farquhar's Beaux Stratagem.
467 Lips busy and eyes fix'd, foot falling slow,
    Arms hanging idly down, hands clasp'd below.
                         COWPER.
491-512 These lines were added in the second edition, in
consequence of the language adopted by some of the actors,
and by their advocates the Critical Reviewers, on the first
appearance of the poem.

What! shall Opinion then, of Nature free, 501
And liberal as the vagrant air, agree
To rust in chains like these, imposed by things
Which, less than nothing, ape the pride of kings?
No—though half-poets with half-players join
To curse the freedom of each honest line;
Though rage and malice dim their faded cheek,
What the Muse freely thinks, she'll freely speak;
With just disdain of every paltry sneer,
Stranger alike to flattery and fear, 510
In purpose fix'd, and to herself a rule,
Public contempt shall wait the public fool.

Austin would always glisten in French silks;
Ackman would Norris be, and Packer Wilks;

---

[513] Austin had been manager of the Chester Theatre, and
was Garrick's factotum; and after his patron's death, retired to Ireland on an easy fortune.

[514] Packer was a worthy man and useful actor, which
qualities secured him an humble engagement at Drury Lane
Theatre; this ironical mention of him, and of his compeer
Ackman, has rescued their names from that oblivion in which
they would otherwise have by this time been involved.

Henry Norris, a celebrated comedian, contemporary with
Betterton and Booth, from his ludicrous representation in
Farquhar's Constant Couple he obtained the nickname of
Jubilee Dicky, and in the first edition of the Spectator, in the
Advertisement of the Beaux Stratagem, he is called Dickey
Scrub. Norris died in the year 1725.

Robert Wilks. This actor's predilection for the stage induced him to quit for it in 1689 a very profitable post in
Ireland, in which his successor in a short period of time accumulated a fortune of £50,000. His first trial was at the
Theatre Royal, Drury Lane, but not thinking himself sufficiently noticed, he returned to Dublin, where he shone without a competitor for five years, when the tragical death of
the accomplished William Mountford, basely murdered by
Charles Lord Mohun and Captain Hill in December, 1691,
from jealousy of Mrs. Bracegirdle's (the celebrated actress)
supposed preference for Mountford, occasioned an opening for

For who, liko Ackman, can with humour pleaso?
Who can, like Packer, charm with sprightly ease?
Higher than all the rest, see Bransby strut,
A mighty Gulliver in Lilliput!
Ludicrous Nature! which at once could show
A man so very high, so very low.   520
   If I forget thee, Blakes, or if I say
Aught hurtful, may I never see thee play.
Let critics, with a supercilious air,
Decry thy various merit, and declare
Frenchman is still at top;—but scorn that rage
Which, in attacking thee, attacks the age.
French follies, universally embraced,
At once provoke our mirth, and form our taste.
   Long from a nation ever hardly used,
At random censured, wantonly abused,   530
Have Britons drawn their sport; with partial view
Form'd general notions from the rascal few;
Condemn'd a people, as for vices known,
Which, from their country banish'd, seek our own.

him on the London stage, where he made his second appearance in 1696, in the character of Lysippus in the Maid's Tragedy,
and in 1714 became joint patentee and manager with Cibber
and Doggett until his death in 1731. His master-pieces were
Prince Hal, Sir Harry Wildair, and Hamlet; in the latter,
Garrick alone came near him.

[517] Bransby, whose uncommon height of stature seems
to have precluded all other notice, had more merit than the
poet appears willing to allow him. His performance of Kent
in Lear, and of Downright in Every Man in his Humour,
evinced a justness of conception that entitled him to more
honourable mention.

[521] Blakes was originally a peruke-maker by trade. His
forte lay in personating the French fop or valet, which he
did with consummate chasteness and accuracy. He died in
1763.

At length, howe'er, the slavish chain is broke,
And Sense, awaken'd, scorns her ancient yoke:
Taught by thee, Moody, we now learn to raise
Mirth from their foibles, from their virtues, praise.

Next came the legion which our summer Bayes
From alleys, here and there, contrived to raise, 540
Flush'd with vast hopes, and certain to succeed,
With wits who cannot write, and scarce can
read.
Veterans no more support the rotten cause,
No more from Elliot's worth they reap applause;
Each on himself determines to rely;
Be Yates disbanded, and let Elliot fly.
Never did play'rs so well an author fit,
To Nature dead, and foes declared to wit.
So loud each tongue, so empty was each head,
So much they talk'd, so very little said, 550
So wondrous dull, and yet so wondrous vain,
At once so willing, and unfit to reign,
That Reason swore, nor would the oath recall,
Their mighty master's soul inform'd them all.

[537] This very respectable actor and amiable man retired
from the stage about the year 1795. In Irish characters he
has never been excelled. He died in 1812.
[539] Alluding to the summer theatre in the Haymarket,
where Murphy's plays were got up and acted under the joint
management of himself and Mr. Foote.
Miss Elliot, a young actress of great merit, made her first
appearance at the Haymarket Theatre in the part of Maria,
in the Citizen, a farce by Murphy, who dedicated it to her.
The sprightly humour and busy situations of the character
were so admirably represented by her, that the applause she
acquired in this part obtained for her an engagement at one
of the winter theatres, which she relinquished at the instance
of the late Duke of Cumberland, the brother of George the
Third. She died in 1769, in the 26th year of her age.

As one with various disappointments sad,
Whom dulness, only, kept from being mad,
Apart from all the rest great Murphy came—
Common to fools and wits the rage of fame.
What though the sons of Nonsense hail him Sire,
Auditor, Author, Manager, and Squire !   560
His restless soul's ambition stops not there ;
To make his triumphs perfect dub him Player.
   In person tall, a figure form'd to please,
If symmetry could charm deprived of ease ;
When motionless he stands, we all approve ;
What pity 'tis the Thing was made to move !
   His voice, in one dull, deep, unvaried sound,
Seems to break forth from caverns under ground ;
From hollow chest the low, sepulchral note
Unwilling heaves, and struggles in his throat. 570
   Could authors butcher'd give an actor grace,
All must to him resign the foremost place.
When he attempts, in some one favourite part,
To ape the feelings of a manly heart,
His honest features the disguise defy,
And his face loudly gives his tongue the lie.
   Still in extremes, he knows no happy mean,
Or raving mad, or stupidly serene.
In cold-wrought scenes the lifeless actor flags ;
In passion, tears the passion into rags.   580
Can none remember ?—Yes—I know all must—

---

560 Murphy undertook, in the Auditor, in concert with
Smollett, who was the editor of the Briton, a systematic
defence of Lord Bute's administration, which commenced
29th November, 1762 ; on the same day was published No. 1
of the Briton ; No. 1 of the North Briton, principally conducted by Wilkes and Churchill, appeared June 5 ; and
No. 1 of the Auditor, June 10.

When in the Moor he ground his teeth to dust,
When o'er the stage he Folly's standard bore,
Whilst Common Sense stood trembling at the door.
How few are found with real talents blest!
Fewer with Nature's gifts contented rest.
Man from his sphere eccentric starts astray;
All hunt for fame, but most mistake the way.
Bred at St. Omer's to the shuffling trade,
The hopeful youth a Jesuit might have made,   590
With various readings stored his empty skull,
Learn'd without sense, and venerably dull;
Or, at some banker's desk, like many more,
Content to tell that two and two make four,
His name had stood in City annals fair,
And prudent Dulness mark'd him for a mayor.
What then could tempt thee, in a critic age,
Such blooming hopes to forfeit on a stage?
Could it be worth thy wondrous waste of pains
To publish to the world thy lack of brains?   600
Or might not reason e'en to thee have shown
Thy greatest praise had been to live unknown?
Yet let not vanity, like thine, despair:
Fortune makes Folly her peculiar care.
A vacant throne high-placed in Smithfield view,
To sacred Dulness and her first-born due,
Thither with haste in happy hour repair,
Thy birth-right claim, nor fear a rival there.
Shuter himself shall own thy juster claim,
And venal Ledgers puff their Murphy's name;   610

[582] Murphy's first attempt on the stage was in 1754 as Othello.
[610] The Public Ledger, a newspaper, conducted by Hugh Kelly.

Whilst Vaughan or Dapper, call him which you
 will,
Shall blow the trumpet, and give out the bill.
There rule secure from critics and from sense,
Nor once shall Genius rise to give offence;
Eternal peace shall bless the happy shore,
And little factions break thy rest no more.

 From Covent Garden crowds promiscuous go,
Whom the Muse knows not, nor desires to know :
Veterans they seem'd, but knew of arms no more
Than if, till that time, arms they never bore :   620
Like Westminster militia train'd to fight,
They scarcely knew the left hand from the right.
Ashamed among such troops to show the head,
Their chiefs were scatter'd, and their heroes fled.

 Sparks at his glass sat comfortably down
To separate frown from smile, and smile from frown.
Smith, the genteel, the airy, and the smart,

<hr />

[611] Thomas Vaughan, a friend of Murphy, the author of
two very indifferent farces, Love's Metamorphosis, and the
Hotel.

[621] The Westminster militia with their metropolitan brethren in arms, the City of London trained bands and lumber
troopers, were the standing joke of their fellow citizens, and
have acquired an enduring fame in their well known representatives, Johnny Gilpin and Major Sturgeon; the latter,
after a brilliant field day, returning to town in the Turnham
Green stage with Captain Cucumber, Lieutenant Pattypan,
and Ensign Tripe, were stopped near the Hammersmith turn-
pike, and robbed and stripped by a single footpad.

[625] Luke Sparks, though no scholar, was a man of strong
intelligence, and knew how to take possession of a character;
but he sometimes gave too much hardness in his manner;
his colouring was coarse, though his outline was generally
exact. He died about 1769.

[627] A very favourite actor in genteel comedy, commonly
called gentleman Smith, and particularly distinguished in

Smith was just gone to school to say his part.
Ross, (a misfortune which we often meet)
Was fast asleep at dear Statira's feet;   630
Statira, with her hero to agree,
Stood on her feet as fast asleep as he.
Macklin, who largely deals in half-form'd sounds,

Charles Surface, in the School for Scandal. He was the
son of a wholesale grocer in the City, educated at Eton, and
from thence removed to Cambridge, which he abruptly left
for the stage, and made his first appearance in the character
of Theodosius in 1753. His chief defect was an unpleasing
monotony of voice and an unwieldy person. He married a
sister of the Earl of Sandwich, whom he survived; and retired from the stage on 9th June 1788, to Bury St. Edmunds.
In the year 1797, he was prevailed upon to act Charles, for
the benefit of his friend King, which he did, notwithstanding
the disadvantages of age and corpulence, with an ease and
elegance that obtained the unanimous plaudits of a crowded
house.

⁶²⁹ David Ross was the son of a gentleman of consideration at Edinburgh, and educated at Westminster School, but
afterwards abandoned by his father, who left him by his will
the sum of one shilling, to be paid to him on the first day of
every month of May, that being his birthday, the more bit-
terly to remind him of his misfortune in being born. He
resorted to the stage, and afterwards submitted to marry the
cast-off mistress of a nobleman for the sake of her annuity.
Late in life he succeeded in invalidating his father's will,
and obtained about £6000. He pleaded guilty to the charge
brought against him by Churchill, and laughed at his punishment over a glass with his friend Bonnel Thornton. His
defects were evidently owing to his love of ease and fondness
for social pleasure; but he sometimes gave proofs that he
was master of abilities to rouse and animate an audience in
the most passionate scenes of our best tragedies.

⁶³⁰ Ross's Statira was Mrs. Palmer, the daughter of Mrs.
Pritchard. She was an actress of very inferior merit, and
was only endured in consequence of her mother's popularity.

⁶³³ Charles Macklin, *alias* M'Laughlin, " the Jew that
Shakspeare drew." The censure bestowed on him by Churchill is just, but his very defects were in his favour in the

Who wantonly transgresses Nature's bounds,
Whose acting's hard, affected, and constrain'd,
Whose features, as each other they disdain'd,
At variance set, inflexible, and coarse,
Ne'er know the workings of united force,
Ne'er kindly soften to each other's aid,
Nor show the mingled powers of light and shade,
No longer for a thankless stage concern'd,   641
To worthier thoughts his mighty genius turn'd,
Harangued, gave lectures, made each simple elf
Almost as good a speaker as himself,
Whilst the whole town, mad with mistaken zeal,
An awkward rage for elocution feel;
Dull cits and grave divines his praise proclaim,
And join with Sheridan's their Macklin's name.
Shuter, who never cared a single pin
Whether he left out nonsense, or put in,   650
Who aim'd at wit, though levell'd in the dark,
The random arrow seldom hit the mark,
At Islington, all by the placid stream

representation of Shylock, Iago, and characters of that
stamp, and in his own plays of the Man of the World and
Love à la Mode. A satisfactory account of his long career
in the theatrical world would include a history of the stage
during the greater part of the last century, he having made
his first appearance in 1726, and his last performance was
Shylock, in the year 1790, though his life was protracted till
February 1797. He had an extraordinarily harsh set of
features, and an unprepossessing countenance, which occasioned Quin to say of him, "If God writes a legible hand,
that fellow is a villain." He was considered an excellent
tutor in the theatrical art, and Barry was in no small degree
indebted to his instructions for his celebrity in Othello.

    648 The biographer of Swift, and father of Richard
Brinsley.

    653 The new river, as it was named, before similar works
were denominated canals, to be since superseded by railways.

Where City swains in lap of Dulness dream,
Where, quiet as her strains, their strains do flow,
That all the patron by the bards may know,
Secret as night, with Rolt's experienced aid,
The plan of future operations laid,
Projected schemes the summer months to cheer,
And spin out happy folly through the year. 660
 But think not, though these dastard chiefs are
  fled,
That Covent Garden troops shall want a head;
Harlequin comes their chief!—See from afar
The hero seated in fantastic car!
Wedded to Novelty, his only arms
Are wooden swords, wands, talismans and charms;
On one side Folly sits, by some call'd Fun,
And on the other his arch-patron, Lun;

[657] Richard Rolt, a poor, low creature, by profession a hackney writer to an attorney, and afterwards a drudge to booksellers, as often as they would trust him with employment. He was supposed to be the author of the Anti Rosciad, and was at this time the chief director of the amusements at Sadler's Wells under Mr. Rosamon, the proprietor of that house. He once went over to Ireland, where he published Dr. Akenside's Pleasures of Imagination as his own work, and under his own name. He died in 1773.

[666] Mr. John Rich had been the manager of Covent Garden theatre, almost fifty years, under the patent granted by Charles the Second, in which he succeeded his father Christopher, and in 1761 he resigned the active part of the duty to his son-in-law Beard. Rich acquired the name of Lun, by his excellent performance of Harlequin. The splendour of his pantomimes, and the agility of his performers drew as great crowds to his theatre as could be collected by all the efforts of the first actors of the time at Drury Lane, and enabled him with an indifferent company of actors to make a stand against the greatest performers of his time. Mr. Rich in the year 1747 first intro-

Behind, for liberty a-thirst in vain,
Sense, helpless captive, drags the galling chain;
Six rude, mis-shapen beasts the chariot draw, 671
Whom Reason loaths, and Nature never saw;
Monsters, with tails of ice and heads of fire;
" Gorgons, and Hydras, and Chimeras dire."
Each was bestrode by full as monstrous wight,
Giant, dwarf, genius, elf, hermaphrodite.
The Town, as usual, met him in full cry;
The Town, as usual, knew no reason why:
But Fashion so directs, and Moderns raise
On Fashion's mould'ring base their transient praise.

    Next, to the field a band of females draw   681
Their force, for Britain owns no Salique law:
Just to their worth, we female rights admit,
Nor bar their claim to empire or to wit.

    First, giggling, plotting, chamber-maids arrive,
Hoydens and romps, led on by General Clive.

duced the pantomime. He was not only the inventor of that
entertainment in England, but likewise the most perfect
harlequin that ever appeared on the English stage. He
died in 1761.

    686 Catherine Clive, a celebrated comic actress, was the
daughter of an Irish gentleman of the name of Raftor, and
in 1732 married G. Clive, Esq. brother of the late Mr. Baron
Clive. From a collision of tempers they soon separated, but
calumny never attempted to aim the slightest arrow at her
fame. A more extensive walk in comedy than that of Mrs.
Clive cannot be imagined; the chambermaid, in every varied
shape which art or nature could lend her; characters of caprice and affectation, from the high-bred lady Fanciful to
the vulgar Mrs. Heidelberg; country girls, romps, hoydens,
and dowdies, superannuated beauties, viragos, and humourists.
To a strong and melodious voice, with an ear for music, she
added all the sprightly action requisite to a number of parts
in ballad farces. Her comic abilities had never been excelled,
in Horace Walpole's opinion. In 1769 Mrs. Clive quitted

In spite of outward blemishes, she shone,
For humour famed, and humour all her own :
Easy, as if at home, the stage she trod,
Nor sought the critic's praise, nor fear'd his rod :
Original in spirit and in ease,   691
She pleased by hiding all attempts to please :
No comic actress ever yet could raise,
On humour's base, more merit or more praise.
   With all the native vigour of sixteen,
Among the merry troop conspicuous seen,
See lively Pope advance in jig, and trip
Corinna, Cherry, Honeycomb, and Snip :
Not without art, but yet to Nature true,
She charms the town with humour just, yet new :
Cheer'd by her promise, we the less deplore   701
The fatal time when Clive shall be no more.

the stage, and lived a retired life upon a competency at
Twickenham in a charming residence on the banks of the
Thames belonging to Horace Walpole, who delighted much
in her society. She died in 1785.
   ⁶⁹⁸ This pleasing actress fully confirmed our author's
prediction, and long survived to contribute to the entertainment of the public. To Mrs. Clive she was indebted for all
that care, instruction, and example could afford, and to her
own docility, talents, and good sense, for availing herself of
the precepts of so experienced and accomplished a performer.
Introduced early on the stage, Miss Pope had the peculiar
merit and advantage of conciliating the friendship of the
most valuable performers of the time. Her obligations to
Mrs. Clive we have already noticed ; with Mrs. Pritchard
and Garrick she was on the most friendly terms, and through
life preserved that strict propriety of conduct which justified
their partiality towards her. Her first appearance was on
27th Oct. 1759, in the character of Corinna in the Confederacy ; and the next in 1760, in Polly Honeycomb. She
retired from the Stage some years before her death, which
occurred in 1812.

Lo ! Vincent comes—with simple grace array'd,
She laughs at paltry arts, and scorns parade:
Nature through her is by reflection shown,
Whilst Gay once more knows Polly for his own.
Talk not to me of diffidence and fear—
I see it all, but must forgive it here ;
Defects like these, which modest terrors cause,
From Impudence itself extort applause.   710
Candour and Reason still take Virtue's part ;
We love e'en foibles in so good a heart.
Let Tommy Arne, with usual pomp of style,
Whose chief, whose only merit's to compile,
Who, meanly pilfering here and there a bit,
Deals music out as Murphy deals out wit,
Publish proposals, laws for taste prescribe,
And chaunt the praise of an Italian tribe ;
Let him reverse kind Nature's first decrees,
And teach e'en Brent a method not to please ; 720
But never shall a truly British age

[703] Mrs. Vincent, afterwards Mrs. Mills, was more admired
as a melodious singer than for her talents as an actress, she
seems by her amiable diffidence to have obtained from our
author at least her full share of commendation. She had in
early life been, during several seasons, a favourite singer at
Marybone Gardens, and died Sept. 1811.

[706] The original performer of Polly Peachum was Miss
Fenton, with whose representation of it, the Duke of Bolton
was so delighted as to take her from the stage and make her
his wife.

[713] Thomas Augustine Arne, the famous musician, and
brother to Mrs. Cibber, was born in 1710, and educated at
Eton. In 1759 he had the degree of doctor of music con-
ferred on him by the University of Oxford. He died in
1778.

[720] Miss Brent, a scholar of Dr. Arne, at her outset made
a tender of her abilities to Garrick at a very moderate salary,
but met with a peremptory refusal. Garrick had good reason

Bear a vile race of eunuchs on the stage;
The boasted work's call'd National in vain,
If one Italian voice pollutes the strain.
Where tyrants rule, and slaves with joy obey,
Let slavish minstrels pour the enervate lay;
To Britons far more noble pleasures spring,
In native notes, whilst Beard and Vincent sing.

Might figure give a title unto fame,
What rival should with Yates dispute her claim?

to repent his hastiness, for Beard immediately engaged her, and she most powerfully contributed to his very successful competition with Drury Lane. Miss Brent was deficient in the beauty as well as the form necessary to represent the amiable simplicity of Polly Peachum; but such were the fascinating powers of her voice, though in her style absolutely wide of the author's original design, (who intended no more than the giving a common ballad tune in the simplest manner), that London seemed to be better pleased with the Beggar's Opera than when the parts were originally acted by Tom Walker and the celebrated Miss Fenton. In vain did Garrick oppose his prime characters in tragedy and comedy to Polly Peachum; she irresistibly attracted all ranks to her performance, and united all suffrages in her favour. Beard followed this blow with the popular opera of Artaxerxes; the public were allured by nothing but the power of sound and sing-song, and Shakespeare and Garrick were obliged to leave the field to Beard and Brent. It is thought that this success of Covent Garden in 1763 contributed not a little to Garrick's determination to visit the Continent that year. Miss Brent afterwards married Mr. Pinto, a celebrated performer on the violin. She survived both her husband and her voice, and incurred much pecuniary distress by the double misfortune.

[728] John Beard married a daughter of Rich, and in 1761 succeeded him in the management of Covent Garden Theatre. He retired from the stage in 1767, after having been some years afflicted with deafness, and died in 1791, at the age of seventy-four years.

[730] Anna Maria Yates, the wife of Richard Yates, who has been mentioned in a preceding note. Her husband was so

But justice may not partial trophies raise,   731
Nor sink the actress in the woman's praise.
Still hand in hand her words and actions go,
And the heart feels more than the features show;
For, through the regions of that beauteous face,
We no variety of passions trace;
Dead to the soft emotions of the heart,
No kindred softness can those eyes impart:
The brow, still fix'd in sorrow's sullen frame,
Void of distinction, marks all parts the same.   740
   What's a fine person, or a beauteous face,
Unless deportment gives them decent grace?
Bless'd with all other requisites to please,
Some want the striking elegance of ease;
The curious eye their awkward movement tires:
They seem like puppets led about by wires.
Others, like statues, in one posture still,
Give great ideas of the workman's skill;
Wond'ring, his art we praise the more we view,
And only grieve he gave not motion too.   750
Weak of themselves are what we beauties call;
It is the manner which gives strength to all;
This teaches every beauty to unite,
And brings them forward in the noblest light:
Happy in this, behold, amidst the throng,

highly incensed with Churchill for presuming to censure his
wife, that he invited him to a tavern, with an intention, as
was supposed, either of expostulating with him on his conduct, or of bringing the matter to a more decisive discussion.
But Mr. George Garrick hearing for what purpose they had
withdrawn, ran to the place of meeting, and, though the
contending parties were much enraged, was so happy as to
reconcile them over a hearty bottle. Mrs. Yates died in
1787.

With transient gleam of grace, Hart sweeps along.
  If all the wonders of external grace,
A person finely turn'd, a mould of face,
Where, union rare, expression's lively force
With beauty's softest magic holds discourse,   760
Attract the eye; if feelings void of art
Rouse the quick passions, and inflame the heart;
If music, sweetly breathing from the tongue,
Captives the ear, Bride must not pass unsung.

756 Mrs. Hart was the daughter of a respectable tradesman
in St. James's, from whose house she eloped with a favoured
lover, and afterwards, by the elegance of her figure, obtained
an engagement at Covent Garden theatre; but being possessed of no other claim to public favour, she grew tired of
the insignificance of her theatrical character, and quitting
the stage, took no farther pains to support any character at
all. She then married one Reddish, an inferior actor, who
was induced to take her for the sake of an annuity of £200,
settled on her by a former admirer. Reddish afterwards
married the widow of George Canning, and mother of the
late Right Honourable George Canning, whom she lived to
see in the plenitude of his power, and who always treated
her with affectionate respect, occasionally visiting her at
Bath, and addressing a letter invariably to her on every Sun-
day throughout the year. She after Reddish's death married
a Mr. Hunn, whom she also survived.

764 Our author considerably over-rated the abilities but
not the personal attractions of this actress, which procured
for her the protection of the wealthy army agent, John Cal-
craft, who occupies a prominent position in the Memoirs of
the celebrated Mrs. Bellamy. He bequeathed to Miss Bride
a large pecuniary legacy and two annuities of £1000 and
£500, the latter to cease should she marry. He also left to
each of his children by her and by Mrs. Bellamy £10,000,
and eventually his son by the latter succeeded to large landed
estates in Lincolnshire and Dorsetshire, and many years represented his own rotten borough of Wareham in Parliament.
In 1770 she forfeited her second annuity by marrying a gentleman of some consideration, and also a member of the then
House of Commons for some other rotten borough.

When fear, which rank ill-nature terms conceit,
By time and custom conquer'd, shall retreat;
When judgment, tutor'd by experience sage,
Shall shoot abroad, and gather strength from age;
When Heaven, in mercy, shall the stage release
From the dull slumbers of a still-life piece;   770
When some stale flower, disgraceful to the walk,
Which long hath hung, though wither'd, on the
    stalk,
Shall kindly drop, then Bride shall make her way,
And merit find a passage to the day;
Brought into action, she at once shall raise
Her own renown, and justify our praise.

    Form'd for the tragic scene, to grace the stage
With rival excellence of love and rage,
Mistress of each soft art, with matchless skill
To turn and wind the passions as she will;   780
To melt the heart with sympathetic woe,
Awake the sigh, and teach the tear to flow;
To put on frenzy's wild, distracted glare,
And freeze the soul with horror and despair;
With just desert enroll'd in endless fame,
Conscious of worth superior, Cibber came.

[771] An unkind allusion to Mrs. Palmer, the daughter of
Mrs. Pritchard, whose listlessness and want of animation
our author has previously animadverted on under the name
of Statira. Her mother's influence obtained for her a position
at the theatre far beyond her ability adequately to sustain.
[786] Mrs. Susannah Maria Cibber was the daughter of Mr.
Arne, an upholsterer in King-street, Covent Garden, and was
sister to the celebrated composer of that name. In 1734 she
married Theophilus Cibber, and became a pupil of his father
Colley, to whose instructions she was considerably indebted
for her future eminence. Her wretched husband literally
sold her honour and his own to a gentleman, against whom

When poor Alicia's madd'ning brains are rack'd,
And strongly imaged griefs her mind distract,
Struck with her grief, I catch the madness too;
My brain turns round, the headless trunk I view!
The roof cracks, shakes, and falls!—new horrors
      rise,   791
And Reason buried in the ruin lies.

Nobly disdainful of each slavish art,
She makes her first attack upon the heart;
Pleased with the summons, it receives her laws,
And all is silence, sympathy, applause.

But when, by fond ambition drawn aside,
Giddy with praise, and puff'd with female pride,
She quits the tragic scene, and, in pretence

be afterwards commenced a suit in the King's Bench, and
recovered ten pounds damages. She continued to live with
that gentleman till her death, on 30 Jan. 1766. Her person was perfectly elegant; for although she somewhat declined beyond the bloom of youth, and even wanted that
embonpoint which sometimes assists in concealing the impression made by the hand of time, yet there was so complete a
symmetry and proportion in the different parts of her
form, that it was impossible to view her figure and not
think her young, or look in her face and not consider
her handsome. Her voice was beyond conception plaintive
and musical, yet far from deficient in the power of express-
ing resentment or disdain; and such equal command of
feature did she possess for the representation of pity or
rage, of pride or complacence, that it would be difficult to
say whether she affected the hearts of an audience most,
when playing the gentle, delicate Celia, or the haughty,
resentful Hermione; in the innocent, love-sick Juliet, or
the forsaken, enraged Alicia. In a word, through every
cast of tragedy she was excellent, and but for Mrs. Pritchard,
supreme. She made some attempts in comedy, but they
were in no degree equal to her efforts in the tragic walk.
Lady Constance, in Shakespeare's King John, was her
favourite part, and in it even Mrs. Pritchard fell below her.

To comic merit breaks down nature's fence, 800
I scarcely can believe my ears or eyes,
Or find out Cibber through the dark disguise.
  Pritchard, by Nature for the stage design'd,

803 Mrs. Hannah Pritchard's maiden name was Vaughan.
She was, when very young, recommended to the notice of
Mr. Booth, who was exceedingly pleased with her manner
of reciting several tragic parts; but not being then in the
management of the theatre, he advised her to apply else-
where. Her first appearance was in one of Fielding's pieces,
in the little Haymarket theatre. Her second attempt was
in Lady Diana Talbot, in Anna Boleyn, at the playhouse in
Goodman's Fields; and soon after she acted at Bartholomew
Fair, where she gained the notice and applause of the public, by her easy, unaffected manner of speaking, and was
greatly caressed and admired for singing in some farce a
droll favourite air, which began with " Sweet, if you love
me, smiling turn." She now obtained an engagement at
Drury Lane; where her graceful person, attractive countenance, expressive yet simple manner, her unembarrassed
deportment and proper action charmed all the spectators.
Rosalind, in As you Like It, at once established her theatrical character: her delivery of dialogue, whether of humour,
wit, or mere sprightliness, was perhaps never equalled. Not
confined to any one walk of acting, she ranged through them
all; and discovered a fund of merit in every distinct class;
her tragic power was eminent, but particularly in characters
which required force of expression and dignity of action.
Churchill has with great discrimination seized her peculiar
excellences, and given a finished portrait of her, in her prime
characters of Lady Macbeth, Zara, and Mrs. Oakly. Her
unblemished conduct in private life justly increased her
favour with all ranks of people, and few actresses were ever
so sincerely beloved and powerfully patronised as Mrs. Pritchard. After having trod the stage six and thirty years,
Mrs. Pritchard.in 1768 resolved to withdraw into retirement,
and spend the remainder of her life at Bath. To this she
was tempted by the prospect of great advantages, which
were to accrue to her from a legacy of one Mr. Thomas
Leonard, an attorney, of Lyon's-Inn, a distant relation, who
died in 1766, and of whose will her brother, Mr. Henry

In person graceful, and in sense refined;
Her art as much as Nature's friend became,
Her voice as free from blemish as her fame;
Who knows so well in majesty to please,
Attemper'd with the graceful charms of ease?
When Congreve's favour'd pantomime to grace,
She comes a captive queen of Moorish race;   810
When love, hate, jealousy, despair and rage,
With wildest tumults in her breast engage,
Still equal to herself is Zara seen;
Her passions are the passions of a Queen.
When she to murder whets the tim'rous thane,
I feel ambition rush through every vein;
Persuasion hangs upon her daring tongue,
My heart grows flint, and every nerve's new strung.
In comedy—"Nay, there," cries Critic, " hold;
Pritchard's for comedy too fat and old: 820
Who can, with patience, bear the gray coquette,
Or force a laugh with over-grown Julett?
Her speech, look, action, humour, all are just,
But then her age and figure give disgust."
Are foibles then, and graces of the mind,
In real life, to size or age confined?

Vaughan, was the executor. But whatever might have
been the intention of the testator by his will, the bulk of his
estate fell to the heirs at law, who were nearer relations.
Mrs. Pritchard took leave of the public in an epilogue written by Mr. Garrick, after the performance of Macbeth for
her benefit; she spoke it with many sobs and tears, which
were increased by the generous feelings of a numerous and
splendid audience. She died at Bath about four months
after, in the fifty-seventh year of her age.
822 A part in the then revived comedy of the Pilgrim, by
Beaumont and Fletcher, in the dramatis personæ of which
Juletta is designated as Alinda's maid, a witty lass,

Do spirits flow, and is good-breeding placed
In any set circumference of waist?
As we grow old, doth affectation cease,
Or gives not age new vigour to caprice?   830
If in originals these things appear,
Why should we bar them in the copy here?
The nice punctilio-mongers of this age,
The grand, minute reformers of the stage,
Slaves to propriety of every kind,
Some standard measure for each part should find,
Which when the best of actors shall exceed,
Let it devolve to one of smaller breed.
All Actors, too, upon the back should bear
Certificate of birth;—time, when;—place, where;
For how can critics rightly fix their worth,   841
Unless they know the minute of their birth?
An audience, too, deceived, may find, too late,
That they have clapp'd an actor out of date.

Figure, I own, at first may give offence,
And harshly strike the eye's too curious sense;
But when perfections of the mind break forth,
Humour's chaste sallies, judgment's solid worth;
When the pure genuine flame by Nature taught,
Springs into sense and every action's thought;   850
Before such merit all objections fly;
Pritchard's genteel, and Garrick's six feet high.

Oft have I, Pritchard, seen thy wond'rous skill,
Confess'd thee great, but find thee greater still;
That worth, which shone in scatter'd rays before,
Collected now, breaks forth with double power.
The Jealous Wife! on that thy trophies raise,

---

⁸⁵⁷ The Jealous Wife, by Colman, was first acted in 1761
with extraordinary success, and still maintains an honour-

Inferior only to the author's praise.

From Dublin, famed in legends of romance
For mighty magic of enchanted lance,   860
With which her heroes arm'd victorious prove,
And, like a flood, rush o'er the land of Love,
Mossop and Barry came.—Names ne'er design'd
By Fate in the same sentence to be join'd.
Raised by the breath of popular acclaim,
They mounted to the pinnacle of fame;
There the weak brain, made giddy with the height,
Spurr'd on the rival chiefs to mortal fight.
Thus sportive boys around some basin's brim
Behold the pipe-drawn bladders circling swim; 870
But if, from lungs more potent, there arise
Two bubbles of a more than common size,
Eager for honour, they for fight prepare,
Bubble meets bubble, and both sink to air.

Mossop, attach'd to military plan,
Still kept his eye fix'd on his right-hand man;

able rank in the list of acting plays. The Reviews animadverted with much severity on the lax morality of some of the
scenes, and with some justice reprehended that part of it which
is taken from the story of Lady Bellaston, in Tom Jones.

875 Henry Mossop. This unfortunate man was the son of
a clergyman, and liberally educated; though ungraceful in
deportment and undignified in action, awkward in his whole
behaviour, and hard in his expression, he was yet in degree of
stage excellence the third actor of his time; a Garrick and a
Barry only were his superiors; in parts of vehemence and rage
he was almost unequalled; and in sentimental gravity, from
the power of his voice and the justness of his elocution, he was
a very commanding speaker. After having been several
years in the service of Mr. Garrick, Mossop in 1760, left it
to go to Dublin, where Barry and Woodward engaged him
at a considerable salary. He had scarcely finished one successful campaign with these new masters, when he unhap-
pily yielded to a strong inclination to become a manager, he

Whilst the mouth measures words with seeming skill,
The right hand labours, and the left lies still ;
For he resolved on scripture-grounds to go,
What the right doth, the left-hand shall not know.
With studied impropriety of speech   881
He soars beyond the hackney critic's reach ;
To epithets allots emphatic state,
Whilst principals, ungraced, like lackeys, wait ;
In ways first trodden by himself excels,
And stands alone in indeclinables ;
Conjunction, preposition, adverb, join
To stamp new vigour on the nervous line ;
In monosyllables his thunders roll,
He, she, it, and, we, ye, they, fright the soul. 890
    In person taller than the common size,
Behold where Barry draws admiring eyes !

accordingly refused the large offer of £1000 a year to relinquish his scheme, and under the patronage of some titled
ladies, " the damaged Quality," as Mrs. Clive with equal
wit and truth styled them, formed a company at the theatre
in Smock Alley.   After struggling in vain for seven or eight
years, with a variety of difficulties, and being reduced at last
to absolute bankruptcy, he left Ireland, and arrived in London not a little impaired in health.   He here endeavoured
to be again engaged at Drury Lane, but Mr. Garrick had
been so offended by the injudicious conduct of Mossop and
his friends, among whom Fitzpatrick rendered himself most
conspicuous, in endeavouring to persuade the public of their
equality as actors, that he met with a decided negative: he
then applied to the managers of Covent Garden, who returned for answer, that their arrangements were so made as
to put it out of their power to employ him.   This answer
was supposed to be made in consequence of a very celebrated
actress having refused to act in any play with this unhappy
man.   He died in a few days after of a broken heart, and in
great poverty, November, 1773.
    892 Spranger Barry was born in Dublin in 1719, and bred
a silversmith, which trade he abandoned for the theatre, and

When labouring passions, in his bosom pent,
Convulsive, rage, and struggling heave for vent,
Spectators, with imagined terrors warm,
Anxious expect the bursting of the storm;
But, all unfit in such a pile to dwell,
His voice comes forth, like Echo from her cell

made his first attempt in the character of Othello in 1744.
In 1747 he came to England, and was engaged at Drury
Lane, which he soon quitted for Covent Garden, and proved
a formidable rival to Garrick, who was the leader of the
other house.   In 1758 he went to Ireland, and jointly with
Woodward was concerned in two new playhouses, one at
Dublin and the other at Cork; these failing, he returned to
England, where he was engaged by Mr. Foote, at the Haymarket; and in 1766 he accepted the proposals of Mr. Garrick, for himself and his wife, at the liberal salary of £1500
per annum.   Mrs. Barry was then gradually rising to that
excellence in her profession which soon ranked her among the
most celebrated actresses.   An increase of £200 a year in
their salary tempted Mr. and Mrs. Barry in the year 1774 to
leave Drury Lane for Covent Garden. An hereditary gout increased upon him at this time, and such were the encroachments it made upon his powers of acting, that his defects
became too visible to the audience.   He died January 10,
1777.   Of all the tragic actors who have trod the stage during the last hundred years, excepting only Garrick, and not
excepting the principal tragedians of our later period, Kem-
ble, Cooke, Young, Kean, and Macready, Mr. Barry appears
to have been the most pleasing, and notwithstanding the
defects which the poet has justly, though perhaps too
severely reprehended, he established in many of his perform-
ances an equality with Garrick, and in Othello and a few
other parts contended for the superiority. His other favourite
characters were, Jaffier, Orestes, Castalio, Phocyas, Varanes,
Essex, Alexander, Romeo, &c.   In all characters of this
stamp, where the lover or hero was to be exhibited, Barry
was *unique;* so much so, that when Mrs. Cibber, whose reputation for love and plaintive tenderness was well known, played
with Garrick, she generally represented his daughter or sister—
with Barry she was always his wife or mistress. He likewise
excelled in many parts of genteel comedy; such as Lord

To swell the tempest needful aid denies,   899
And all adown the stage in feeble murmurs dies.

What man, like Barry, with such pains, can err
In elocution, action, character?
What man could give, if Barry was not here,
Such well applauded tenderness to Lear?
Who else can speak so very, very fine,
That sense may kindly end with every line?

Some dozen lines before the ghost is there,
Behold him for the solemn scene prepare:
See how he frames his eyes, poises each limb,
Puts the whole body into proper trim:—   910
From whence we learn, with no great stretch of art,
Five lines hence comes a ghost, and, ha! a start.

When he appears most perfect, still we find
Something which jars upon and hurts the mind:
Whatever lights upon a part are thrown,
We see too plainly they are not his own:
No flame from Nature ever yet he caught,
Nor knew a feeling which he was not taught:
He raised his trophies on the base of art,   919
And conn'd his passions, as he conn'd his part.

Quin, from afar, lured by the scent of fame,
A stage leviathan, put in his claim,

Townly, Young Bevill, &c. The Bastard in King John
was another exclusive character of his, which Garrick attempted in vain—not having either sufficiency of figure or
of heroic jocularity.

921 Correctly as Churchill seems to have appreciated the
merit of the actor, he has not done justice to the man; for
under a rough exterior James Quin possessed a heart full
of the milk of human kindness. He was born in London
in 1693; his father married a reputed widow, who, after
bearing him this son, was claimed by her first husband,
who returned from abroad, though supposed to have been

Pupil of Betterton and Booth. Alone,
Sullen he walk'd, and deem'd the chair his own:
For how should moderns, mushrooms of the day,
Who ne'er those masters knew, know how to play?
Gray-bearded veterans, who, with partial tongue

dead some years. By this misfortune James lost his father's estate, being deemed illegitimate. He was intended for the law, but studied Shakespeare more than the statutes, and soon displayed his theatric powers at Mr. Rich's theatre, in the character of Falstaff; he continued to be for many years the unrivalled representative of the humorous knight, no one having approached his excellence in that part except, perhaps, Mr. Henderson. At the conclusion of the second season Mr. Quin was engaged at very high terms to perform at Drury Lane, and there he maintained the highest rank till the appearance of Garrick in 1741. Quin, who had hitherto been esteemed the first actor in tragedy, could not conceal his annoyance at the great success of his rival. After he had seen Garrick's Richard, he declared " that if the young fellow was right, he and the rest of the players had been all wrong;" and upon being told that Goodman's Fields theatre was crowded every night to see the new actor, he said " that Garrick was a new religion; Whitefield was followed for a time; but they would all come to church again." Quin enjoyed the intimacy of Pope and of Thomson, who calls him in the Castle of Indolence " the Æsopus of the age." " The commencement of his friendship with the latter," says Dr. Johnson, " is very honourable to Quin, who is reported to have delivered Thomson (then known to him only by his genius) from an arrest, by a very considerable present: and its continuance was honourable to both; for friendship is not always the sequel of obligation." The season of 1741 concluded Quin's engagement at Drury Lane, and he went over to Dublin with Mrs. Clive, Ryan, and others. He there played Cato and Othello with increasing reputation. In 1742, Quin returned to Covent Garden, to oppose Garrick, but with no great success: he afterwards, however, formed a very lucrative engagement with him, and it was agreed by these eminent actors that certain parts should be assumed by them alternately, particularly Richard III. and Othello; but Quin soon

Extol the times when they themselves were young;
Who, having lost all relish for the stage,
See not their own defects, but lash the age,   930
Received, with joyful murmurs of applause,
Their darling chief, and lined his favourite cause.

found his reputation decreasing, while that of Garrick aug-
mented. Quin had been strongly patronized by Frederick
Prince of Wales, and was employed to instruct the royal
children in a correct pronunciation. The dignified propriety
and grace of diction which marked George the Third's first
speech to parliament being mentioned to Quin, he exultingly
exclaimed, "I taught the boy." His last performance was
in the character of Falstaff, March 19, 1753, after which he
retired on a large annuity to Bath, where he died in 1766,
the same year as Mrs. Cibber.

923 Thomas Betterton, the Garrick of the seventeenth century, was born in 1635; he soon attained a great degree of
excellence on the stage, but never received a larger salary
than £4 per week. He died April 28, 1710, and was
buried in Westminster Abbey with much pomp; and great
honour was paid his memory by his friend Sir Richard
Steele, who has related in the Tatler, in the most dignified and pathetic manner, the history of the ceremonial.
Pope, when a mere boy, was introduced to Betterton, who
sat to him for his picture, which Pope drew in oil. It is no
easy task to do justice to the merits of judgment, voice,
and person, which were conspicuous in this actor, who
shone alike in Hotspur, and in Macbeth, in Falstaff, and in
Hamlet. The latter, however, was his masterpiece. In
the traditional history of the stage it is said that Betterton
took every particle of Hamlet from Sir William Davenant,
who had seen Taylor, who was taught by Shakespeare.
The full melody of Betterton's voice possessed so powerful a
charm, as to give grace and dignity to the wildest rhapso-
dies of Lee's Alexander; and what would in any other actor
have appeared the most ludicrous expressions of tumidity
and rant, received a flowing elegance from Betterton which
charmed the ears of his auditors.

923 Barton Booth, an eminent actor of the old school, of
an honourable family, nearly related to the Earls of War-

Far be it from the candid Muse to tread
Insulting o'er the ashes of the dead;
But, just to living merit, she maintains,
And dares the test, whilst Garrick's genius reigns;
Ancients, in vain, endeavour to excel,
Happily praised, if they could act as well.
But, though prescription's force we disallow,
Nor to antiquity submissive bow;   940
Though we deny imaginary grace,
Founded on accidents of time and place,
Yet real worth of every growth shall bear
Due praise; nor must we, Quin, forget thee there.

rington, was educated at Westminster under Dr. Busby, and
was much applauded in the part of Pamphilus in the Andria
at the annual Latin play. He was intended for the church,
but disappointed his parents by engaging himself at the early
age of seventeen to the manager of the Dublin theatre;
from thence, after some ineffectual attempts to draw him
from the stage, he was introduced to Mr. Betterton, who
took him under his protection and tuition. His first performance in London was in 1701, in the part of Maximus
in Lord Rochester's Valentinian, and in 1712 he reached the
summit of his art in Cato, for his admirable performance
of which, the managers presented him with fifty guineas,
and the Whigs and Tories who professed to feel an equal
interest in the plot, made collections on one night in the
boxes, each of them to that amount, which they presented
to him in purses, the one party as a slight acknowledgment
of his "honest opposition to a perpetual dictator," and the
other for his "dying so bravely in the cause of liberty."
His first wife, whom he married in 1704, was a daughter
of Sir William Barkham, Bart. of Norfolk; she dying without issue, he, in 1719, married Miss Hester Santlow, the
celebrated actress, who survived him. He died in 1733, at
about fifty years of age, leaving no issue. Booth is said to
have formed himself upon Betterton, as Quin did upon Booth.
Othello was his masterpiece; but even in that part he was
inferior to his master

His words bore sterling weight; nervous and strong,
In manly tides of sense they roll'd along :
Happy in art, he chiefly had pretence
To keep up numbers, yet not forfeit sense ;
No actor ever greater heights could reach
In all the labour'd artifice of speech.   950

    Speech ! is that all ?—And shall an actor found
An universal fame on partial ground ?
Parrots themselves speak properly by rote,
And, in six months, my dog shall howl by note.
I laugh at those who, when the stage they tread,
Neglect the heart, to compliment the head ;
With strict propriety their care 's confined
To weigh out words, while passion halts behind :
To syllable-dissectors they appeal ;
Allow them accent, cadence,—Fools may feel ; 960
But, spite of all the criticising elves,
Those who would make us feel, must feel themselves.

    His eyes, in gloomy socket taught to roll,
Proclaim'd the sullen " habit of his soul :"
Heavy and phlegmatic he trod the stage,
Too proud for tenderness, too dull for rage.
When Hector's lovely widow shines in tears,
Or Rowe's gay rake dependent virtue jeers,
With the same cast of features he is seen

---

964 Rage on, ye winds; burst, clouds, and waters, roar.
    You bear a just resemblance to my fortune,
    And suit the gloomy habit of my soul.
The part of Zanga in Dr. Young's Revenge, in which these
lines occur, was a favourite character with Quin, as it had
been with Mossop.
967.8 Andromache, in the tragedy of the Distressed Mother,
adapted by Ambrose Philips from the French of Racine; and
Lothario, in the Fair Penitent.

To chide the libertine, and court the queen. 970
From the tame scene, which without passion flows,
With just desert his reputation rose;
Nor less he pleased, when on some surly plan
He was at once the actor and the man.
  In Brute he shone unequall'd: all agree
Garrick's not half so great a brute as he.
When Cato's labour'd scenes are brought to view,
With equal praise the actor labour'd too;
For still you'll find, trace passions to their root,
Small difference 'twixt the Stoic and the Brute.
In fancied scenes, as in life's real plan, 981
He could not, for a moment, sink the man.
In whate'er cast his character was laid,
Self still, like oil, upon the surface play'd.
Nature, in spite of all his skill, crept in:
Horatio, Dorax, Falstaff,—still 'twas Quin.
  Next follows Sheridan;—a doubtful name,
As yet unsettled in the rank of fame:

---

975 Sir John Brute in Vanbrugh's Provoked Wife.
986 Dorax, the rough soldier in Dryden's Don Sebastian.
987 Thomas Sheridan was born at Quilca in Ireland, in
1721. After a classical education, he in 1743 appeared on
the stage in Dublin, and acquired considerable eminence as
a tragedian, particularly in the character of Cato. In the
situation of manager he became very unpopular in that city,
owing to his attempts to prevent any spectators intruding
behind the scenes; and, being compelled to embark for England, was engaged during one season at Covent Garden.
In 1756 he revisited Dublin, where the animosity against
him had subsided, and was received with great applause.
However he soon quitted the Irish stage and commenced
lecturing on elocution, in which he met with signal success;
and was honoured by the university of Dublin with the degree of M.A. At the accession of George the Third a pension was granted to him, and in 1763 he read a course of

This, fondly lavish in his praises grown,
Gives him all merit ; that allows him none ;   990
Between them both, we'll steer the middle course,
Nor, loving praise, rob Judgment of her force.
　　Just his conceptions, natural and great ;
His feelings strong, his words enforced with weight.
Was speech-famed Quin himself to hear him speak,
Envy would drive the colour from his cheek ;
But step-dame Nature, niggard of her grace,
Denied the social powers of voice and face.
Fix'd in one frame of features, glare of eye,
Passions, like chaos, in confusion lie :   1000
In vain the wonders of his skill are tried
To form distinctions Nature hath denied.
His voice no touch of harmony admits,
Irregularly deep, and shrill by fits.
The two extremes appear like man and wife,
Coupled together for the sake of strife.
　　His action's always strong, but sometimes such,
That candour must declare he acts too much.
Why must impatience fall three paces back ?
Why paces three return to the attack ?   1010
Why is the right leg, too, forbid to stir,
Unless in motion semicircular ?
Why must the hero with the Nailor vie,
And hurl the close-clench'd fist at nose or eye ?
In royal John, with Philip angry grown,
I thought he would have knock'd poor Davies down.

elegant lectures on elocution to numerous audiences in the
universities of Oxford and Cambridge. In 1778 he compiled a Dictionary of the English language with respect
chiefly to its orthoepy. He published his Life of Swift in
1784, and died in 1788.

Inhuman tyrant! was it not a shame
To fright a king so harmless and so tame?
But, spite of all defects, his glorics rise,   1019
And art, by judgment form'd, with nature vies.
Behold him sound the depth of Hubert's soul,
Whilst in his own contending passions roll;
View the whole scene, with critic judgment scan,
And then deny him merit if you can.
Where he falls short, 'tis Nature's fault alone;
Where he succeeds, the merit's all his own.
    Last Garrick came.—Behind him throng a train

1027 David Garrick was the son of Peter Garrick of Lich-
field, a captain in the army. He was born in 1716. In
1737, he with his townsman and instructor Dr. Samuel
Johnson, came to London to seek his fortune, where he first
entered himself of Lincoln's Inn, with a view to the Bar, and
afterwards entered into partnership with his brother Peter in
the wine trade. In 1741, after experiencing some slights
from the managers of Drury Lane and Covent Garden, he
determined to make trial of his theatrical qualifications at
the playhouse in Goodman's Fields, under the direction of
Mr. Giffard. The part he chose for his first appearance was
that of Richard the Third, in which he displayed so clear a
conception of the character, such power of execution, and an
union of talent so varied and extensive, that he soon
established his reputation as the first actor of the age. In
the whole range of low comedy he blended such a knowledge
of art with the simplicity of nature, as made all the minutiæ
of the picture complete. His Abel Drugger was as perfect
in conception and execution as his Lear. His fame spread
through every part of the town with the greatest rapidity;
and Goodman's Fields theatre, which had been frequented
only by the inhabitants of the city, became the resort of
fashion, and was honoured with the notice of all ranks and
orders of people. At Goodman's Fields Mr. Garrick re-
mained but one season, and then removed to Drury Lane,
where he continued till Fleetwood's mismanagement and
want of prudence brought that theatre to the brink of
ruin. Rich of Covent Garden availed himself of the folly

Of snarling critics, ignorant as vain.

One finds out,—"He's of stature somewhat low—
Your hero always should be tall you know,— 1030
True natural greatness all consists in height,"
Produce your voucher, Critic.—" Serjeant Kite."

Another can't forgive the paltry arts

of his brother manager, and engaged Garrick in his service;
here he continued only one year, when Rich refusing him
an adequate share in the profits, Garrick closed with Lacy,
then the sole proprietor of the Drury Lane theatre, for a
moiety of the patent at £8000, which sum by a strict
attention to economy he had accumulated. This transaction
took place in 1747, and his joint management with Lacy
continued with uninterrupted cordiality and success, until the
death of the latter in 1773, when the whole management
devolved on the survivor.

In June, 1749, Garrick married Mademoiselle Violetta, a
native of Vienna and a famous dancer, first to the Queen of
George the Second, then at the playhouse; she was of un-
exceptionable moral character, and a protégé of Dorothy,
Countess of Burlington; she was a beautiful woman, and was
in such favour at Burlington House, that the tickets for her
benefit were designed by Kent and engraved by Vertue. She
merited and secured the attachment of Garrick, and the respect
of his friends and of a large circle of society; she survived
him forty-three years, dying in October, 1822, at the advanced
age of ninety.

At length an event took place which the admirers of theatrical entertainments had long expected with concern, and
now viewed with regret. Mr. Garrick, at a period when
his powers had suffered little injury from time, and in the
height of his fame and popularity, determined to relinquish
his connexion with the stage, and retire to the honourable
enjoyment of a large fortune [not less than £140,000]
acquired in the course of nearly forty years spent in the service of the public. His last appearance was in the character
of Don Felix, in the play of the Wonder, acted 10th June,
1776, for the benefit of a charity. He died on the 20th of
January, 1779.

1032 The recruiting serjeant in Farquhar's lively comedy
of the Recruiting Officer.

By which he makes his way to shallow hearts;
Mere pieces of finesse, traps for applause.—
"Avaunt! unnatural start, affected pause."

For me, by Nature form'd to judge with phlegm,
I can't acquit by wholesale, nor condemn.
The best things carried to excess are wrong;
The start may be too frequent, pause too long;
But, only used in proper time and place,   1041
Severest judgment must allow them grace.

If bunglers, form'd on Imitation's plan,
Just in the way that monkeys mimic man,
Their copied scene with mangled arts disgrace,
And pause and start with the same vacant face,
We join the critic laugh; those tricks we scorn
Which spoil the scenes they mean them to adorn;
But when, from Nature's pure and genuine source,
These strokes of acting flow with generous force,
When in the features all the soul's portray'd,   1051
And passions, such as Garrick's, are display'd,
To me they seem from quickest feelings caught,
Each start is nature, and each pause is thought.

When reason yields to passion's wild alarms,
And the whole state of man is up in arms,
What but a critic could condemn the player
For pausing here, when cool sense pauses there?
Whilst, working from the heart, the fire I trace,
And mark it strongly flaming to the face;   1060
Whilst in each sound I hear the very man,
I can't catch words, and pity those who can.

[1062] Horace Walpole, in a letter to Sir Horace Mann,
dated 26 May, 1742, thus reported his opinion of Garrick at
that early but brilliant period of his career. "But all the
run is now after Garrick, a wine merchant, who is turned

Let wits, like spiders, from the tortured brain
Fine-draw the critic-web with curious pain ;
The gods,—a kindness I with thanks must pay,—
Have form'd me of a coarser kind of clay,
Nor stung with envy, nor with spleen diseased,
A poor dull creature, still with Nature pleased :
Hence to thy praises, Garrick, I agree,
And, pleased with Nature, must be pleased with
     thee.   1070
Now might I tell, how silence reign'd throughout,
And deep attention hush'd the rabble rout ;
How every claimant, tortured with desire,
Was pale as ashes, or as red as fire ;
But loose to fame, the Muse more simply acts,
Rejects all flourish, and relates mere facts.
    The judges, as the several parties came,
With temper heard, with judgment weigh'd each
     claim,
And, in their sentence happily agreed,   1079
In name of both great Shakespeare thus decreed :
  " If manly sense, if Nature link'd with art ;
If thorough knowledge of the human heart ;
If powers of acting vast and unconfined ;
If fewest faults with greatest beauties join'd ;
If strong expression, and strange powers which lie
Within the magic circle of the eye ;
If feelings which few hearts, like his, can know,
And which no face so well as his can show,

---

player at Goodman's Fields. He plays all parts, and is a
very good mimic. His acting I have seen, and may say to
you who will not tell it again here, I see nothing wonderful
in it, but it is heresy to say so ; the Duke of Argyle says he
is superior to Betterton."

Deserve the preference;—Garrick! take the chair,
Nor quit it—till thou place an equal there." 1090

1090 Dr. Johnson, with his usual force of expression, paid
a just tribute to the memory of his deceased friend. "At
this man's (Mr. Walmsley's) table I enjoyed many cheerful
and instructive hours, with companions such as are not often
to be found; with one who has lengthened, and one who has
gladdened life; with Dr. James, whose skill in physic will
be long remembered; and with David Garrick, whom I
hoped to have gratified with this character of our common
friend; but, what are the hopes of man! I am disappointed
by that stroke of death which has eclipsed the gaiety of nations, and impoverished the public stock of harmless pleasure."—*Life of* EDMUND SMITH.

SUPPLEMENTAL NOTES TO THE ROSCIAD.

THE sensation occasioned by the publication of the Rosciad may in some degree be estimated by the swarm of poems and pamphlets to which it gave rise: subjoined are the titles of a few only of the best, where almost all were bad.

The Churchiliad, or a few modest questions addressed to the Reverend Author of the Rosciad.

An Epistle to the Author of the Rosciad and the Apology. Thus noticed in the Monthly Review:—

An exhortation to renounce satire and
to the admiring throng
In sweetest notes pour forth the moral song,
ding dong.

The Smithfield Rosciad. By the Author.

An Epistle to C. Churchill, Author of the Rosciad, by D. Hayes, Esq.

An Epistle to C. Churchill, Author of the Rosciad, by R. Lloyd.

The Triumvirate, a poetical portrait taken from the life, and finished after the manner of Swift. By Veritas.

A Parody on the Rosciad of Churchill.

The Anti-Rosciad. By the Author. (This was written by Dr. Thomas Morell, as he informed Mr. Steevens).

The Rosciad of Covent Garden. By the Author. (H. J. Pye).

The Apology, addressed to the Reviewers. By — Esq. author of the Rosciad of Covent Garden.

The Battle of the Players. By the Author.

The Four Farthing Candles, &c. &c.

THE APOLOGY.

ADDRESSED TO THE CRITICAL REVIEWERS.

THIS poem, which was published in April, 1761, was occasioned by the very extraordinary critique upon the Rosciad by the Critical Review soon after the publication of that poem. The Monthly Review cautiously abstained from all mention of it, until a second edition proclaimed the author's name, when it received reluctant praise for its merits, and defects were studiously exposed. The charge of unprovoked hostility cannot therefore in this instance be imputed with justice to our author.

Smollett, the editor of, and principal contributor to the Critical Review, exculpated himself from the charge of being the author of the critique on the Rosciad, in a letter to Mr. Garrick; but so warm was Churchill in his temper, and so prone to take offence, that besides satirising the writer of the Journal, he extended his resentment to Archibald Hamilton, the printer. Their being both Scotchmen certainly did not operate in mitigation of their punishment.

The feverish anxiety of Garrick in consequence of the altered tone respecting him in the Apology, from what it was in the Rosciad, is characteristically displayed in the following propitiatory letter to Lloyd, who most probably exercised his soothing influence over his capricious friend, and effected a truce, if not a cordial peace between the bard and the too sensitive actor.

Hampton, Friday.

DEAR SIR,—Whenever I am happy in the acquaintance of a man of genius and letters, I never let any mean ill-grounded suspicions creep into my mind to disturb that happiness : whatever he says. I am inclined and bound to

believe, and, therefore, I must desire you not to vex yourself with unnecessary delicacy upon my account. I see and
read so much of Mr. Churchill's spirit, without having the
pleasure of his acquaintance, that I am persuaded that his
genius disdains any direction, and that resolutions once
taken by him will withstand the warmest importunities of
his friends. At the first reading of his Apology, I was so
charmed and raised with the power of his writing, that I
really forgot that I was delighted when I ought to have
been alarmed; this puts me in mind of the Highland officer,
who was so warmed and elevated by the heat of the battle
that he had forgot, till he was reminded by the smarting,
that he had received no less than eleven wounds in different
parts of his body. All I have to say, or will say upon the
occasion is this: if Mr. Churchill has attacked his pasteboard
Majesty of Drury Lane from resentment, I should be sorry
for it, though I am conscious it is ill-founded; if he has attacked me merely because I am the *Punch of the Puppet-shew*,
I sha'nt turn my back upon him and salute him in Punch's
fashion; but make myself easy with this thought—that my
situation made the attack necessary, and that it would have
been a pity that so much strong high-coloured poetry should
have been thrown away, either in *justice* or in *friendship*, on so
insignificant a person as myself. In his *Rosciad* he raised
me too high, in his Apology he may have sunk me too low;
he has done as the Israelites did, made an idol of a calf, and
now *the idol dwindles to a calf again.* He has thought fit a
few weeks ago to declare me the best Actor of my time
(which, by the bye, is no great compliment, if there is as
much truth as wit in his Apology), and I will shew the superiority I have over my brethren upon this occasion, by
seeming at least that I am not dissatisfied, and appear as I
once saw a poor soldier on the parade, who was acting a
pleasantry of countenance, while his back was most wofully
striped with the cat-o'-nine-tails. To be a little serious—
you mentioned to me sometime ago, that Mr. Churchill was
displeased with me—you must have known whether justly
or not—if the first, you should certainly have opened your
heart to me and have heard *my* Apology—if the last, you
should as a common friend to both have vindicated me, and
then I might have escaped *his* Apology; but be it this, or
that, or t'other, I am still his great admirer, and, Dear Sir,
Your sincere Friend, and most humble Servant,

To Mr. Lloyd.   D. GARRICK.

The original of the above is one of a very valuable collection of contemporary autograph letters which belonged to the late Mr. Pickering, and appears to have been reclaimed by Garrick, by whom it is thus indorsed:—A letter from me to Lloyd about Churchill's Apology.

> Tristitiam et Metus
> Tradam protervis in mare *Criticum*[1]
> Portare ventis.
>
> HORACE, Od. 26.

AUGHS not the heart when giants, big
    with pride,
    Assume the pompous port, the martial
    stride;
O'er arm Herculean heave the enormous shield,
Vast as a weaver's beam the javelin wield;
With the loud voice of thundering Jove defy
And dare to single combat—What?—A fly.
    And laugh we less when giant names, which
        shine   ,
Establish'd, as it were, by right divine,
Critics, whom every captive art adores,
To whom glad Science pours forth all her stores; 10
Who high in letter'd reputation sit,
And hold, Astræa-like, the scales of wit,
With partial rage rush forth,—Oh! shame to tell!
To crush a bard just bursting from the shell?
    Great are his perils in this stormy time
Who rashly ventures on a sea of rhyme:
Around vast surges roll, winds envious blow,

[1] So printed in the 2nd, 5th, and 6th 4to. editions evidently a pun is intended.

And jealous rocks and quicksands lurk below :
Greatly his foes he dreads, but more his friends ;
He hurts me most who lavishly commends.   20
    Look through the world—in every other trade
The same employment's cause of kindness made,
At least appearance of good-will creates,
And every fool puffs off the fool he hates :
Cobblers with cobblers smoke away the night,
And in the common cause e'en players unite :
Authors alone, with more than savage rage,
Unnatural war with brother authors wage.
The pride of Nature would as soon admit
Competitors in empire as in wit ;   30
Onward they rush at Fame's imperious call,
And, less than greatest, would not be at all.
    Smit with the love of honour,—or the pence,—
O'errun with wit, and destitute of sense,
Should any novice in the rhyming trade
With lawless pen the realms of verse invade,
Forth from the court, where sceptred sages sit,
Abused with praise, and flatter'd into wit ;
Where in lethargic majesty they reign,
And what they won by dulness, still maintain,   40
Legions of factious authors throng at once,
Fool beckons fool, and dunce awakens dunce.
To Hamilton's the ready lies repair,—
Ne'er was lie made which was not welcome there—
Thence, on maturer judgment's anvil wrought,
The polish'd falsehood's into public brought.
Quick-circulating slanders mirth afford ;

---

[43] Foote observed to some one who praised Hamilton as a
well read man, " I grant you he reads a great many proofs,
but they are no great proofs of his reading."

And reputation bleeds in every word.
   A critic was of old a glorious name,
Whose sanction handed merit up to fame ;   50
Beauties as well as faults he brought to view,
His judgment great, and great his candour too ;
No servile rules drew sickly taste aside ;
Secure he walk'd, for Nature was his guide.
But now, O, strange reverse! our critics bawl
In praise of candour with a heart of gall ;
Conscious of guilt, and fearful of the light,
They lurk enshrouded in the veil of night ;
Safe from detection, seize the unwary prey,
And stab, like bravoes, all who come that way. 60
   When first my Muse, perhaps more bold than wise,
Bade the rude trifle into light arise,
Little she thought such tempests would ensue ;
Less, that those tempests would be raised by you.
The thunder's fury rends the towering oak,
Rosciads; like shrubs, might 'scape the fatal stroke.
Vain thought! a critic's fury knows no bound ;
Drawcansir-like, he deals destruction round ;
Nor can we hope he will a stranger spare,
Who gives no quarter to his friend Voltaire.   70
   Unhappy Genius! placed by partial Fate
With a free spirit in a slavish state ;
Where the reluctant Muse, oppress'd by kings,
Or droops in silence, or in fetters sings.
In vain thy dauntless fortitude hath borne
The bigot's furious zeal, and tyrant's scorn.
Why didst thou safe from home-bred dangers steer,
Reserved to perish more ignobly here ?

[59] Some editions have "detraction" for "detection."
[70] This refers to Dr. Smollett.

Thus, when, the Julian tyrant's pride to swell,
Rome with her Pompey at Pharsalia fell,   80
The vanquish'd chief escaped from Cæsar's hand,
To die by ruffians in a foreign land.
    How could these self-elected monarchs raise
So large an empire on so small a base?
In what retreat, inglorious and unknown,
Did Genius sleep when Dulness seized the throne?
Whence, absolute now grown, and free from awe,
She to the subject world dispenses law.
Without her license not a letter stirs,
And all the captive criss-cross-row is hers.   90
The Stagyrite, who rules from Nature drew,
Opinions gave, but gave his reasons too.
Our great Dictators take a shorter way—
Who shall dispute what the Reviewers say?
Their word's sufficient; and to ask a reason,
In such a state as theirs, is downright treason.
True judgment now with them alone can dwell;
Like Church of Rome, they're grown infallible.
Dull, superstitious readers they deceive,
Who pin their easy faith on critic's sleeve,   100
And, knowing nothing, every thing believe.
But why repine we that these puny elves
Shoot into giants?—we may thank ourselves:
Fools that we are, like Israel's fools of yore,
The calf ourselves have fashion'd we adore.
But let true reason once resume her reign,
This god shall dwindle to a calf again.
    Founded on arts which shun the face of day,
By the same arts they still maintain their sway.

    90 A corruption of Christ-cross-row, an old name for the
Alphabet.

Wrapp'd in mysterious secrecy they rise, 110
And, as they are unknown, are safe and wise.
At whomsoever aim'd, howe'er severe,
The envenom'd slander flies, no names appear:
Prudence forbids that step;—then all might know,
And on more equal terms engage the foe.
But now, what Quixote of the age would care
To wage a war with dirt, and fight with air!
By interest join'd, the expert confederates stand,
And play the game into each other's hand:
The vile abuse, in turn by all denied, 120
Is bandied up and down from side to side:
It flies—hey!—presto!—like a juggler's ball,
Till it belongs to nobody at all.
   All men and things they know, themselves un-
       known,
And publish every name—except their own.
Nor think this strange—secure from vulgar eyes,
The nameless author passes in disguise;
But veteran critics are not so deceived,
If veteran critics are to be believed.
Once seen, they know an author evermore, 130
Nay, swear to hands they never saw before.
Thus in the Rosciad, beyond chance or doubt,
They by the writing found the writers out.
"That's Lloyd's—his manner there you plainly
       trace,
And all the Actor stares you in the face.
By Colman that was written—on my life,
The strongest symptoms of the Jealous Wife.
That little disingenuous piece of spite,
Churchill, a wretch unknown! perhaps might write."
How doth it make judicious readers smile, 140

When authors are detected by their style!
Though every one, who knows this author, knows
He shifts his style much oftener than his clothes.
    Whence could arise this mighty critic spleen,
The Muse a trifler, and her theme so mean?
What had I done, that angry heaven should send
The bitterest foe where most I wish'd a friend?
Oft hath my tongue been wanton at thy name,
And hail'd the honours of thy matchless fame.
For me let hoary Fielding bite the ground,   150
So nobler Pickle stand superbly bound;
From Livy's temples tear th' historic crown,
Which with more justice blooms upon thine own.
Compared with thee, be all life-writers dumb,
But he who wrote the Life of Tommy Thumb.
Who ever read the Regicide, but swore
The author wrote as man ne'er wrote before?
Others for plots and under-plots may call,
Here's the right method—have no plot at all.
Who can so often in his cause engage   160
The tiny pathos of the Grecian stage,
Whilst horrors rise, and tears spontaneous flow
At tragic Ha! and no less tragic Oh!
To praise his nervous weakness all agree,
And then, for sweetness, who so sweet as he!
Too big for utterance when sorrows swell,
The too big sorrows flowing tears must tell;

---

[156] Very early in life Dr. Smollett wrote a tragedy, entitled the Regicide, founded on the story of the assassination of James the First of Scotland, which, with all his interest, he could never get represented on the stage; he afterwards published it by subscription with no great success. He has alluded to this and other of his theatrical transactions in the story of Melopoyne in Roderic Random.

But when those flowing tears shall cease to flow,
Why—then the voice must speak again, you know.
    Rude and unskilful in the poet's trade,   170
I kept no Naïads by me ready made;
Ne'er did I colours high in air advance,
Torn from the bleeding fopperies of France;
No flimsy linsey-woolsey scenes I wrote,
With patches here and there, like Joseph's coat.
Me humbler themes befit: secure, for me,
Let play-wrights smuggle nonsense duty free;
Secure, for me, ye lambs, ye lambkins! bound,
And frisk and frolic o'er the fairy ground:
Secure, for me, thou pretty little fawn!   180
Lick Sylvia's hand, and crop the flowery lawn;
Uncensured let the gentle breezes rove
Through the green umbrage of the enchanted grove:
Secure, for me, let foppish Nature smile,
And play the coxcomb in the Desert Isle.
    The stage I chose—a subject fair and free—
'Tis yours—'tis mine—'tis public property.
All common exhibitions open lie
For praise or censure to the common eye.
Hence are a thousand hackney writers fed;   190
Hence Monthly Critics earn their daily bread.
This is a general tax which all must pay,
From those who scribble, down to those who play.
Actors, a venal crew, receive support
From public bounty for the public sport.
To clap or hiss all have an equal claim,
The cobbler's and his lordship's right the same.
All join for their subsistence; all expect

[185] The Desert Island, a dramatic tale in three acts, by
A. Murphy, 1760, borrowed from a drama of Metastasio.

Free leave to praise their worth, their faults correct.
When active Pickle Smithfield stage ascends,   200
The three days' wonder of his laughing friends,
Each, or as judgment or as fancy guides,
The lively witling praises or derides.
And where's the mighty difference, tell me where,
Betwixt a Merry Andrew and a player?
    The strolling tribe, a despicable race!
Like wandering Arabs, shift from place to place.
Vagrants by law, to justice open laid,
They tremble, of the beadle's lash afraid;
And, fawning, cringe for wretched means of life
To Madam Mayoress, or his Worship's wife.   211
    The mighty monarch, in theatric sack,
Carries his whole regalia at his back;
His royal consort heads the female band,
And leads the heir apparent in her hand;
The pannier'd ass creeps on with conscious pride,
Bearing a future prince on either side.
No choice musicians in this troop are found
To varnish nonsense with the charms of sound;
No swords, no daggers, not one poison'd bowl;
No lightning flashes here, no thunders roll;   221
No guards to swell the monarch's train are shown;
The monarch here must be a host alone:
No solemn pomp, no slow processions here;
No Ammon's entry, and no Juliet's bier.

[208] By 17 G. II. c. 5. "All common players of interludes,
and all persons who for hire or reward, act or cause to be
acted any interlude or entertainment of the stage, or any
part therein, not being authorized by law, shall be deemed
rogues and vagabonds, and be punished accordingly." This
statute has been altered and qualified by several subsequent
enactments.

By need compell'd to prostitute his art,
The varied actor flies from part to part;
And, strange disgrace to all theatric pride!
His character is shifted with his side.
Question and answer he by turns must be,   230
Like that small wit in modern tragedy,
Who, to patch up his fame—or fill his purse—
Still pilfers wretched plans, and makes them worse;
Like gypsies, lest the stolen brat be known,
Defacing first, then claiming for his own.
In shabby state they strut, and tatter'd robe,
The scene a blanket, and a barn the globe:
No high conceits their moderate wishes raise,
Content with humble profit, humble praise.
Let dowdies simper, and let bumpkins stare,   240
The strolling pageant hero treads in air:
Pleased, for his hour he to mankind gives law,
And snores the next out on a truss of straw.
But if kind fortune, who sometimes we know
Can take a hero from a puppet-show,
In mood propitious should her favourite call
On royal stage in royal pomp to bawl,
Forgetful of himself he rears the head,
And scorns the dunghill where he first was bred.
Conversing now with well dress'd kings and queens,
With gods and goddesses behind the scenes,   251
He sweats beneath the terror-nodding plume,
Taught by mock honours real pride t'assume.

---

²⁶ A ludicrous representation of the distresses of itinerant players had been given by Hogarth, in his engraving published in 1738, of Strolling Actresses dressing in a barn, of which piece Mr. Walpole observed, that for wit and imagination it was the best of all the artist's works.

On this great stage, the world, no monarch e'er
Was half so haughty as a monarch player.
Doth it more move our anger or our mirth
To see these things, the lowest sons of earth,
Presume, with self-sufficient knowledge graced,
To rule in letters, and preside in taste?
The town's decisions they no more admit;   260
Themselves alone the arbiters of wit;
And scorn the jurisdiction of that court
To which they owe their being and support.
Actors, like monks of old, now sacred grown,
Must be attack'd by no fools but their own.
Let the vain tyrant sit amidst his guards,

²⁶⁰ Churchill appears to have been goaded into this additional attack upon actors in general, by the absurd clamour they raised at his treatment of them in the Rosciad, and by his suspicion that they had influenced the Critical Reviewers, and had retained some hirelings to write the Anti-Rosciad, Churchilliad, and other poems with which the press then teemed in their vindication.

²⁶⁶ These sarcastic lines were in general supposed to have been aimed at Mr. Garrick, and were not aimed in vain; he felt all the force of them, and was rendered exceedingly unhappy at having, by some indiscreet reflections on the author of the Rosciad, provoked a writer at once so irritable and so powerful. The offence given was a suggestion he had dropped, that the author of the Rosciad had become his panegyrist principally with a view to the freedom of the theatre. The unworthy insinuation was thus immediately resented by the Poet. To ensure a reconciliation, Garrick wrote a letter to Churchill, which comprehended an apology for himself and the players, full of encomiums upon the satirist's uncommon vein of poetry, and concluding with deprecating his future wrath. This epistle Garrick read to a friend, expecting his approbation of it in very ample terms, but here he was disappointed; he was told that as Churchill had attacked him on very slight or scarce any provocation, it was too great a condescension on his part to write such a laboured vindication of his conduct, and to adopt a tone of expostu-

His puny green-room wits and venal bards,
Who meanly tremble at the puppet's frown,
And for a play-house freedom lose their own ;
In spite of new-made laws, and new-made kings,
The free-born Muse with liberal spirit sings.   271
Bow down, ye slaves ! before these idols fall !
Let Genius stoop to them who've none at all !
Ne'er will I flatter, cringe, or bend the knee
To those who, slaves to all, are slaves to me.
     Actors, as actors, are a lawful game,
The poet's right, and who shall bar his claim ?
And if, o'erweening of their little skill,
When they have left the stage they're actors still ;
If to the subject world they still give laws,   280
With paper crowns, and sceptres made of straws ;
If they in cellar or in garret roar,
And kings one night, are kings for evermore ;
Shall not bold truth, e'en there, pursue her theme,
And wake the coxcomb from his golden dream ?
Or if, well worthy of a better fate,
They rise superior to their present state ;
If, with each social virtue graced, they blend
The gay companion and the faithful friend ;
If they, like Pritchard, join in private life   290
The tender parent and the virtuous wife ;
Shall not our verse their praise with pleasure speak,

lation in which many of the expressions were of too humili-
ating and even degrading a nature for any man of spirit to
submit to, and that the writer of the Rosciad, who was a man
of quick discernment and of an undaunted mind, would not
think the better of him for such an apology. They were afterwards reconciled by the mediation of Robert Lloyd ; and
Churchill frequently visited Garrick both at Hampton and
in town, but would never accept of any play-house freedom,
from him, or from any other manager or actor.

Though Mimics bark, and Envy split her cheek?
No honest worth's beneath the Muse's praise;
No greatness can above her censure raise;
Station and wealth to her are trifling things;
She stoops to actors, and she soars to kings.
 Is there a man, in vice and folly bred,
To sense of honour as to virtue dead,
Whom ties nor human nor divine can bind 300
Alien from God, and foe to all mankind;
Who spares no character; whose every word,
Bitter as gall, and sharper than the sword,
Cuts to the quick; whose thoughts with rancour
  swell;
Whose tongue on earth performs the work of hell?
If there be such a monster, the Reviews
Shall find him holding forth against abuse.
" Attack profession!—'tis a deadly breach!—
The Christian laws another lesson teach:—
Unto the end should charity endure. 310
And candour hide those faults it cannot cure."
Thus Candour's maxims flow from Rancour's throat,
As devils, to serve their purpose, Scripture quote.
 The Muse's office was by Heaven design'd
To please, improve, instruct, reform mankind;
To make dejected Virtue nobly rise
Above the towering pitch of splendid Vice;
To make pale Vice, abash'd, her head hang down,
And, trembling, crouch at Virtue's awful frown.
Now arm'd with wrath, she bids eternal shame, 320
With strictest justice, brand the villain's name;
Now in the milder garb of Ridicule
She sports, and pleases while she wounds the fool.

  [299] Intended for Smollett.

Her shape is often varied ; but her aim,
To prop the cause of Virtue, still the same,
In praise of mercy let the guilty bawl ;
When Vice and Folly for correction call,
Silence the mark of weakness justly bears,
And is partaker of the crimes it spares.
But if the Muse, too cruel in her mirth,   330
With harsh reflections wounds the man of worth ;
If wantonly she deviates from her plan,
And quits the actor to expose the man ;
Ashamed, she marks that passage with a blot,
And hates the line where candour was forgot.
But what is candour, what is humour's vein,
Though judgment join to consecrate the strain,
If curious numbers will not aid afford,
Nor choicest music play in every word ?
Verses must run, to charm a modern ear,   340
From all harsh, rugged interruptions clear.
Soft let them breathe, as Zephyr's balmy breeze,
Smooth let their current flow, as summer seas,
Perfect then only deem'd when they dispense
A happy, tuneful vacancy of sense.
Italian fathers thus, with barbarous rage,
Fit helpless infants for the squeaking stage :
Deaf to the calls of pity, Nature wound,
And mangle vigour for the sake of sound.
Henceforth farewell, then, feverish thirst of fame ; 350
Farewell the longings for a poet's name ;   `
Perish my Muse—a wish 'bove all severe
To him who ever held the Muses dear—

[333] Churchill, much to his credit, blotted out several lines,
which, in the first edition of the Rosciad, were of a nature
personally injurious to the character of Mr. John Palmer.

If e'er her labours weaken, to refine,
The generous roughness of a nervous line.

Others affect the stiff and swelling phrase ;
Their Muse must walk in stilts, and strut in stays;
The sense they murder, and the words transpose,
Lest poetry approach too near to prose.
See tortured Reason how they pare and trim, 360
And, like Procrustes, stretch, or lop the limb.

Waller, whose praise succeeding bards rehearse,
Parent of harmony in English verse,
Whose tuneful Muse in sweetest accents flows,
In couplets first taught straggling sense to close.

In polish'd numbers and majestic sound,
Where shall thy rival, Pope! be ever found ?
But whilst each line with equal beauty flows,
E'en excellence, unvaried, tedious grows.
Nature, through all her works, in great degree, 370
Borrows a blessing from variety.
Music itself her needful aid requires
To rouse the soul, and wake our dying fires.
Still in one key, the nightingale would tease ;
Still in one key, not Brent would always please.

Here let me bend, great Dryden, at thy shrine,

---

[367] Our author, who had studiously formed himself on the
model of Dryden, was always a warm advocate for the
superiority of that poet over Pope. Davies gives us the following anecdote on the subject :—" Churchill held Pope so
cheap that one of his most intimate friends assured me, that
he had some thoughts of attacking his poetry ; and another
gentleman informed me that, in a convivial hour, he wished
the bard of Twickenham was alive, that he might have an
opportunity to make him bring forth all his art of poetry ;
for he would not only have a struggle with him for pre-
eminence, but endeavour to break his heart." Davies adds,
" this must be considered as a wild effusion over a bottle."

Thou dearest name to all the tuneful nine.
What if some dull lines in cold order creep,
And with his theme the poet seems to sleep?
Still, when his subject rises proud to view,   380
With equal strength the poet rises too:
With strong invention, noblest vigour fraught,
Thought still springs up and rises out of thought;
Numbers ennobling numbers in their course,
In varied sweetness flow, in varied force;
The powers of genius and of judgment join,
And the whole Art of Poetry is thine.

But what are numbers, what are bards, to me,
Forbid to tread the paths of poesy?
" A sacred Muse should consecrate her pen;   390
Priests must not hear nor see like other men :
Far higher themes should her ambition claim :
Behold where Sternhold points the way to fame."

Whilst, with mistaken zeal dull bigots burn,
Let Reason for a moment take her turn.
When coffee-sages hold discourse with kings,
And blindly walk in paper leading-strings,
What if a man delight to pass his time
In spinning reason into harmless rhyme,
Or sometimes boldly venture to the play?   400
Say, where's the crime?—great man of prudence,
       say?

390 On this passage the Critical Reviewers elegantly observed in vindication of themselves, "that they never in-
quired whether the author was a priest or a publican, a
curate or a cobbler; whether he spent his time in squabbling
with the players behind the scenes at the theatre, or in pray-
ing his bible among the old women in Westminster."

No two on earth in all things can agree;
All have some darling singularity:
Women and men, as well as girls and boys,
In gew-gaws take delight, and sigh for toys.
Your sceptres and your crowns, and such like
   things,
Are but a better kind of toys for kings.
In things indifferent Reason bids us choose,
Whether the whim's a monkey or a Muse.
 What the grave triflers on this busy scene,   410
When they make use of this word Reason, mean,
I know not; but according to my plan,
'Tis Lord Chief-Justice in the court of man,
Equally form'd to rule in age and youth,
The friend of Virtue, and the guide to truth.
To her I bow, whose sacred power I feel;
To her decision make my last appeal;
Condemn'd by her, applauding worlds in vain
Should tempt me to take up the pen again:
By her absolved, my course I'll still pursue: 420
If Reason's for me, God is for me too.

NIGHT.

AN EPISTLE TO ROBERT LLOYD.

THIS poem was published in October, 1761. Its title may probably have been suggested by Dr. Armstrong's "Day, an Epistle to J. Wilkes, of Aylesbury, Esq." then lately published, without the consent of the author, who was with the English army in Germany; from whence it was written in easy loose verse, with little regard to the matter, and less to the manner. In his epistle Dr. Armstrong ventured to censure Churchill, who expressed much resentment at the attack, and would never be reconciled with the author of it. The principal object of Night was to exculpate the poet and the friend to whom it is addressed, from the censure of the world on the score of those irregularities in conduct, which the celebrity of the foregoing poems rendered more conspicuous in the author of them, by inducing those who smarted under his lash to make researches into his private character, and by publishing exaggerated statements of his improprieties of behaviour, to deaden the force of the blow they could not parry. His propensity to late hours, and his employment of them in genial converse with his friends, he here avows; and great examples in ancient and modern times will certainly rescue his taste from the charge of singularity. Had he not been himself so severe a censor, his private irregularities would have been softened down to the eccentricities of genius, and his midnight parties would have been dignified with the amiable attributes of social enjoyment, " the feast of reason and the flow of soul;" instead of which, they were blazoned abroad as the orgies of brutal intemperance, and the scenes of vulgar and depraved gratification.

NIGHT.*

Contrarius evehor orbi.—OVID. Met. lib. ii.

WHEN foes insult, and prudent friends
    dispense,
    In pity's strains, the worst of inso-
    lence,
Oft with thee, Lloyd, I steal an hour from grief,
And in thy social converse find relief.
The mind, of solitude impatient grown,
Loves any sorrows rather than her own.
   Let slaves to business, bodies without soul,
Important blanks in Nature's mighty roll,
Solemnize nonsense in the day's broad glare:
We Night prefer, which heals or hides our care. 10
   Rogues justified, and by success made bold,
Dull fools and coxcombs sanctified by gold,
Freely may bask in fortune's partial ray,
And spread their feathers opening to the day;
But threadbare Merit dares not shew the head
Till vain Prosperity retires to bed.
Misfortunes, like the owl, avoid the light;

* "This Night, like many others at this time of the year,
is very cold, long, dark, and dirty, which will not induce
many to walk out in it."—CRITICAL REVIEW, Dec. 1761.

The sons of Care are always sons of Night.

The wretch bred up in method's drowsy school,
Whose only merit is to err by rule,　　　　20
Who ne'er through heat of blood was tripping
　　　caught,
Nor guilty deem'd of one eccentric thought;
Whose soul directed to no use is seen,
Unless to move the body's dull machine,
Which, clockwork-like, with the same equal pace,
Still travels on through life's insipid space,
Turns up his eyes to think that there should be,
Among God's creatures, two such things as we;
Then for his nightcap calls, and thanks the powers
Which kindly gave him grace to keep good hours.

Good hours—fine words—but was it ever seen 31
That all men could agree in what they mean?
Florio, who many years a course hath run
In downright opposition to the sun,
Expatiates on good hours, their cause defends
With as much vigour as our prudent friends.
The uncertain term no settled notion brings,
But still in different mouths means different things;
Each takes the phrase in his own private view;
With prudence it is ten, with Florio two.　　　40

Go on, ye fools, who talk for talking's sake,
Without distinguishing, distinctions make;
Shine forth in native folly, native pride,
Make yourselves rules to all the world beside;

18　　　What have we with *day* to do?
　　　Sons of Care, 'twas made for you.

This is the more popular doctrine, and we believe most
commonly governs the distribution of the four-and-twenty
hours.

Reason, collected in herself, disdains
The slavish yoke of arbitrary chains ;
Steady and true each circumstance she weighs,
Nor to bare words inglorious tribute pays.
Men of sense live exempt from vulgar awe,
And Reason to herself alone is law :   50
That freedom she enjoys with liberal mind,
Which she as freely grants to all mankind.
No idol-titled name her reverence stirs,
No hour she blindly to the rest prefers ;
All are alike, if they're alike employ'd,
And all are good if virtuously enjoy'd.
    Let the sage Doctor (think him one we know)
With scraps of ancient learning overflow ;
In all the dignity of wig declare   `
The fatal consequence of midnight air ;   60
How damps and vapours, as it were by stealth,
Undermine life, and sap the walls of health :
For me let Galen moulder on the shelf ;
I'll live, and be physician to myself.
While soul is join'd to body, whether fate
Allot a longer or a shorter date,
I'll make them live, as brother should with brother,
And keep them in good humour with each other.
    The surest road to health, say what they will,
Is never to suppose we shall be ill.   70
Most of those evils we poor mortals know,
From doctors and imagination flow.
Hence, to old women with your boasted rules !
Stale traps, and only sacred now to fools ;
As well may sons of physic hope to find
One medicine, as one hour, for all mankind.
    If Rupert after ten is out of bed,

The fool next morning can't hold up his head;
What reason this which me to bed must call,
Whose head, thank Heaven, never aches at all? 80
In different courses different tempers run;
He hates the moon: I sicken at the sun.
Wound up at twelve at noon, his clock goes right;
Mine better goes, wound up at twelve at night.
　Then in oblivion's grateful cup I drown
The galling sneer, the supercilious frown,
The strange reserve, the proud, affected state
Of upstart knaves grown rich, and fools grown great.
No more that abject wretch disturbs my rest,
Who meanly overlooks a friend distressed. 90
Purblind to poverty the worldling goes,
And scarce sees rags an inch beyond his nose,
But from a crowd can single out his grace,
And cringe and creep to fools who strut in lace.
　Whether those classic regions are survey'd
Where we in earliest youth together stray'd,
Where hand in hand we trod the flowery shore,
Though now thy happier genius runs before;
When we conspired a thankless wretch to raise,
And taught a stump to shoot with pilfer'd praise, 100

---

[99] The Rev. William Sellon, minister of St. James's,
Clerkenwell, and lecturer of St. Andrew's Holborn and of the
Magdalen, the person alluded to in these lines, is again
satirised in the Ghost, under the name of Plausible.
By the assistance of his clever contemporaries at Westminster school, Churchill, Lloyd, and Thornton, he contrived to acquire more reputation there, than his native
dulness warranted; but on quitting that seminary, he
forgot the obligation, and treated his friends with ingra-
titude. A few years after he became a famous preacher,
" From Holborn e'en to C'erkenwell," Ghost, B. iii. l. 741.

Who once for reverend merit famous grown,
Gratefully strove to kick his maker down;
Or if more general arguments engage,
The court or camp, the pulpit, bar, or stage;
If half-bred surgeons, whom men doctors call,
And lawyers, who were never bred at all,
Those mighty letter'd monsters of the earth,
Our pity move, or exercise our mirth;
Or if in tittle-tattle, toothpick way,
Our rambling thoughts with easy freedom stray, 110
A gainer still thy friend himself must find,
His grief suspended, and improved his mind.

Whilst peaceful slumbers bless the homely bed
Where virtue, self-approved, reclines her head;
Whilst vice beneath imagined horrors mourns,
And conscience plants the villain's couch with
        thorns,
Impatient of restraint, the active mind,
No more by servile prejudice confined, ·
Leaps from her seat, as waken'd from a trance,
And darts through Nature at a single glance; 120
Then we our friends, our foes, ourselves, survey,
And see by Night what fools we are by day.

Stripp'd of her gaudy plumes and vain disguise,
See where ambition mean and loathsome lies;
Reflection with relentless hand pulls down
The tyrant's bloody wreath and ravish'd crown.
In vain he tells of battles bravely won,
Of nations conquer'd, and of worlds undone;
Triumphs like these but ill with manhood suit,
And sink the conqueror beneath the brute.   130
But if, in searching round the world, we find
Some generous youth, the friend of all mankind,

Whose anger, like the bolt of Jove, is sped
In terrors only at the guilty head,
Whose mercies, like heaven's dew, refreshing fall
In general love and charity to all,
Pleased we behold such worth on any throne,
And doubly pleased we find it on our own.
    Through a false medium things are shewn by
      day;
Pomp, wealth, and titles judgment lead astray. 140
How many from appearance borrow state,
Whom Night disdains to number with the great!
Must not we laugh to see yon lordling proud
Snuff up vile incense from a fawning crowd?
Whilst in his beam surrounding clients play,
Like insects in the sun's enlivening ray,
Whilst, Jehu-like, he drives at furious rate,
And seems the only charioteer of state,
Talking himself into a little god,
And ruling empires with a single nod;   150
Who would not think, to hear him law dispense,
That he had interest, and that they had sense?
Injurious thought! beneath Night's honest shade,
When pomp is buried, and false colours fade,
Plainly we see, at that impartial hour,
Them dupes to pride, and him the tool of power.
    God help the man condemn'd by cruel fate
To court the seeming, or the real great!
Much sorrow shall he feel, and suffer more
Than any slave who labours at the oar: 160
By slavish methods must he learn to please,
By smooth-tongued flattery, that cursed court-
    disease;
Supple to every wayward mood strike sail,

And shift with shifting humour's peevish gale.
To nature dead he must adopt vile art,
And wear a smile, with anguish in his heart.
A sense of honour would destroy his schemes,
And Conscience ne'er must speak unless in dreams.
When he hath tamely borne, for many years,
Cold looks, forbidding frowns, contemptuous sneers;
When he at last expects, good easy man !   171
To reap the profits of his labour'd plan,
Some cringing lackey, or rapacious whore,
To favours of the great the surest door ;
Some catamite, or pimp, in credit grown,
Who tempts another's wife, or sells his own,
Steps 'cross his hopes, the promised boon denies,
And for some minion's minion claims the prize.
    Foe to restraint, unpractised in deceit,
Too resolute, from nature's active heat,   180
To brook affronts, and tamely pass them by,
Too proud to flatter, too sincere to lie ;
Too plain to please, too honest to be great,
Give me, kind Heaven, an humbler, happier state ;
Far from the place where men with pride deceive,
Where rascals promise, and where fools believe ;
Far from the walk of folly, vice, and strife,
Calm, independent, let me steal through life,
Nor one vain wish my steady thoughts beguile
To fear his lordship's frown, or court his smile.
Unfit for greatness, I her snares defy,   191
And look on riches with untainted eye ;
To others let the glittering baubles fall,
Content shall place us far above them all.
    Spectators only, on this bustling stage,
We see what vain designs mankind engage :

Vice after vice with ardour they pursue,
And one old folly brings forth twenty new.
Perplex'd with trifles through the vale of life,
Man strives 'gainst man, without a cause for strife;
Armies embattled meet, and thousands bleed   201
For some vile spot, where fifty cannot feed.
Squirrels for nuts contend, and, wrong or right,
For the world's empire kings ambitious fight.
What odds?—to us 'tis all the self-same thing,
A nut, a world, a squirrel, and a king.

Britons, like Roman spirits famed of old,
Are cast by nature in a patriot mould;
No private joy, no private grief, they know;
Their soul's engross'd by public weal or woe;   210
Inglorious ease, like ours, they greatly scorn;
Let care with nobler wreaths their brows adorn:
Gladly they toil beneath the statesman's pains,
Give them but credit for a statesman's brains.
All would be deem'd, e'en from the cradle, fit
To rule in politics as well as wit.
The grave, the gay, the fopling, and the dunce,
Start up (God bless us!) statesmen all at once.

His mighty charge of souls the priest forgets,
The court-bred lord his promises and debts;   220
Soldiers their fame, misers forget their pelf,
The rake his mistress, and the fop himself,
Whilst thoughts of higher moment claim their care,
And their wise heads the weight of kingdoms bear.

Females themselves the glorious ardour feel,
And boast an equal or a greater zeal;
From nymph to nymph the state-infection flies,
Swells in her breast, and sparkles in her eyes.
O'erwhelm'd by politics lie malice, pride,

Envy, and twenty other faults beside.   230
No more their little fluttering hearts confess
A passion for applause, or rage for dress ;
No more they pant for public raree-shows,
Or lose one thought on monkies or on beaus :
Coquettes no more pursue the jilting plan,
And lustful prudes forget to rail at man :
The darling theme Cecilia's self will choose,
Nor thinks of scandal whilst she talks of news.
    The cit, a Common-Councilman by place,
Ten thousand mighty nothings in his face,   240
By situation as by nature great,
With nice precision parcels out the state ;
Proves and disproves, affirms and then denies,
Objects himself, and to himself replies ;
Wielding aloft the politician rod,
Makes Pitt by turns a devil and a god ;
Maintains, e'en to the very teeth of power,
The same thing right and wrong in half an hour :
Now all is well, now he suspects a plot,
And plainly proves, whatever is, is not :   250
Fearfully wise, he shakes his empty head,
And deals out empires as he deals out thread ;
His useless scales are in a corner flung,
And Europe's balance hangs upon his tongue.
    Peace to such triflers, be our happier plan
To pass through life as easy as we can.
Who's in or out, who moves this grand machine,
Nor stirs my curiosity nor spleen.
Secrets of state no more I wish to know
Than secret movements of a puppet-show :   260
Let but the puppets move, I've my desire,
Unseen the hand which guides the master-wire.

What is't to us, if taxes rise or fall?
Thanks to our fortune, we pay none at all.
Let muckworms, who in dirty acres deal,
Lament those hardships which we cannot feel.
His grace, who smarts, may bellow if he please,
But must I bellow too, who sit at ease?
By custom safe, the poet's numbers flow
Free as the light and air some years ago.   270
No statesman e'er will find it worth his pains
To tax our labours, and excise our brains.
Burthens like these, vile earthly buildings bear;
No tribute's laid on castles in the air.

  Let then the flames of war destructive reign,
And England's terrors awe imperious Spain;
Let every venal clan and neutral tribe
Learn to receive conditions, not prescribe;
Let each new year call loud for new supplies,
And tax on tax with double burthen rise;   280
Exempt we sit, by no rude cares oppress'd,
And, having little, are with little bless'd.

  270 An additional tax on windows had then just been imposed by parliament, to commence from the 5th of April,
1762; that day many housekeepers put up their dead lights,
or outside shutters, and one citizen more poetic than his
neighbours, expressed his displeasure by inscribing on his
shutter the following couplet, of which it may be truly said,
facit indignatio versum :

    "These are those dismal taxing days of yore,
    Which our forefathers never saw before."

  277 Alluding to the precautions adopted by government
after the rebellion of 1745, and to some difficulties which
occurred in carrying into effect Mr. Pitt's measure, proposed in 1757, for raising 2000 men in the Highlands of
Scotland for the British service in America.

All real ills in dark oblivion lie,
And joys, by fancy form'd, their place supply;
Night's laughing hours unheeded slip away,
Nor one dull thought foretels approach of day.
Thus have we lived, and whilst the fates afford
Plain plenty to supply the frugal board;
Whilst Mirth with Decency, his lovely bride,   289
And wine's gay god, with Temperance by his side,
Their welcome visit pay; whilst Health attends
The narrow circle of our chosen friends;
Whilst frank good-humour consecrates the treat,
And woman makes society complete,
Thus will we live, though in our teeth are hurl'd
Those hackney strumpets, Prudence and the World.
Prudence, of old a sacred term, implied
Virtue, with godlike wisdom for her guide,
But now in general use is known to mean
The stalking-horse of vice, and folly's screen.   300
The sense perverted we retain the name;
Hypocrisy and Prudence are the same.
A tutor once, more read in men than books,
A kind of crafty knowledge in his looks,
Demurely sly, with high preferment bless'd,
His favourite pupil in these words address'd:
    " Wouldst thou, my son, be wise and virtuous
            deem'd,
By all mankind a prodigy esteem'd?
Be this thy rule; be what men *prudent* call;
Prudence, almighty Prudence, gives thee all.   310
Keep up appearances; there lies the test;
The world will give thee credit for the rest.
Outward be fair, however foul within;
Sin if thou wilt, but then in secret sin.

This maxim's into common favour grown,—
Vice is no longer vice, unless 'tis known.
Virtue indeed may barefaced take the field;
But vice is virtue when 'tis well conceal'd.
Should raging passion drive thee to a whore,
Let Prudence lead thee to a postern door;⁣ 320
Stay out all night, but take especial care
That Prudence bring thee back to early prayer.
As one with watching and with study faint,
Reel in a drunkard, and reel out a saint."

With joy the youth this useful lesson heard,
And in his memory stored each precious word,
Successfully pursued the plan, and now,
"Room for my Lord—Virtue, stand by and bow."
And is this all—is this the worldling's art,
To mask, but not amend a vicious heart?⁣ 330
Shall lukewarm caution and demeanour grave
For wise and good stamp every supple knave?
Shall wretches, whom no real virtue warms,
Gild fair their names and states with empty forms,
While Virtue seeks in vain the wish'd for prize,
Because, disdaining ill, she hates disguise;
Because she frankly pours forth all her store,
Seems what she is, and scorns to pass for more?
Well—be it so—let vile dissemblers hold⁣ 339
Unenvied power, and boast their dear bought gold;
Me neither power shall tempt, nor thirst of pelf,
To flatter others, or deny myself;
Might the whole world be placed within my span,
I would not be that thing, that prudent man.

" What !" cries Sir Pliant, " would you then oppose
Yourself, alone, against a host of foes?

Let not conceit, and peevish lust to rail,
Above all sense of interest prevail.
Throw off, for shame ! this petulance of wit ;
Be wise, be modest, and for once submit: 350
Too hard the task 'gainst multitudes to fight ;
You must be wrong ; the World is in the right."
    What is this World?—a term which men have got
To signify, not one in ten knows what ;
A term, which with no more precision passes
To point out herds of men than herds of asses ;
In common use no more it means, we find,
Than many fools in same opinions join'd.
    Can numbers then change nature's stated laws ?
Can numbers make the worse the better cause ?
Vice must be vice, virtue be virtue still,   361
Though thousands rail at good and practise ill.
Wouldst thou defend the Gaul's destructive rage,
Because vast nations on his part engage ?
Though to support the rebel Cæsar's cause
Tumultuous legions arm against the laws ;
Though Scandal would our patriot's name impeach,
And rails at virtues which she cannot reach,
What honest man but would with joy submit
To bleed with Cato, and retire with Pitt ?   370

370 Mr. Pitt, in September, 1761, indignant at the repeated insults offered to this country by Spain, proposed to
the cabinet an immediate rupture with that court ; in this
proposition he was supported by Lord Temple, but was opposed by Lord Bute, and all the other members of the min-
istry : upon which Mr. Pitt and Lord Temple took their
leaves, and their written advice on the subject being rejected
by his majesty, they resigned their seals of office into his
hands on the 5th of October following. Lord Temple was
dismissed from the Lord Leiutenancy of Bucks on the 7th
of May, and Lord Le Despencer succeeded him on the 9th.

Stedfast and true to virtue's sacred laws,
Unmoved by vulgar censure or applause,
Let the World talk, my Friend ; that World, we
know,
Which calls us guilty, cannot make us so.
Unawed by numbers, follow Nature's plan ;

Upon this event an article appeared in the London Gazette,
announcing their resignation, the appointment of the Earl of
Egremont, as Mr. Pitt's successor in the situation of one of
the principal Secretaries of State, and that, in consideration
of the great and important services of Mr. Pitt, his majesty
was pleased to grant to the Lady Hester Pitt the Barony of
Chatham [4 Dec. 1761]; and also to confer upon William
Pitt, Esq., an annuity of £3000 during his own life, and
that of his wife and of their eldest son.

The moment this intelligence was published Mr. Pitt's
character was assailed with the utmost malignity and by all
the hired servants of the administration, and by some mistaken zealots of the opposite faction. They branded him in
various newspapers and pamphlets with the names of pen-
sioner, apostate, deserter, and loaded him with every term
of reproach. This occasioned a temporary diminution of his
popularity; but in a few weeks the prejudice began to sub-
side, and public feeling ran in a contrary direction. When
he went into the city on the ensuing Lord Mayor's Day, he
was honoured in all the streets through which he passed
with unbounded applause, and soon after several cities and
towns presented him with addresses, thanking him for his
important services, and lamenting the cause of his resignation.

All doubts respecting the propriety of his conduct were
dispelled by the declaration of war against Spain, which his
successors were compelled to make on the 2nd of January,
1762, though they postponed that measure until the insults
of the court of Spain became so notorious that even Lord
Bute confessed they could be no longer concealed.

Thus came by constraint, without dignity, and above three
months after an opportunity for essentially crippling the
enemy had elapsed, that declaration of war which would
have been issued with *eclat* by Mr. Pitt in September.

Mr. Pitt, in July 1766, irrecoverably forfeited his popula-

Assert the rights, or quit the name of man.
Consider well, weigh strictly right and wrong;
Resolve not quick, but once resolved, be strong.
In spite of dulness, and in spite of wit,
If to thyself thou canst thyself acquit,   380
Rather stand up, assured with conscious pride,
Alone, than err with millions on thy side.

rity by his coalition with the very men against whom he
had hitherto directed all the powers of his commanding
eloquence. He was created Earl of Chatham, and, with the
office of Lord Privy Seal, took the general control over the
measures of government. Mr. Townshend and General
Conway were his managers in the House of Commons. His
noble brother-in-law, Lord Temple, and his intimate friend,
Lord Rockingham, not only refused to hold any situation
under him, but peremptorily declined any interview or personal intercourse with him. He felt deeply the loss of Lord
Temple, whose gracious affability procured him the esteem of
all ranks of people, while the splendour of his own talents com-
manded only their admiration. This preyed upon his mind
while his body was a victim to the gout, and the conduct of
his new associates in office did not contribute to alleviate his
uneasiness. In 1768 he resigned, was reconciled to Lord
Temple, and retired to Hayes. He now limited his political
exertions to a punctual attendance in the House of Lords.
Notwithstanding the animated opposition he offered, until
his death in 1778, to most of the measures of government,
and particularly to the American war, he could never regain
the confidence of the people.

THE PROPHECY OF FAMINE.

A SCOTS PASTORAL.

INSCRIBED TO JOHN WILKES, ESQ.

MR. WILKES said of this poem before its appearance in January, 1763, "that he was sure it would
take, as it was at once personal, poetical, and political:" his
prediction was accomplished. The Prophecy of Famine almost exceeded the Rosciad in popularity, and in extent of
circulation; and, like that poem, incited a number of inferior
writers to draw their pens in praise, censure, or imitation.
The titles of these productions are preserved in the periodical
publications of the day, but the works themselves sleep with
their fathers.   Of such productions and their authors,
Churchill might with propriety have said with Lord Shaftes-
bury, "that he would never reply unless he should hear
of them or their works in any good company a twelvemonth
after."

In a letter to Wilkes, previous to the publication of this
poem, Churchill writes: "Think not that the Scottish
Eclogue totally stands still, or that I can ever be unmindful
of anything which I think will give Wilkes pleasure, and
which I am certain will do me honour in having his name
prefixed. The present state of it however stands thus—it is
split into two poems—the Scottish Eclogue, which will be
inscribed to you in the pastoral way—and another poem,
which I think will be a strong one, immediately addressed
by way of Epistle to you—this way they will be both of a
piece, otherwise it would have been

'Delphinum sylvis appingit, fluctibus aprum.'

The Pastoral begins thus, and I believe will be out soon,

but nothing comes out till I begin to be pleased with it myself:—

> ' When Cupid first instructs,' &c.

The other runs thus:—

> ' From solemn thought,' &c.

> ' Can Wilkes?—I know thou canst—retreat awhile,
> Learn pity's lesson, and disdain to smile.'

> . ' Oft have I heard thee,' &c."

This plan our author altered, and embodied the two
intended poems in the following acrimonious satire.

This must be considered as our author's first political
poem. Before he was concerned in the North Briton, he
paid very little attention to the management of the political
machine, but once engaged in what he considered the sacred
cause of liberty, he was sincere and strenuous. He was ac-
tuated by that love of liberty which generally inspires men
of genius.

Churchill omitted no opportunity of displaying his invete-
rate animosity against the whole Scottish nation; and highly
pleased with the extraordinary success of this poem, he
dressed his younger son in a Scotch plaid like a High-
lander, and carried him everywhere in that garb: the boy
being once asked by a gentleman, why he was clothed in
such a manner? answered with great vivacity—" Sir, my
father hates the Scotch, and does it to plague them."

THE PROPHECY OF FAMINE.

Carmina tum melius, cum venerit ipse, canemus.[1]

DR. KING, Oxon.

WHEN Cupid first instructs his darts to fly
From the sly corner of some cook-maid's
eye,
The stripling raw, just enter'd in his
teens,
Receives the wound, and wonders what it means;
His heart, like dripping, melts, and new desire
Within him stirs, each time she stirs the fire;
Trembling and blushing, he the fair one views,
And fain would speak, but can't—without a Muse.
So to the sacred mount he takes his way,   9
Prunes his young wings, and tunes his infant lay;
His oaten reed to rural ditties frames,
To flocks and rocks, to hills and rills, proclaims,
In simplest notes, and all unpolish'd strains,
The loves of nymphs, and eke the loves of swains.
Clad, as your nymphs were always clad of yore,
In rustic weeds—a cook-maid now no more—
Beneath an aged oak Lardella lies,
Green moss her couch; her canopy the skies.
From aromatic shrubs the roguish gale

---

[1] This heading appears in the 4to. editions. In Tooke's
edition, 1804, the following heading is first printed:—

Nos patriam fugimus. VIRGIL.

We all get out of our country as fast as we can.

Steals young perfumes, and wafts them through
    the vale.   20
The youth, turn'd swain, and skill'd in rustic lays,
Fast by her side his amorous descant plays.
Herds low, flocks bleat, pies chatter, ravens
    scream,
And the full chorus dies a-down the stream.
The streams, with music freighted, as they pass
Present the fair Lardella with a glass,
And Zephyr, to complete the love-sick plan,
Waves his light wings, and serves her for a fan.
   But when maturer Judgment takes the lead,
These childish toys on Reason's altar bleed;   30
Form'd after some great man, whose name breeds
    awe,
Whose every sentence Fashion makes a law;
Who on mere credit his vain trophies rears,
And founds his merit on our servile fears;
Then we discard the workings of the heart,
And nature's banish'd by mechanic art;
Then, deeply read, our reading must be shown;
Vain is that knowledge which remains unknown:
Then Ostentation marches to our aid,
And letter'd Pride stalks forth in full parade;   40
Beneath their care behold the work refine,
Pointed each sentence, polish'd every line;
Trifles are dignified, and taught to wear
The robes of ancients with a modern air;
Nonsense with classic ornaments is graced,
And passes current with the stamp of taste.
   Then the rude Theocrite is ransack'd o'er,
And courtly Maro call'd from Mincio's shore;
Sicilian Muses on our mountains roam,

Easy and free as if they were at home;   50
Nymphs, Naiads, Nereids, Dryads, Satyrs, Fauns,
Sport in our floods, and trip it o'er our lawns;
Flowers which once flourish'd fair in Greece and
    Rome,
More fair revive in England's meads to bloom;
Skies without cloud exotic suns adorn,
And roses blush, but blush without a thorn;
Landscapes unknown to dowdy Nature rise,
And new creations strike our wond'ring eyes.

    For bards like these, who neither sing nor say,
Grave without thought, and without feeling gay, 60
Whose numbers in one even tenor flow,
Attuned to pleasure, and attuned to woe;
Who, if plain Common-sense her visit pays,
And mars one couplet in their happy lays,
As at some ghost affrighted, start and stare,
And ask the meaning of her coming there ;—
For bards like these a wreath shall Mason bring,
Lined with the softest down of Folly's wing;
In Love's pagoda shall they ever doze,
And Gisbal kindly rock them to repose;   70

[67] William Mason, author of Elfrida, Caractacus, and an
Elegy on the death of the Countess of Coventry, was the
intimate friend and the executor of Gray, to whom, and to
whose memory and fame, he was enthusiastically devoted.
. His Life of Gray, prefixed to an edition of his works, suggested to Boswell the form of his Life of Johnson.   Mason,
through the patronage of the Holdernesse family, obtained
considerable church preferment, and died Precentor of York,
April 5, 1797, aged 71.
[70] " Gisbal, an Hyperborean tale, translated from the
fragments of Ossian, the son of Fingal."   The stupidity of
this attack upon Scotland, can only be equalled by its scur-
rility.

My Lord ———— to letters as to faith most true—
At once their patron and example too—
Shall quaintly fashion his love-labour'd dreams,
Sigh with sad winds, and weep with weeping
      streams ;
Curious in grief, (for real grief, we know,
Is curious to dress up the tale of woe)
From the green umbrage of some Druid's seat
Shall his own works in his own way repeat.
   Me, whom no Muse of heavenly birth inspires,
No judgment tempers when rash genius fires ;   80
Who boast no merit but mere knack of rhyme,
Short gleams of sense, and satire out of time;
Who cannot follow where trim fancy leads
By prattling streams, o'er flower-empurpled meads;
Who often, but without success, have pray'd
For apt Alliteration's artful aid ;
Who would, but cannot, with a master's skill,
Coin fine new epithets, which mean no ill ;
Me, thus uncouth, thus every way unfit
For pacing poesy, and ambling wit,   90
Taste with contempt beholds, nor deigns to place
Amongst the lowest of her favour'd race.
   Thou, Nature, art my goddess—to thy law
Myself I dedicate—hence, slavish awe,
Which bends to fashion, and obeys the rules
Imposed at first, and since observed by fools !

---

[74] A harsh censure of Lord Lyttelton's Monody on his
wife; which, though, like all his productions, highly laboured, contains many beauties. He was also the author of
a History of Henry the Second—a labour of twenty years.
The allusion to faith refers to his Lordship's essay on the
conversion of St. Paul.

Hence those vile tricks which mar fair Nature's hue,
And bring the sober matron forth to view,
With all that artificial, tawdry glare
Which virtue scorns, and none but strumpets wear!
Sick of those pomps, those vanities, that waste 101
Of toil, which critics now mistake for taste;
Of false refinements sick, and labour'd case,
Which art, too thinly veil'd, forbids to please,
By Nature's charms (inglorious truth!) subdued,
However plain her dress, and 'haviour rude,
To northern climes my happier course I steer,
Climes where the goddess reigns throughout the
        year;
Where, undisturb'd by Art's rebellious plan,
She rules the loyal laird, and faithful clan.   110

To that rare soil, where virtues clust'ring grow,
What mighty blessings doth not England owe!
What waggon-loads of courage, wealth, and sense,
Doth each revolving day import from thence!
To us she gives, disinterested friend!
Faith without fraud, and Stuarts without end.
When we prosperity's rich trappings wear,
Come not her generous sons and take a share?
And if, by some disastrous turn of fate,
Change should ensue, and ruin seize the state, 120

110 Ironically alluding to the then recent rebellion of 1745,
and to the disaffection of several entire clans, one of which,
the M'Gregors, was compelled by Act of Parliament to
relinquish its name, as all were to discontinue the national
dress.
116 Stuart, the family name of Lord Bute: it was noticed
by the opposition papers of the day, that out of sixteen
names in one list of gazette promotions there were eleven
Stuarts and four M'Kenzies.

Shall we not find, safe in that hallow'd ground,
Such refuge as the holy martyr found?
　　Nor less our debt in science, though denied
By the weak slaves of prejudice and pride.
Thence came the Ramsays, names of worthy note,
Of whom one paints, as well as t'other wrote;
Thence, Home, disbanded from the sons of prayer
For loving plays, though no dull dean was there;

[125] Allan Ramsay, author of the Gentle Shepherd, and father of the well-known painter. The poet died in 1758; the painter in 1784. Dr. Johnson bore testimony to the colloquial talents of the younger Ramsay; and in a letter to Sir Joshua Reynolds, in Aug. 1784, writes, "Poor Ramsay! on which side soever I turn, mortality presents its formidable frown. I no sooner lost sight of dear Allan, than I am told I shall see him no more." On the subject of Mr. Ramsay's talent for conversation, Mr. Northcote has related that Reynolds often observed that Ramsay was the most sensible man of all the living artists.

[127] John Home, the author of the play of Douglas, on which alone his reputation now rests. Douglas was first acted at Edinburgh in 1756, with great success; when the uproar made by the fanatical Scotch clergy against a minister's turning dramatist compelled Home to resign his living. Lord Bute then became his great friend and patron, and introduced him to the Prince of Wales, who settled on him a pension of a hundred a year. He afterwards obtained another place; and his Douglas had great success at Covent Garden Theatre—a good fortune which did not befal any of his subsequent pieces. He lived to a great age.

[128] Dr. Zachary Pearce, Bishop of Rochester and Dean of Westminster, when the name of our author appeared to the second edition of the Rosciad, reprimanded him for writing on a subject so totally inconsistent with his profession: Churchill replied, "that if he was so culpable, the translator of Longinus (Dr. Pearce) could not be entirely blameless." The Bishop immediately shifted the ground of reprehension, and desired him to alter his mode of dressing, and not affect in his appearance the gaiety of a layman, when he ought to assume the gravity becoming his sacred function. These

Thence issued forth, at great Macpherson's call,
That old, new, epic pastoral, Fingal;   130

animadversions being again enforced by the Dean in his
official capacity, at the instance of the parishioners of St.
John the Evangelist, Churchill, in Jan. 1763, resigned the
lectureship of that parish.

[129] James Macpherson, born in 1738, published in 1760
Fragments of Ancient Poetry. These fragments, which were
declared to be genuine remains of ancient Scottish poetry, at
their first appearance delighted many readers; and some
good judges, especially Dr. Blair, were extremely warm in
their praise. As other specimens were said to exist, a subscription was set on foot to enable Mr. Macpherson to quit
the family in which he was tutor, and undertake a mission
into the Highlands and western isles, to secure what might
remain of the works of the ancient bards, particularly those
of Ossian the son of Fingal. He engaged in the undertaking,
and in 1762 and '63 produced the Epic poems of Fingal
Temora, the authenticity of which occasioned so much con-
troversy. Dr. Johnson entertained no doubt that they were
forged; in consequence of which, Macpherson wrote him
a very insolent letter, which drew forth the following answer
from the Doctor:

Mr. James Macpherson,—I received your foolish and im-
pudent letter.—Any violence that shall be attempted upon
me, I will do my best to repel; and what I cannot do for
myself the law shall do for me; for I will not be hindered
from exposing what I think a cheat by the menaces of a ruffian.
What would you have me retract? I thought your work an
imposition; I think so still; and for my opinion I have
given reasons which I here dare you to refute. Your abilities, since your Homer, are not so formidable; and what I
hear of your morality inclines me to credit rather what you
shall prove than what you shall say.

SAM. JOHNSON.

Mr. Macpherson published a contemptible translation of
the Iliad, and was not more successful in his attempts in
historical and controversial writing. He sat in parliament
many years for the borough of Camelford, and died in 1796,
possessed of great wealth, the fruit of his East India agen-
cies and connections.

Thence Malloch, friend alike of church and state,
Of Christ and Liberty, by grateful Fate
Raised to rewards, which, in a pious reign,
All daring infidels should seek in vain ;
Thence simple bards, by simple prudence taught,
To this wise town by simple patrons brought,

[131] David Mallett or Malloch, as he first called himself,
was the son of a small innkeeper in Crieff, and was born about
1698. At his outset in life he was through penury compelled to be janitor of the high school at Edinburgh; he
afterwards became tutor to the sons of the Duke of Montrose,
with whom he travelled, and on his return settled in London, where he became an author by profession. Here his
literary reputation grew so high, that the Duchess of Marlborough left him and Mr. Glover £1000 between them to
write the life of the great duke her husband; but clogged
the bequest with a condition that the work should be approved by her executors; and even added the humorous in-
junction, that it should not contain a single line of verse.
Mr. Glover declining the task, the £1000 became the property of Mallett, who, however, never executed the commis-
sion. On his death the papers which had been intrusted to
him were restored to the family, and being with others of no
less value deposited at Blenheim, were regularly arranged
by order of the late duke, and constituted the stores, whence
Mr. Coxe compiled his elaborate history of the illustrious
statesman and warrior. In the political disputes of his time,
Mr. Mallett took part with his countryman, Lord Bute; to
serve whom he wrote his tragedy of Elvira. He was re-
warded by his noble patron with the office of keeper of the
book of entries for ships in the port of London, to which he
was appointed in 1763. He enjoyed also a considerable
pension which had been bestowed on him for his success in
turning the public vengeance upon Admiral Byng, by means
of a letter of accusation signed "*A plain man.*" Towards
the end of his life he went to France; but finding his health
declining he returned to England, and died in 1765. As
a writer, Mallett holds a very inferior rank. Dr. Johnson
remarked of him that he was the only Scot whom Scotsmen
did not commend.

In simple manner utter simple lays,
And take, with simple pensions, simple praise.
    Waft me, some muse, to Tweed's inspiring
       stream,
Where all the little Loves and Graces dream ; 140
Where, slowly winding, the dull waters creep,
And seem themselves to own the power of sleep ;
Where on the surface lead, like feathers, swims ;
There let me bathe my yet unhallow'd limbs,
As once a Syrian bathed in Jordan's flood,
Wash off my native stains, correct that blood
Which mutinies at call of English pride,
And, deaf to prudence, rolls a patriot tide.
    From solemn thought which overhangs the brow,
Of patriot care, when things are—God knows how;
From nice trim points, where Honour, slave to rule,
In compliment to folly plays the fool ; 152
From those gay scenes, where mirth exalts his
      power,
And easy humour wings the laughing hour ;
From those soft, better moments, when desire,
Beats high, and all the world of man's on fire ;
When mutual ardours of the melting fair
More than repay us for whole years of care,
At Friendship's summons will my Wilkes retreat,
And see, once seen before, that ancient seat, 160
That ancient seat, where majesty display'd
Her ensigns, long before the world was made !
    Mean, narrow maxims which enslave mankind,
Ne'er from its bias warp thy settled mind :
Not duped by party nor opinion's slave,
Those faculties which bounteous nature gave
Thy honest spirit into practice brings,

Nor courts the smile, nor dreads the frown of
    kings,
Let rude, licentious Englishmen comply
With tumult's voice, and curse they know not why;
Unwilling to condemn, thy soul disdains   171
To wear vile faction's arbitrary chains,
And strictly weighs, in apprehension clear,
Things as they are, and not as they appear.
With thee good-humour tempers lively wit;
Enthron'd with judgment, candour loves to sit,
And nature gave thee, open to distress,
A heart to pity, and a hand to bless.
    Oft have I heard thee mourn the wretched lot
Of the poor, mean, despised, insulted Scot,   180
Who, might calm reason credit idle tales,
By rancour forged where prejudice prevails,
Or starves at home, or practises, through fear
Of starving, arts which damn all conscience here.
When scribblers, to the charge by interest led,
The fierce North Briton foaming at their head,
Pour forth invectives, deaf to candour's call,
And, injured by one alien, rail at all;
On northern Pisgah when they take their stand,
To mark the weakness of that Holy Land,   190
With needless truths their libels to adorn,
And hang a nation up to public scorn,
Thy generous soul condemns the frantic rage,
And hates the faithful, but ill-natured page.
    The Scots are poor, cries surly English pride;

[186] The Earl of Bute having been induced to patronize
the publication of a paper called the Briton, by Smollett,
provoked a retaliatory attack by Wilkes, assisted by
Churchill and others, under the name of the North Briton.

True is the charge, nor by themselves denied.
Are they not then in strictest reason clear,
Who wisely come to mend their fortunes here?
If, by low, supple arts successful grown,
They sapp'd our vigour to increase their own; 200
If, mean in want, and insolent in power,
They only fawn'd more surely to devour,
Roused by such wrongs should reason take alarm,
And e'en the Muse for public safety arm:
But if they own ingenuous virtue's sway,
And follow where true honour points the way;
If they revere the hand by which they're fed,
And bless the donors for their daily bread,
Or by vast debts of higher import bound,
Are always humble, always grateful found; 210
If they, directed by Paul's holy pen,
Become discreetly all things to all men,
That all men may become all things to them,
Envy may hate, but justice can't condemn.
" Into our places, states, and beds they creep;"
They've sense to get what we want sense to keep.
Once, be the hour accursed, accursed the place!
I ventured to blaspheme the chosen race.
Into those traps, which men, call'd patriots, laid,
By specious arts unwarily betray'd, 220
Madly I leagued against that sacred earth,
Vile parricide! which gave a parent birth:
But shall I meanly error's path pursue,
When heavenly truth presents her friendly clue?
Once plunged in ill, shall I go farther in?
To make the oath, was rash: to keep it, sin.
Backward I tread the paths I trod before,
And calm reflection hates what passion swore.

Converted, (blessed are the souls which know
Those pleasures which from true conversion flow,
Whether to reason, who now rules my breast,   231
Or to pure faith, like Lyttelton and West)
Past crimes to expiate, be my present aim
To raise new trophies to the Scottish name;
To make (what can the proudest Muse do more?)
E'en faction's sons her brighter worth adore;
To make her glories stamp'd with honest rhymes,
In fullest tide roll down to latest times.
　　" Presumptuous wretch! and shall a Muse like
　　　thine,
An English Muse, the meanest of the nine,   240
Attempt a theme like this? Can her weak strain
• Expect indulgence from the mighty Thane?
Should he from toils of government retire,
And for a moment fan the poet's fire;
Should he of sciences the moral friend,
Each curious, each important search suspend,
Leave unassisted Hill of herbs to tell,
And all the wonders of a cockleshell,
Having the Lord's good grace before his eyes,
Would not the Home step forth and gain the prize?

---

232 George Lord Lyttelton, author of the history of
Henry II. and Gilbert West, the translator of Pindar. The
former, who had been a sceptic in his earlier years,
received at Wickham in Kent, in the house of Mr. West,
that conviction which produced his celebrated "Disser-
tation on the conversion and apostolic mission of Paul."
Mr. West was much in the intimacy of Mr. Pitt, and enjoyed some lucrative appointments under government. For
his "Observations on the Resurrection," which appeared in
1747, he received from Oxford by diploma, the degree of
LL.D. He died in 1756. His friend Lord Lyttelton survived him upwards of seventeen years.

Or if this wreath of honour might adorn   251
The humble brows of one in England born,
Presumptuous still thy daring must appear ;
Vain all thy towering hopes whilst I am here."
  Thus spake a form, by silken smile, and tone
Dull and unvaried, for the Laureate known,
Folly's chief friend, Decorum's eldest son,
In every party found, and yet of none.
This airy substance, this substantial shade,
Abash'd I heard, and with respect obey'd.   261
  From themes too lofty for a bard so mean,
Discretion beckons to an humbler scene ;
The restless fever of ambition laid,
Calm I retire, and seek the sylvan shade.
Now be the Muse disrobed of all her pride,

[256] William Whitehead was the son of a tradesman in
Cambridge, and a member of Clare Hall. He accompanied
Lords Nuneham and Villiers, sons of the Earls of Harcourt
and Jersey, in their travels on the continent; and after their
return, kept up an uninterrupted intercourse with these
noble familes, living constantly with one or the other of
them. Through their interest he in 1757, on the death of
Colley Cibber, was appointed Poet Laureate, and also obtained the badge of secretary and registrar of the order of the
Bath. Churchill's resentment was probably excited against
Whitehead by the publication by the latter, in 1762, of
his " Charge to the Poets," in which, however, the satire
was so general, that we have found it difficult to discover
anything offensive to him; but after that period all
Churchill's productions abounded with severe attacks upon
the Laureate. Whitehead adhered to a precept which he
had laid down, and made no reply. Churchill's animadversions however had such an effect upon Mr. Garrick, who
dreaded being again involved in a dispute with so powerful
an enemy, that he would not venture to produce upon the
stage a tragedy offered to him by Whitehead. The Laureate
died in 1785, at the age of 70.

Be all the glare of verse by truth supplied,
And if plain nature pours a simple strain,
Which Bute may praise, and Ossian not disdain,
Ossian, sublimest, simplest bard of all,
Whom English infidels, Macpherson call,   270
Then round my head shall Honour's ensigns wave,
And pensions mark me for a willing slave.
    Two boys, whose birth, beyond all question,
       springs
From great and glorious, though forgotten, kings,
Shepherds, of Scottish lineage, born and bred
On the same bleak and barren mountain's head,
By niggard nature doom'd on the same rocks
To spin out life, and starve themselves and flocks,
Fresh as the morning, which, enrobed in mist,
The mountain's top with usual dulness kiss'd,   280
Jockey and Sawney to their labours rose;
Soon clad I ween, where nature needs no clothes;
Where, from their youth enured to winter-skies,
Dress and her vain refinements they despise.
    Jockey, whose manly, high-boned cheeks to
      crown,
With freckles spotted, flamed the golden down,
With meikle art could on the bag-pipes play,
E'en from the rising to the setting day;
Sawney as long without remorse could bawl
Home's madrigals, and ditties from Fingal: 290
Oft' at his strains, all natural though rude,
The Highland lass forgot her want of food,
And, whilst she scratch'd her lover into rest,
Sunk pleased, though hungry, on her Sawney's
      breast.
    Far as the eye could reach, no tree was seen,

Earth, clad in russet, scorn'd the lively green:
The plague of locusts they secure defy,
For in three hours a grasshopper must die:
No living thing, whate'er its food, feasts there,
But the cameleon, who can feast on air.   300
No birds, except as birds of passage, flew;
No bee was known to hum, no dove to coo:
No streams, as amber smooth, as amber clear,
Were seen to glide, or heard to warble here:
Rebellion's spring, which through the country ran,
Furnish'd, with bitter draughts, the steady clan:
No flowers embalm'd the air, but one white rose,
Which, on the tenth of June, by instinct blows;
By instinct blows at morn, and when the shades
Of drizzly eve prevail, by instinct fades.   310
    One, and but one poor solitary cave,
Too sparing of her favours, nature gave;
That one alone (hard tax on Scottish pride!)
Shelter at once for man and beast supplied.
There snares without entangling briars spread,
And thistles, arm'd against the invader's head,
Stood in close ranks, all entrance to oppose;
Thistles now held more precious than the rose.
All creatures which, on nature's earliest plan,
Were form'd to loath, and to be loath'd by man; 320
Which owed their birth to nastiness and spite,
Deadly to touch, and hateful to the sight;
Creatures, which when admitted in the ark
Their saviour shunn'd, and rankled in the dark,
Found place within: marking her noisome road

307 The white rose, the emblem of the Jacobites, was
worn by them on the 10th of June, in honour of the pretender's birth-day.

With poison's trail, here crawl'd the bloated toad :
There webs were spread of more than common size,
And half-starved spiders prey'd on half-starved
    flies :
In quest of food, efts strove in vain to crawl ;
Slugs, pinch'd with hunger, smear'd the slimy
    wall :   330
The cave around with hissing serpents rung ;
On the damp roof unhealthy vapour hung ;
And Famine, by her children always known,
As proud as poor, here fix'd her native throne.
    Here, for the sullen sky was overcast,
And summer shrunk beneath a wintry blast ;
A native blast, which, arm'd with hail and rain,
Beat unrelenting on the naked swain,
The boys for shelter made ; behind, the sheep,
Of which those shepherds every day *take keep*, 340
Sickly crept on, and with complainings rude,
On nature seem'd to call, and bleat for food.

JOCKEY.

    Sith to this cave, by tempest, we're confined,
And within *ken* our flocks, under the wind,
Safe from the pelting of this perilous storm,
Are laid *emong* yon' thistles, dry and warm,
What, Sawney, if by Shepherds' art we try
To mock the rigour of this cruel sky ?
What if we tune some merry roundelay ?
Well dost thou sing, nor ill doth Jockey play. 350

SAWNEY.

    Ah ! Jockey, ill advisest thou, I wis,
To think of songs at such a time as this :

Sooner shall herbage crown these barren rocks,
Sooner shall fleeces clothe these ragged flocks,
Sooner shall want seize shepherds of the south,
And we forget to live from hand to mouth,
Than Sawney, out of season, shall impart
The songs of gladness with an aching heart.

JOCKEY.

Still have I known thee for a silly swain;
Of things past help what boots it to complain? 360
Nothing but mirth can conquer fortune's spite;
No sky is heavy if the heart be light:
Patience is sorrow's salve: what can't be cured,
So Donald right areeds, must be endured.

SAWNEY.

Full silly swain, I wot, is Jockey now.
How didst thow bear thy Maggy's falsehood? how,
When with a foreign loon she stole away,
Didst thou forswear thy pipe and shepherd's lay!
Where was thy boasted wisdom then, when I
Applied those proverbs, which you now apply? 370

JOCKEY.

O she was bonny! all the Highlands round
Was there a rival to my Maggy found?
More precious (though that precious is to all)
Than the rare med'cine which we Brimstone call,
Or that choice plant, so grateful to the nose,
Which, in I know not what far country, grows,
Was Maggy unto me: dear do I rue
A lass so fair should ever prove untrue.

SAWNEY.

Whether with pipe or song to charm the ear,
Through all the land did Jamie find a peer?   380
Cursed be that year by every honest Scot,
And in the shepherd's calendar forgot,
That fatal year when Jamie, hapless swain!
In evil hour forsook the peaceful plain:
Jamie, when our young laird discreetly fled,
Was seized, and hang'd till he was dead, dead, dead.

JOCKEY.

Full sorely may we all lament that day,
For all were losers in the deadly fray.
Five brothers had I; on the Scottish plains,
Well dost thou know were none more hopeful
    swains;   390
Five brothers there I lost, in manhood's pride;
.Two in the field, and three on gibbets died:
Ah! silly swains! to follow war's alarms;
Ah! what hath shepherds' life to do with arms?

SAWNEY.

Mention it not—there saw I strangers clad
In all the honours of our ravish'd plaid;
Saw the Ferrara, too, our nation's pride,
Unwilling grace the awkward victor's side.
There fell our choicest youth, and from that day
Mote never Sawney tune the merry lay;   400
Bless'd those which fell! cursed those which still
    survive,
To mourn fifteen renew'd in forty-five.

Thus plain'd the boys, when from her throne of
    turf,
With boils emboss'd, and overgrown with scurf,
Vile humours, which, in life's corrupted well,
Mix'd at the birth not abstinence could quell,
Pale Famine rear'd the head; her eager eyes,
Where hunger e'en to madness seem'd to rise,
Speaking aloud her throes and pangs of heart,
Strain'd to get loose, and from their orbs to start:
Her hollow cheeks were each a deep-sunk cell, 411
Where wretchedness and horror loved to dwell:
With double rows of useless teeth supplied,
Her mouth from ear to ear extended wide,
Which, when for want of food her entrails pined,
She oped, and cursing, swallow'd nought but wind:
All shrivell'd was her skin; and here and there,
Making their way by force, her bones lay bare:
Such filthy sight to hide from human view,
O'er her foul limbs a tatter'd plaid she threw. 420
    " Cease," cried the goddess, " cease, despairing
    swains !
And from a parent hear what Jove ordains:
" Pent in this barren corner of the isle,
Where partial fortune never deign'd to smile;
Like nature's bastards, reaping for our share
What was rejected by the lawful heir;
Unknown amongst the nations of the earth,
Or only known to raise contempt and mirth;
Long free, because the race of Roman braves
Thought it not worth their while to make us slaves;
Then into bondage by that nation brought,   431
Whose ruin we for ages vainly sought;
Whom still with unslacked hate we view, and still,

The power of mischief lost, retain the will ;
Consider'd as the refuse of mankind,
A mass till the last moment left behind,
Which frugal nature doubted, as it lay,
Whether to stamp with life or throw away ;
Which, form'd in haste, was planted in this nook,
But never enter'd in creation's book ;   440
Branded as traitors who for love of gold
Would sell their God, as once their king they sold.
Long have we borne this mighty weight of ill,
These vile injurious taunts, and bear them still ;
But times of happier note are now at hand,
And the full promise of a better land :
There, like the sons of Israel, having trod,
For the fix'd term of years ordain'd by God,
A barren desert, we shall seize rich plains,   449
Where milk with honey flows, and plenty reigns :
With some few natives join'd, some pliant few,
Who worship interest and our track pursue ;
There shall we though the wretched people grieve,
Ravage at large, nor ask the owners' leave.
  "For us, the earth shall bring forth her increase,
For us, the flocks shall wear a golden fleece ;
Fat beeves shall yield us dainties not our own,
And the grape bleed a nectar yet unknown :
For our advantage shall their harvests grow,
And Scotsman reap what they disdain'd to sow :
For us, the sun shall climb the eastern hill ;   461

---

440 Cleveland, in his famous couplet on Scotland, intro-
duces an allusion to Scripture equally severe :

  "Had Cain been Scot, God had reversed his doom,
Not forced him wander, but confined him home."

For us, the rain shall fall, the dew distil:
When to our wishes nature cannot rise,
Art shall be task'd to grant us fresh supplies;
His brawny arm shall drudging labour strain,
And for our pleasure suffer daily pain:
Trade shall for us exert her utmost powers,
Hers all the toil, and all the profit ours:
For us, the oak shall from his native steep
Descend, and fearless travel through the deep:
The sail of commerce, for our use unfurl'd,   471
Shall waft the treasures of each distant world:
For us, sublimer heights shall science reach;
For us, their statesmen plot, their churchmen
          preach:
Their noblest limbs of council we'll disjoint,
And, mocking, new ones of our own appoint:
Devouring War, imprison'd in the North,
Shall, at our call, in horrid pomp break forth,
And when, his chariot-wheels with thunder hung.
Fell Discord braying with her brazen tongue,   480
Death in the van, with Anger, Hate, and Fear,
And Desolation stalking in the rear,
Revenge, by Justice guided, in his train,
He drives impetuous o'er the trembling plain,
Shall, at our bidding, quit his lawful prey,
And to meek, gentle, generous Peace give way.
    "Think not, my Sons, that this so bless'd estate
Stands at a distance on the roll of fate;
Already big with hopes of future sway,
E'en from this cave I scent my destined prey.   490
Think not, that this dominion o'er a race
Whose former deeds shall time's last annals grace,
In the rough face of peril must be sought,

And with the lives of thousands dearly bought :
No—fool'd by cunning, by that happy art
Which laughs to scorn the blundering hero's heart,
Into the snare shall our kind neighbours fall
With open eyes, and fondly give us all.
    " When Rome, to prop her sinking empire, bore
Their choicest levies to a foreign shore,   500
What if we seized, like a destroying flood,
Their widow'd plains, and fill'd the realm with
        blood,
Gave an unbounded loose to manly rage,
And, scorning mercy, spared nor sex, nor age ?
When, for our interest too mighty grown,
Monarchs of warlike bent possess'd the throne,
What if we strove divisions to foment,
And spread the flames of civil discontent,
Assisted those who 'gainst their king made head,
And gave the traitors refuge when they fled ?   510
When restless Glory bade her sons advance,
And pitch'd her standard in the fields of France,
What if, disdaining oaths, an empty sound,
By which our nation never shall be bound,
Bravely we taught unmuzzled war to roam,
Through the weak land, and brought cheap laurels
        home ?
When the bold traitors leagued for the defence
Of law, religion, liberty, and sense,
When they against their lawful monarch rose,
And dared the Lord's anointed to oppose,   520
What if we still revered the banish'd race,
And strove the royal vagrants to replace,
With fierce rebellions shook the unsettled state,
And greatly dared, though cross'd by partial fate ?

These facts, which might, where wisdom held the
    sway,
Awake the very stones to bar our way,
There shall be nothing, nor one trace remain
In the dull region of an English brain ;   [move,
Bless'd with that faith which mountains can re-
First they shall dupes, next saints, last martyrs,
    prove.   530
  " Already is this game of fate begun
Under the sanction of my darling son ;
That son, of nature royal as his name,
Is destined to redeem our race from shame :
His boundless power, beyond example great,
Shall make the rough way smooth, the crooked
    straight ;
Shall for our ease the raging floods restrain,
And sink the mountain level to the plain.
Discord, whom in a cavern under ground
With massy fetters their late patriot bound ;   540
Where her own flesh the furious hag might tear,
And vent her curses to the vacant air ;
Where, that she never might be heard of more,
He planted Loyalty to guard the door,
For better purpose shall our chief release,
Disguise her for a time, and call her peace.
  " Lured by that name, fine engine of deceit!
Shall the weak English help themselves to cheat ;

546 The splendid victories obtained under Mr. Pitt's
administration had, like those of the Duke of Marlborough,
infused a warlike spirit into the nation, which indisposed it
towards the greatest of all blessings. The peace of 1763,
was compared to that of Utrecht, and became the constant
subject of intemperate abuse with the leaders of opposition ;
on the discussion of the preliminary articles, in the House of

To gain our love, with honours shall they grace
The old adherents of the Stuart race,   550
Who, pointed out no matter by what name,
Tories or Jacobites, are still the same ;
To soothe our rage the temporising brood
Shall break the ties of truth and gratitude,
Against their saviour venom'd falsehoods frame,
And brand with calumny our William's name :
To win our grace, (rare argument of wit !)
To our untainted faith shall they commit
(Our faith which, in extremest perils tried,
Disdain'd, and still disdains to change her side) 560
That sacred Majesty they all approve,
Who most enjoys, and best deserves their love."

Lords, the Earl of Bute entered into a spirited vindication of
them, and concluded his speech with declaring, "That he
wished no other epitaph to be inscribed upon his tomb, than,
that he was the adviser of that peace, on the merits of which
their lordships were then called upon to decide."

AN EPISTLE TO WILLIAM HOGARTH.

PUBLISHED IN JULY 1763.

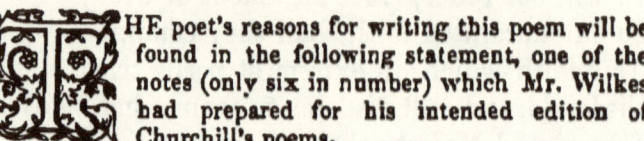

HE poet's reasons for writing this poem will be found in the following statement, one of the notes (only six in number) which Mr. Wilkes had prepared for his intended edition of Churchill's poems.

"The Scottish minister had been attacked in a variety of political papers; the North Briton in particular waged open war with him. Some of the numbers had been ascribed to Mr. Wilkes, others to Mr. Churchill and Mr. Lloyd. Mr. Hogarth had for several years lived on terms of friendship if not of intimacy with Mr. Wilkes. As the Buckinghamshire regiment of militia, which this gentleman had the honour of commanding, had been for some months at Winchester, guarding the French prisoners, the Colonel was there on that duty. A friend wrote to him, that Mr. Hogarth intended soon to publish a political print of the *Times*, in which Mr. Pitt, Lord Temple, Mr. Churchill, and himself, were held out to the public as objects of ridicule. Mr. Wilkes, on this notice, remonstrated by two of their common friends to Mr. Hogarth, that such a proceeding would not only be unfriendly in the highest degree, but extremely injudicious; for such a pencil ought to be universal and moral, to speak to all ages and all nations, not to be dipped in the dirt of the faction of a day, of an insignificant part of the country, when it might command the admiration of the whole. An answer was sent, that neither Mr. Wilkes nor Mr. Churchill was attacked in the *Times*, though Lord Temple and Mr. Pitt were, and that the print would soon appear. A second message soon after told Mr. Hogarth that Mr. Wilkes would never think it worth his while to take notice of any reflections on himself; but when his friends were attacked, he found himself wounded in the most sensible part, and would as well as he could revenge their cause; adding, that if he thought the North Briton would insert what he should send, he would make an appeal to the public on the very Saturday following the publication of the print. The *Times* soon after appeared, and on the Saturday following No. XVII. of the North Briton. If Mr. Wilkes did write that paper, he kept his word better with Mr. Hogarth than the painter had done with him.

" When Mr. Wilkes was the second time brought from the Tower to Westminster Hall, Mr. Hogarth skulked behind in a corner of the gallery of the court of Common Pleas; and while the Lord Chief Justice Pratt, with the eloquence and courage of old Rome, was enforcing the great principles of Magna Charta and the English constitution; while every breast from his caught the holy flame of liberty, the painter was employed in caricaturing the person of the man, while all the rest of his fellow-citizens were animated in his cause; for they knew it to be their own cause, of their country, and of its laws. It was declared to be so a few hours after by the unanimous sentence of the judges of that court; and they were all present. The print of Mr. Wilkes was soon after published, drawn from the life by William Hogarth. It must be allowed to be an excellent compound caricatura, or a caricatura of what nature had already caricatured. I know but one short apology to be made for this gentleman, or, to speak more properly, for the person of Mr. Wilkes; it is, that he did not make himself,' and that he never was solicitous about the *case* of his soul (as Shakespeare calls it) only so far as to keep it clean and in health. I never heard that he once hung over the glassy stream, like another Narcissus, admiring the image in it, nor that he ever stole an amorous look at his counterfeit in a side mirror. His form, such as it is, ought to give him no pain, while it is capable of giving so much pleasure to others. I believe he finds himself tolerably happy in the clay cottage to which he is *tenant for life,* because he has learned to keep it in pretty good order; while the share of health and animal spirits which Heaven has given him shall hold out, I can scarcely imagine he will be one moment peevish about the outside of so precarious, so temporary a habitation, or will ever be brought to own, ' Ingenium Galbæ male habitat:' ' Monsieur est mal logé.' "

Ut Pictura, Poesis.—HOR.

MONGST the sons of men how few are
known
Who dare be just to merit not their
own!
Superior virtue and superior sense
To knaves and fools will always give offence;
Nay, men of real worth can scarcely bear,
So nice is jealousy, a rival there.
Be wicked as thou wilt; do all that's base;
Proclaim thyself the monster of thy race:
Let Vice and Folly thy black soul divide;
Be proud with meanness, and be mean with pride.
Deaf to the voice of Faith and Honour, fall   11
From side to side, yet be of none at all:
Spurn all those charities, those sacred ties,
Which Nature, in her bounty, good as wise,
To work our safety, and ensure her plan,
Contrived to bind and rivet man to man:
Lift against Virtue Power's oppressive rod;
Betray thy country, and deny thy God;
And, in one general, comprehensive line,
To group, which volumes scarcely could define,   20
Whate'er of sin and dulness can be said,
Join to a Fox's heart a Dashwood's head;

[22] Henry Fox, afterwards Lord Holland, Paymaster-
General of the Forces during the whole of the war under
Lord Bute's administration, of which he was one of the
ablest advocates in the House of Commons. From some

Yet may'st thou pass unnoticed in the throng,
And, free from envy, safely sneak along:
The rigid saint, by whom no mercy's shown
To saints whose lives are better than his own,
Shall spare thy crimes; and Wit, who never once
Forgave a brother, shall forgive a dunce.
    But should thy soul, form'd in some luckless
      hour,
Vile interest scorn, nor madly grasp at power; 30
Should love of fame, in every noble mind
A brave disease, with love of virtue join'd,
Spur thee to deeds of pith, where courage, tried
In Reason's court, is amply justified;
Or, fond of knowledge, and averse to strife,
Shouldst thou prefer the calmer walk of life;
Shouldst thou, by pale and sickly study led,
Pursue coy Science to the fountain-head;
Virtue thy guide, and public good thy end,

alleged inaccuracies in his accounts while Paymaster, he
was stigmatized as "the defaulter of unaccounted millions."
Soon after the peace of Paris, Sir John Phillips moved in
the House of Commons, "that a committee be appointed to
take into consideration the several estimates and accounts
presented to the House, either in the present or in any former session of parliament, which relate to the application or
expenditure of the public money since the commencement of
the late war." The House of Commons came to this resolution on the 22nd of February, 1763: on the 17th of April
following Mr. Fox was created Lord Holland, and in a very
short time after retired for a season to France. He died
1 July, 1774.
  [22] Sir Francis Dashwood, afterwards [1763] Lord Le
Despencer, a zealous revolution Tory, intimately connected
with the court of Leicester house. On Lord Bute's coming
into power, he succeeded Mr. Legge in the Chancellorship
of the Exchequer, and Lord Temple in the Colonelcy of the
Buckinghamshire militia. He died in 1781.

Should every thought to our improvement tend, 40
To curb the passions, to enlarge the mind,
Purge the sick weal, and humanize mankind;
Rage in her eye, and malice in her breast,
Redoubled Horror grinning on her crest,
Fiercer each snake, and sharper every dart,
Quick from her cell shall maddening Envy start;
Then shalt thou find, but find, alas! too late,
How vain is worth! how short is glory's date!
Then shalt thou find, whilst friends with foes con-
   spire
To give more proof than virtue would desire, 50
Thy danger chiefly lies in acting well;
No crime's so great as daring to excel.

 Whilst Satire thus, disdaining mean control,
Urged the free dictates of an honest soul,
Candour, who, with the charity of Paul,
Still thinks the best, whene'er she thinks at all,
With the sweet milk of human kindness bless'd,
The furious ardour of my zeal repress'd.
 " Canst thou," with more than usual warmth,
   she cried,
" Thy malice to indulge, and feed thy pride; 60
Canst thou, severe by nature as thou art,
With all that wondrous rancour in thy heart,
Delight to torture truth ten thousand ways,
To spin detraction forth from themes of praise,
To make Vice sit, for purposes of strife,
And draw the hag much larger than the life;
To make the good seem bad, the bad seem worse,
And represent our nature as our curse?
 " Doth not humanity condemn that zeal
Which tends to aggravate and not to heal? 70

Doth not discretion warn thee of disgrace,
And danger, grinning, stare thee in the face,
Loud as the drum which, spreading terror round,
From emptiness acquires the power of sound?
Doth not the voice of Norton strike thy ear,
And the pale Mansfield chill thy soul with fear?
Dost thou, fond man, believe thyself secure,
Because thou'rt honest, and because thou'rt poor?
Dost thou on law and liberty depend?
Turn, turn thy eyes, and view thy injured friend.
Art thou beyond the ruffian gripe of power,   81
When Wilkes, prejudged, is sentenced to the
    Tower?

[75] Sir Fletcher Norton was Attorney-General from 1763 to 1765; Speaker of the House of Commons from 1770 to 1780; and was created a peer in 1782 by the title of Lord Grantley. One of the most remarkable passages of his life was his attempt, in the House of Commons, to prove that our colonies in America were directly represented in parliament by the members for the county of Kent; the charters of each of the provinces reciting them to be part and parcel of the manor of Greenwich. When Speaker of the House of Commons, Sir Fletcher Norton distinguished himself by a singular speech to the king, on presenting for the royal assent in 1777 the bill for granting a large sum in aid of the civil list. This speech he concluded with these words: "This, Sire, they have done in the well-grounded confidence that you will apply wisely what they have granted liberally." Mr. Rigby having severely censured this address, the House came to a resolution, upon the motion of Mr. C. J. Fox, "That the Speaker did express with just and proper energy the sentiments of this House;" and passed a vote of thanks to him for his conduct on the occasion. He died in 1789.

[82] The North Briton was discontinued upon the resignation of Lord Bute in April 1763, having gained a complete victory over that minister. Not contented with this success, it menaced his successors, and recommenced on Saturday the

Dost thou by privilege exemption claim,
When privilege is little more than name?
Or to prerogative (that glorious ground
On which state scoundrels oft have safety found)

23rd of April with the famous No. XLV, which charged
the king's speech, made at the close of the session, with con-
veying a direct falsehood. The author obtained his end by
becoming the object of an illegal prosecution. A general
warrant, signed by and under the seal of Lord Halifax, was
issued to apprehend the author, printers, and publishers of
that seditious and treasonable paper. On the 29th of April
1763, late at night, the messengers entered the house of
Mr. Wilkes, and produced their warrant, with the terms of
which he refused to comply; but on their return the next
morning he was compelled to accompany them to the office
of the Secretary of State, whence he was committed close
prisoner to the Tower, his papers having been previously
seized and sealed, and all access to his person strictly pro-
hibited. On his examination, Wilkes, with great presence of
mind, screened our author, his fellow-labourer in the political
vineyard, from a similar prosecution; though it afterwards
appeared, by the evidence of Kearsley, the original publisher of the North Briton, that Mr. Charles Churchill received a part of the profits arising from its sale.
    Mr. Wilkes, immediately on his commitment, applied to
the Court of Common Pleas for a habeas corpus, and, after
several attempts on the part of the law officers of the crown
to evade the force of that writ, was brought up to the court
on the 3rd and 6th days of May. After due deliberation,
the Chief Justice ordered his discharge on his claim of privilege as a member of the House of Commons, such privilege
having been violated by his apprehension and committal to
the Tower for a supposed offence involving neither treason,
felony, nor even a breach of the peace. In the next term an
information was filed against him as the author of No. XLV,
to which he refused to answer, on his former plea of privilege. In November a message was sent by the king to the
House of Commons, by George Grenville, Chancellor of the
Exchequer, informing the House of the proceedings that had
been taken against Mr. Wilkes, and that his Majesty had,
out of regard to their privileges, directed copies of the libel,

Dost thou pretend, and there a sanction find,
Unpunish'd, thus to libel human-kind?
" When poverty, the poet's constant crime,
Compell'd thee, all unfit, to trade in rhyme,   90

the examinations, &c, to be laid before them for their consideration. The House upon this immediately resolved, by a majority of 273 against 111, "That the paper entitled the North Briton, No. XLV. was a false, scandalous, and seditious libel, containing expressions of the most unexampled insolence and contumely towards his Majesty, the grossest aspersions on both houses of parliament, and the most audacious defiance of the authority of the whole legislature; and most manifestly tending to alienate the affections of the people from his Majesty, to withdraw them from their obedience to the laws of the realm, and to excite them to traitorous insurrections." And thereupon it was resolved, "That privilege of parliament does not extend to the writing and publishing seditious libels, and that the North Briton, No. XLV. is a false, scandalous, and seditious libel." It was accordingly ordered to be burnt at the Royal Exchange by the common hangman, which was carried into execution with great difficulty by Mr. Sheriff Harley. With respect to No. XLV. Churchill never saw a line of it previous to the publication, though he narrowly escaped being taken into custody by the messengers under the general warrant against the persons concerned in the North Briton. He called at Mr. Wilkes' house while they were in possession of it; but that wily demagogue, by addressing him as "Thompson" (his person being entirely unknown to the messengers), gave him an opportunity of withdrawing unmolested.

During the Christmas vacation Mr. Wilkes retired to France; on the 16th of January, 1764, a day fixed for his appearance in the House of Commons, the Speaker produced a letter from Mr. Wilkes, inclosing medical certificates of the ill state of his health, in consequence of a wound he had received in his duel with Mr. Martin, as an apology for his absence. The House nevertheless voted Mr. Wilkes guilty of a contempt of their authority, proceeded to hear evidence on the charge against him, and on the 29th of January, 1764, after a long and vehement debate, resolved, "That John

Had not romantic notions turn'd thy head,
Hadst thou not valued honour more than bread;
Had Interest, pliant Interest, been thy guide,
And had not Prudence been debauch'd by Pride,
In flattery's stream thou wouldst have dipp'd thy
　　pen,
Applied to great and not to honest men ;
Nor should conviction have seduced thy heart
To take the weaker though the better part.
　What but rank folly, for thy curse decreed,
Could into Satire's barren path mislead,　　　100
When, open to thy view, before thee lay
Soul-soothing Panegyric's flowery way ?
There might the Muse have saunter'd at her ease,
And, pleasing others, learn'd herself to please ;
Lords should have listen'd to the sugar'd treat,
And ladies, simpering, own'd it vastly sweet ;
Rogues, in thy prudent verse with virtue graced,
Fools mark'd by thee as prodigies of taste,
Must have forbid, pouring preferments down,
Such wit, such truth as thine to quit the gown.
Thy sacred brethren too (for they no less　　　111
Than laymen, bring their offerings to success)

Had hail'd thee good if great, and paid the vow
Sincere as that they pay to God; whilst thou
In lawn hadst whisper'd to a sleeping crowd,
As dull as Rochester, and half as proud.

    Peace, Candour—wisely hadst thou said, and well
Could Interest in this breast one moment dwell;
Could she, with prospect of success, oppose
The firm resolves which from conviction rose. 120
I cannot truckle to a fool of state,
Nor take a favour from the man I hate:
Free leave have others by such means to shine;
I scorn their practice; they may laugh at mine.

    But, in this charge, forgetful of thyself,
Thou hast assumed the maxims of that elf
Whom God in wrath for man's dishonour framed,
Cunning in heaven, amongst us Prudence named,
That servile prudence, which I leave to those
Who dare not be my friends, can't be my foes. 130

    Had I, with cruel and oppressive rhymes,
Pursued and turn'd misfortunes into crimes;
Had I, when Virtue gasping lay and low,
Join'd tyrant Vice, and added woe to woe;
Had I made Modesty in blushes speak,
And drawn the tear down beauty's sacred cheek;
Had I (damn'd then) in thought debased my lays,
To wound that sex which honour bids me praise;
Had I, from vengeance, by base views betray'd,
In endless night sunk injured Ayliffe's shade; 140
Had I (which satirists of mighty name,

---

[116] See note on l. 128 of the preceding poem.
[140] John Ayliffe was originally steward in the Ilchester
family, but was promoted by Lord Holland to the situation
of Commissary of the Musters. Considerable as were the

Renown'd in rhyme, revered for moral fame,
Have done before, whom justice shall pursue
In future verse) brought forth to public view
A noble friend, and made his foibles known,
Because his worth was greater than my own;
Had I spared those (so Prudence had decreed)
Whom, God so help me at my greatest need,
I ne'er will spare, those vipers to their king
Who smooth their looks, and flatter whilst they
    sting;   150
Or had I not taught patriot zeal to boast

emoluments of this office, they proved unequal to the ex-
penses of his establishment, and he had recourse to several
nefarious practices to support it. A long course of villany
was terminated by his execution at Tyburn in 1759; the
crime for which he suffered was forging Lord Holland's
name to a valuable lease to himself. Although Ayliffe, in
his defence, made some very injurious insinuations against
his patron, Lord Holland treated him with the utmost kindness and forbearance during his trial and subsequent imprisonment. He sent him money and provisions; payed his
chamber rent from the time of his incarceration till his
death; sent his own physician to attend him; and hired a
special keeper to take care of him, so that he might not be
ironed. He also consented to a postponement of the trial,
and suppressed two distinct confessions of forgery delibe-
rately made by Ayliffe. The latter expected till the last
moment a pardon, which it was reported had been promised
him by a friend, provided he would undertake not to re-
veal some important transactions he had been privy to; with
this condition he complied, but his friend, no doubt, thought
the fulfilment of the sentence would be the best pledge of his
secrecy.

    Churchill was only prevented by death from publishing a
poem he had more than once advertised, entitled "An Elegy,
or Ayliffe's Ghost." A reverend emissary was employed by
a noble Lord to ward off the threatened blow; but Churchill
was not to be bribed, and death alone deprived the world
of the promised satire.

[145] Alluding to Pope's attack on Addison

Of those who flatter least, but love him most;
Had I thus sinn'd, my stubborn soul should bend
At Candour's voice, and take, as from a friend,
The deep rebuke ; myself should be the first
To hate myself, and stamp my Muse accurst.
    But shall my arm—forbid it, manly pride,
Forbid it, reason, warring on my side—
For vengeance lifted high, the stroke forbear,
And hang suspended in the desert air ;   160
Or to my trembling side unnerved sink down,
Palsied, forsooth, by Candour's half-made frown ?
When Justice bids me on, shall I delay,
Because insipid Candour bars my way ?
When she, of all alike the puling friend,
Would disappoint my satire's noblest end ;
When she to villains would a sanction give,
And shelter those who are not fit to live ;
When she would screen the guilty from a blush,
And bids me spare whom Reason bids me crush ;
All leagues with Candour proudly I resign ;   171
She cannot be for Honour's turn, nor mine.
    Yet come, cold monitor ! half foe, half friend
Whom Vice can't fear, whom Virtue can't com-
       mend ;
Come, Candour, by thy dull indifference known,
Thou equal-blooded judge, thou luke-warm drone,
Who, fashion'd without feelings, dost expect
We call that virtue which we know defect ;
Come, and observe the nature of our crimes,
The gross and rank complexion of the times ; 180
Observe it well, and then review my plan,
Praise if you will, or censure if you can.
    Whilst Vice, presumptuous, lords it as in sport,

And Piety is only known at court ;
Whilst wretched Liberty expiring lies
Beneath the fatal burthen of Excise ;
Whilst nobles act, without one touch of shame,
What men of humble rank would blush to name ;
Whilst Honour's placed in highest point of view,
Worshipp'd by those who justice never knew ; 190
Whilst bubbles of distinction waste in play
The hours of rest, and blunder through the day ;
With dice and cards opprobrious vigils keep,
Then turn to ruin empires in their sleep ;
Whilst fathers, by relentless passion led,
Doom worthy, injured sons to beg their bread,
Merely with ill-got, ill-saved wealth to grace
An alien, abject, poor, proud, upstart race ;
Whilst Martin flatters only to betray,
And Webb gives up his dirty soul for pay ; 200
Whilst titles serve to hush a villain's fears ;

[196] Thomas Potter, Esq., one of our author's companions, and a man of splendid but misdirected talents, was disinherited by his father, the Archbishop of Canterbury, on account of his unprincipled and dissolute conduct. He also offended his father by a very unequal, if not disgraceful, marriage. Mr. Potter was M. P. for Aylesbury, which seat he vacated on being appointed one of the Vice-Treasurers of Ireland. With some address he contrived to get his friend Wilkes to succeed him at Aylesbury, whilst he himself came in for Okehampton, vacated by Mr. Pitt, who succeeded Lord Northington at Bath.

[199] Samuel Martin, Esq. F.R.S. M.P. for Camelford; the hero of the Duellist.

[200] Philip Carteret Webb, Esq. F.A.S., M.P. for Haslemere, Solicitor to the Treasury, by his active exertions in the proceedings against Wilkes rendered himself very obnoxious to the popular party. He was an eminent antiquary, and his collection of MSS, coins, marble busts, bronzes, and other curious works of art, were very valuable.

Whilst peers are agents made, and agents peers ;
Whilst base betrayers are themselves betray'd,
And makers ruin'd by the thing they made ;
Whilst C——, false to God and man, for gold,
Like the old traitor who a Saviour sold,
To shame his master, friend, and father, gives ;
Whilst Bute remains in power, whilst Holland lives,
Can Satire want a subject, where Disdain,   200
By Virtue fired, may point her sharpest strain ?
Where, clothed with thunder, Truth may roll along,
And Candour justify the rage of song ?

Such things, such men before thee, such an age,
Where Rancour, great as thine, may glut her rage,
And sicken e'en to surfeit; where the pride
Of Satire, pouring down in fullest tide,
May spread wide vengeance round, yet all the while
Justice behold the ruin with a smile ;
Whilst I, thy foe misdeem'd, cannot condemn
Nor disapprove that rage I wish to stem,   220
Wilt thou, degenerate and corrupted, choose
To soil the credit of thy haughty Muse?
With fallacy, most infamous, to stain

<hr />

205 Churchill occasionally threw out an initial by way of
exciting the curiosity of the reader, who was at liberty to
apply the cap to any head it might fit.

206 Lord Bute's administration commenced on the 29th of
May, 1762, and terminated with his resignation on the 8th
of April, 1763, when he was succeeded by Mr. Grenville.
Lord Sandwich succeeded Mr. Grenville as First Lord of the
Admiralty. Lord Bute, however, though nominally out of the
administration, was thought to possess all-powerful influence
at this time, an influence which Lord Chatham asserted was
greater than that of the throne itself.

206 Henry Fox, first Lord Holland. *See* the Notes to
" Epistle to Hogarth," l. 140, and " The Duellist," Book I.
l. 128.

Her truth, and render all her anger vain?
When I beheld thee, incorrect, but bold,
A various comment on the stage unfold;
When players on players before thy satire fell,
And poor Reviews conspired thy wrath to swell;
When states and statesmen next became thy care,
And only kings were safe if thou wast there,   230
Thy every word I weigh'd in judgment's scale,
And in thy every word found truth prevail.
Why dost thou now to falsehood meanly fly?
Not even Candour can forgive a lie.
 Bad as men are, why should thy frantic rhymes
Traffic in slander, and invent new crimes?
Crimes which, existing only in thy mind,
Weak spleen brings forth to blacken all mankind.
By pleasing hopes we lure the human heart
To practise virtue, and improve in art;   240
To thwart these ends (which, proud of honest fame,
A noble Muse would cherish and inflame)
Thy drudge contrives, and in our full career
Sicklies our hopes with the pale hue of fear;
Tells us that all our labours are in vain;
That what we seek we never can obtain;
That, dead to virtue, lost to Nature's plan,
Envy possesses the whole race of man;
That worth is criminal, and danger lies,
Danger extreme, in being good and wise.   250
 'Tis a rank falsehood; search the world around,
There cannot be so vile a monster found,
Not one so vile, on whom suspicions fall
Of that gross guilt which you impute to all.
Approved by those who disobey her laws,
Virtue from vice itself extorts applause:

Her very foes bear witness to her state;
They will not love her, but they cannot hate.
Hate Virtue for herself! with spite pursue
Merit for merit's sake ! might this be true   260
I would renounce my nature with disdain,
And with the beasts that perish graze the plain;
Might this be true, had we so far fill'd up
The measure of our crimes, and from the cup
Of guilt so deeply drank, as not to find,
Thirsting for sin, one drop, one dreg behind,
Quick ruin must involve this flaming ball,
And Providence in justice crush us all.
None but the damn'd, and amongst them the worst,
Those who for double guilt are doubly curst,   270
Can be so lost; nor can the worst of all
At once into such deep damnation fall;
By painful, slow degrees they reach this crime,
Which e'en in hell must be a work of time.

Cease, then, thy guilty rage, thou wayward son,
With the foul gall of discontent o'errun;
List to my voice—be honest, if you can,
Nor slander Nature in her favourite man.
But if thy spirit, resolute in ill,
Once having err'd, persists in error still,   280
Go on at large, no longer worth my care,
And freely vent those blasphemies in air,
Which I would stamp as false, tho' on the tongue
Of angels the injurious slander hung.

Duped by thy vanity, (that cunning elf
Who snares the coxcomb to deceive himself)
Or blinded by thy rage, didst thou believe
That we too, coolly, would ourselves deceive ?
That we, as sterling, falsehood would admit,

Because 'twas season'd with some little wit? 290
When fiction rises pleasing to the eye,
Men will believe, because they love the lie;
But Truth herself, if clouded with a frown,
Must have some solemn proof to pass her down.
Hast thou, maintaining that which must disgrace
And bring into contempt the human race;
Hast thou, or canst thou, in Truth's sacred court,
To save thy credit, and thy cause support,
Produce one proof, make out one real ground, 299
On which so great, so gross a charge to found?
Nay, dost thou know one man (let that appear,
From wilful falsehood I'll proclaim thee clear),
One man so lost, to nature so untrue,
From whom this general charge thy rashness drew?
On this foundation shalt thou stand or fall—
Prove that in one which you have charged on all.
Reason determines, and it must be done;
'Mongst men or past or present name me one.
    Hogarth.—I take thee, Candour, at thy word,
Accept thy proffer'd terms, and will be heard. 310
Thee have I heard with virulence declaim,
Nothing retain'd of Candour but the name;
By thee have I been charged in angry strains
With that mean falsehood which my soul disdains—
Hogarth, stand forth.—Nay, hang not thus aloof—
Now, Candour, now thou shalt receive such proof,
Such damning proof, that henceforth thou shalt fear
To tax my wrath, and own my conduct clear—
Hogarth, stand forth—I dare thee to be tried
In that great court where Conscience must preside;
At that most solemn bar hold up thy hand; 321
Think before whom, on what account, you stand—

Speak, but consider well—from first to last
Review thy life, weigh every action past ;
Nay—you shall have no reason to complain—
Take longer time, and view them o'er again ;
Canst thou remember from thy earliest youth,
And as thy God must judge thee, speak the truth,
A single instance where, self laid aside,
And justice taking place of fear and pride,   330
Thou with an equal eye didst genius view,
And give to merit what was merit's due ?
Genius and merit are a sure offence,
And thy soul sickens at the name of sense.
Is any one so foolish to succeed,
On Envy's altar he is doom'd to bleed ;
Hogarth, a guilty pleasure in his eyes,
The place of executioner supplies :
See how he glotes, enjoys the sacred feast,
And proves himself by cruelty a priest.   340
    Whilst the weak artist, to thy whims a slave,
Would bury all those powers which nature gave ;
Would suffer blank concealment to obscure
Those rays thy jealousy could not endure ;
To feed thy vanity would rust unknown,
And to secure thy credit blast his own,
In Hogarth he was sure to find a friend ;
He could not fear, and therefore might commend :
But when his spirit, roused by honest shame,
Shook off that lethargy, and soar'd to fame ;   350
When, with the pride of man, resolved and strong,
He scorn'd those fears which did his honour wrong,
And, on himself determined to rely,
Brought forth his labours to the public eye,
No friend in thee could such a rebel know ;

He had desert, and Hogarth was his foe.
Souls of a timorous cast, of petty name
In Envy's court, not yet quite dead to shame,
May some remorse, some qualms of conscience feel,
And suffer honour to abate their zeal ;   360
But the man truly and completely great
Allows no rule of action but his hate ;
Through every bar he bravely breaks his way,
Passion his principle, and parts his prey.
Mediums in vice and virtue speak a mind
Within the pale of temperance confined ;
The daring spirit scorns her narrow schemes,
And, good or bad, is always in extremes.
Man's practice duly weigh'd, through every age
On the same plan hath Envy form'd her rage.   370
'Gainst those whom fortune hath our rivals made,
In way of science, and in way of trade,
Stung with mean jealousy, she arms her spite,
First works, then views their ruin with delight.
Our Hogarth here a grand improver shines,
And nobly on the general plan refines ;
He like himself o'erleaps the servile bound ;
Worth is his mark, wherever worth is found.
Should painters only his vast wrath suffice ?
Genius in every walk is lawful prize :   380
'Tis a gross insult to his o'ergrown state ;
His love to merit is to feel his hate.
When Wilkes, our countryman, our common
            friend,
Arose, his king, his country to defend ;
When tools of power he bared to public view,
And from their holes the sneaking cowards drew ;
When Rancour found it far beyond her reach

To soil his honour, and his truth impeach;
What could induce thee, at a time and place   389
Where manly foes had blush'd to shew their face,
To make that effort which must damn thy name,
And sink thee deep, deep in thy grave with shame?
Did virtue move thee? No; 'twas pride, rank pride,
And if thou hadst not done it, thou hadst died.
Malice (who, disappointed of her end,
Whether to work the bane of foe or friend,
Preys on herself, and, driven to the stake,
Gives Virtue that revenge she scorns to take)
Had killed thee, tottering on life's utmost verge,
Had Wilkes and Liberty escaped thy scourge.   400
   When that Great Charter, which our fathers
      bought
With their best blood, was into question brought;
When, big with ruin, o'er each English head
Vile Slavery hung suspended by a thread;
When Liberty, all trembling and aghast,
Fear'd for the future, knowing what was past;
When every breast was chill'd with deep despair,
Till Reason pointed out that Pratt was there;

---

[405] Charles Pratt, Earl Camden, Chief Justice of the Common Pleas, in which situation his cool, deliberate, persuasive eloquence, his thorough knowledge of the constitution, and manly defence of its principles, afforded the best check to the alarming encroachments of administration, and the most effective counterpoise to the influence of Lord Mansfield.

When Wilkes, in consequence of the warrant granted by Lord Halifax against the authors, &c. of the North Briton, No. XLV. was taken into custody, it was Lord Chief Justice Pratt who delivered the unanimous opinion of the Court, that as he had not been guilty of treason, felony, or a breach of the peace, the privilege of parliament had been flagrantly violated by his imprisonment, and ordered him to be discharged.

Lurking, most ruffian-like, behind a screen,
So placed all things to see, himself unseen,   410
Virtue, with due contempt, saw Hogarth stand,
The murderous pencil in his palsied hand.
What was the cause of Liberty to him,
Or what was Honour? let them sink or swim,
So he may gratify, without control,
The mean resentments of his selfish soul.
Let freedom perish; if to freedom true,
In the same ruin Wilkes may perish too.
    With all the symptoms of assured decay,
With age and sickness pinch'd and worn away,   420
Pale, quivering lips, lank cheeks, and faltering
        tongue,
The spirits out of tune, the nerves unstrung,
Thy body shrivell'd up, thy dim eyes sunk
Within their sockets deep, thy weak hams shrunk,
The body's weight unable to sustain,
The stream of life scarce trembling thro' the vein,
More than half kill'd by honest truths which fell,
Thro' thy own fault, from men who wish'd thee well,
Canst thou, e'en thus, thy thoughts to vengeance
        give,
And, dead to all things else, to malice live?   430
Hence, Dotard, to thy closet; shut thee in;
By deep repentance wash away thy sin;
From haunts of men to shame and sorrow fly,
And, on the verge of death, learn how to die.
    Vain exhortation! wash the Ethiop white,
Discharge the leopard's spots, turn day to night,
Control the course of Nature, bid the deep
Hush at thy pigmy voice her waves to sleep,
Perform things passing strange, yet own thy art

Too weak to work a change in such a heart.   440
That envy, which was woven in the frame
At first, will to the last remain the same.
Reason may droop, may die: but Envy's rage
Improves by time, and gathers strength from age.
Some, and not few, vain triflers with the pen,
Unread, unpractised in the ways of men,
Tell us that Envy, who, with giant stride,
Stalks through the vale of life by Virtue's side,
Retreats when she hath drawn her latest breath,
And calmly hears her praises after death.   450
To such observers Hogarth gives the lie;
Worth may be hearsed, but Envy cannot die;
Within the mansion of his gloomy breast,
A mansion suited well to such a guest,
Immortal, unimpair'd, she rears her head,
And damns alike the living and the dead.
    Oft have I known thee, Hogarth, weak and vain,
Thyself the idol of thy awkward strain,
Through the dull measure of a summer's day,
In phrase most vile, prate long, long hours away, 460
Whilst friends with friends all gaping sit, and gaze
To hear a Hogarth babble Hogarth's praise;
But if athwart thee Interruption came,
And mention'd with respect some ancient's name,
Some ancient's name who, in the days of yore,
The crown of art with greatest honour wore.
How have I seen thy coward cheek turn pale,
And blank confusion seize thy mangled tale!
How hath thy jealousy to madness grown,
And deemed his praise injurious to thy own!   470
Then without mercy did thy wrath make way,
And arts and artists all became thy prey;

Then didst thou trample on establish'd rules,
And proudly levell'd all the ancient schools,
Condemn'd those works, with praise through ages
    graced,
Which you had never seen, or could not taste;
" But would mankind have true perfection shewn,
It must be found in labours of my own.
I dare to challenge, in one single piece,
The united force of Italy and Greece."   480
Thy eager hand the curtain then undrew,
And brought the boasted master-piece to view.
Spare thy remarks—say not a single word—
The picture seen, why is the painter heard?
Call not up shame and anger in our cheeks;
Without a comment Sigismunda speaks.

[486] The subject of Hogarth's painting was taken from
Dryden's admirable translation of Boccaccio's Sigismunda
and Guiscardo. Sigismunda is represented in the act of
receiving, in a rich golden goblet, the heart of her murdered
lover, presented to her by her father's order.

> " Or not amazed, or hiding her surprise,
> She sternly on the bearer fixed her eyes;
> Then thus: Tell Tancred, on his daughter's part,
> The gold, though precious, equals not the heart."

This picture, which proved a source of much mortification
and pecuniary loss to the painter, was undertaken by him
at the earnest request of Sir Richard Grosvenor, afterwards
Earl of Grosvenor, in the year of 1759, at a time when
Hogarth had fully determined to leave off painting, finding
engraving a much more profitable pursuit. Sir Richard, who
was immensely rich, had offered whatever sum the artist
should himself require for his work. In the meantime Sir
Richard had fallen into the clutches of some interested
picture dealers, who induced the baronet to evince some dis-
inclination to complete his engagement. This alarmed
Hogarth, who immediately wrote a letter to Sir Richard,

Poor Sigismunda! what a fate is thine!
Dryden, the great high-priest of all the Nine,
Revived thy name, gave what a Muse could give,
And in his numbers bade thy memory live;   490
Gave thee those soft sensations which might move
And warm the coldest anchorite to love;
Gave thee that virtue, which could curb desire,
Refine and consecrate love's headstrong fire;
Gave thee those griefs, which made the Stoic feel,
And call'd compassion forth from hearts of steel;
Gave thee that firmness, which our sex may shame,
And make man bow to woman's juster claim;
So that our tears, which from compassion flow,
Seem to debase thy dignity of woe.   500
But, O, how much unlike! how fallen! how
        changed!
How much from Nature and herself estranged!
How totally deprived of all the powers
To shew her feelings, and awaken ours,
Doth Sigismunda now devoted stand,

giving him full liberty to take or reject the picture, but re-
minding him at the same time of the terms upon which it
was undertaken. A shuffling and hypocritical answer was
returned by Sir Richard, to which Hogarth replied; and
the correspondence ended with the painting being left upon
his hands.

That Sigismund, like most of Hogarth's serious compositions, was a failure is undoubted; but still it hardly merited
the severe criticism of Walpole. "Hogarth's Sigismunda,"
says Walpole, "has no sober grief, no dignity of suppressed
anguish, no involuntary tear, no settled meditation on the
fate she meant to meet, no amorous warmth turned holy by
despair; in short, all is wanting that should have been
there, all is there that such a story would have banished
from a mind capable of conceiving such complicated woo
woe felt at once so sternly and so tenderly."

The helpless victim of a dauber's hand!
But why, my Hogarth, such a progress made,
So rare a pattern for the sign-post trade;
In the full force, and whirlwind of thy pride,
Why was heroic painting laid aside?   51(
Why is it not resumed? thy friends at court,
Men all in place and power, crave thy support;
Be grateful then for once, and through the field
Of politics, thy epic pencil wield;
Maintain the cause, which they, good lack! avow,
And would maintain too, but they know not how.
Through every pannel let thy virtue tell
How Bute prevail'd, how Pitt and Temple fell!
How England's sons (whom they conspired to bless
Against our will, with insolent success)   520
Approve their fall, and with addresses run,
How got God knows, to hail the Scottish sun?
Point out our fame in war, when vengeance, hurl'd
From the strong arm of Justice, shook the world;
Thine, and thy country's honour to increase,
Point out the honours of succeeding peace;
Our moderation, Christian-like, display,
Shew, what we got, and what we gave away;
In colours, dull and heavy as the tale,
Let a state-chaos through the whole prevail.   530
But, of events regardless, whilst the Muse,
Perhaps with too much heat, her theme pursues;
Whilst her quick spirits rouse at Freedom's call,
And every drop of blood is turn'd to gall;
Whilst a dear country, and an injured friend
Urge my strong anger to the bitterest end;
Whilst honest trophies to revenge are raised,

518 See Night, l. 370, note.

Let not one real virtue pass unpraised;
Justice with equal course bids Satire flow,
And loves the virtue of her greatest foe.   540
  O ! that I here could that rare virtue mean
Which scorns the rule of envy, pride, and spleen;
Which springs not from the labour'd works of art,
But hath its rise from Nature in the heart;
Which in itself with happiness is crown'd,
And spreads with joy the blessing all around !
But truth forbids, and in these simple lays,
Contented with a different kind of praise,
Must Hogarth stand; that praise which genius
        gives,
In which to latest time the artist lives,   550
But not the man; which, rightly understood,
May make us great, but cannot make us good :
That praise be Hogarth's; freely let him wear
The wreath which Genius wove, and planted there:
Foe as I am, should Envy tear it down,
Myself would labour to replace the crown.
  In walks of humour, in that cast of style
Which, probing to the quick, yet makes us smile ,
In comedy, thy natural road to fame,
Nor let me call it by a meaner name,   560
Where a beginning, middle, and an end,
Are aptly joined; where parts on parts depend,
Each made for each, as bodies for their soul,
So as to form one true and perfect whole ;
Where a plain story to the eye is told,

---

565 In corroboration of the poet's view, Lamb places
Hogarth in the first rank of AUTHORS; " I was pleased with
the reply of a gentleman who being asked which book he
esteemed most in his library, answered Shakespeare; being

Which we conceive the moment we behold,
Hogarth unrivall'd stands, and shall engage
Unrivall'd praise to the most distant age.

How couldst thou then to shame perversely run
And tread that path which Nature bade thee shun?
Why did ambition overleap her rules,   571
And thy vast parts become the sport of fools?
By different methods different men excel;
But where is he who can do all things well?
Humour thy province, for some monstrous crime
Pride struck thee with the frenzy of sublime;
But, when the work was finish'd, could thy mind
So partial be, and to herself so blind,
What with contempt all view'd, to view with awe,
Nor see those faults which every blockhead saw?
Blush, thou vain man! and if desire of fame,   581
Founded on real art, thy thoughts inflame,
To quick destruction Sigismunda give,
And let her memory die, that thine may live.

But should fond Candour, for her mercy sake,
With pity view, and pardon this mistake;
Or should Oblivion, to thy wish most kind,
Wipe off that stain, nor leave one trace behind;
Of arts despised, of artists, by thy frown
Awed from just hopes of rising worth kept down,
Of all thy meanness through this mortal race,   591
Canst thou the living memory erase?
Or shall not vengeance follow to the grave,
And give back just that measure which you gave?

asked which he esteemed next best, replied Hogarth. His
graphic representations are indeed BOOKS, they have the
teeming fruitful suggestive meaning of *words*. Other pictures we look at—his prints we read."

With so much merit, and so much success,
With so much power to curse, so much to bless,
Would he have been man's friend, instead of foe,
Hogarth had been a little god below.
Why then, like savage giants, famed of old,
Of whom in Scripture story we are told,   600
Dost thou in cruelty that strength employ,
Which Nature meant to save, not to destroy ?
Why dost thou, all in horrid pomp array'd,
Sit grinning o'er the ruins thou hast made ?
Most rank ill-nature must applaud thy art,
But even Candour must condemn thy heart.
   For me, who, warm and zealous for my friend,
In spite of railing thousands will commend,
And no less warm and zealous against my foes,
Spite of commending thousands, will oppose,   610
I dare thy worst, with scorn behold thy rage,
But with an eye of pity view thy age,
Thy feeble age ! in which, as in a glass,
We see how men to dissolution pass.
Thou wretched being, whom, on reason's plan,
So changed, so lost, I cannot call a man,
What could persuade thee, at this time of life,
To launch afresh into the sea of strife ?
Better for thee, scarce crawling on the earth,
Almost as much a child as at thy birth,   620
To have resign'd in peace thy parting breath,
And sunk unnoticed in the arms of Death.
Why would thy gray, gray hairs resentment brave,
Thus to go down with sorrow to the grave ?
Now, by my soul, it makes me blush to know,
My spirits could descend to such a foe :
Whatever cause the vengeance might provoke,

It seems rank cowardice to give the stroke.

Sure 'tis a curse which angry fates impose,
To mortify man's arrogance, that those   630
Who're fashion'd of some better sort of clay,
Much sooner than the common herd decay.
What bitter pangs must humbled Genius feel,
In their last hours, to view a Swift and Steele!
How must ill-boding horrors fill her breast
When she beholds men mark'd above the rest
For qualities most dear, plunged from that height,
And sunk, deep sunk, in second childhood's night!
Are men, indeed, such things? and are the best
More subject to this evil than the rest,   640
To drivel out whole years of idiot breath,
And sit the monuments of living death!
O, galling circumstance to human pride!
Abasing thought! but not to be denied.
With curious art the brain, too finely wrought,
Preys on herself, and is destroy'd by thought.
Constant attention wears the active mind,
Blots out our powers, and leaves a blank behind.
But let not youth, to insolence allied,
In heat of blood, in full career of pride,   650
Possess'd of genius, with unhallow'd rage
Mock the infirmities of reverend age:
The greatest genius to this fate may bow;
Reynolds, in time, may be like Hogarth now.

654 Sir Joshua Reynolds, fortunately for the world and for
himself, did not accomplish this anticipation. He died in
1791, with a reputation still undiminished, though scarcely
susceptible of increase.

SUPPLEMENTAL NOTE.

The Rev. T. Morell first apprized the painter of the publication of this satire; who retaliated by his print of "The Bruiser," representing Churchill as a bear dressed canonically, holding a pot of porter in his right paw, and a club in his left. On the notches of the club are written, lie 1, lie 2, &c. Another figure is a pug dog, supposed to be meant for Hogarth himself, discharging water on the epistle. In the centre is a prison begging box, standing on a folio, the title of which is "Great George Street," (where Wilkes resided), "A list of the subscribers to the North Briton." Under it is another book, the title of which is "A New Way to Pay Old Debts," a comedy by Massinger, alluding to Wilkes's debts, which were defrayed by the subscriptions to the North Briton. Hogarth afterwards made the following additions; in the form of a framed picture he represented a pyramid, on the side of which is a Cheshire cheese; round it is written £3000 per annum, and at the foot reclines a Roman veteran, in allusion to Mr. Pitt's resignation and pension. The cheese is meant to ridicule Wilkes for having said, "he would rather subsist on a Cheshire cheese and a shoulder of mutton, than submit to the implacable enemies of his country." In the centre stands Hogarth himself, whipping a dancing bear which he holds in a string. At the side of the bear is a monkey, meant for Wilkes, riding on a mopstick, at the head of which is a cap of liberty. The monkey is undergoing the same discipline as the bear. Behind the monkey is a man, having no distinguishable lineaments of face, playing upon a violin, apparently designed for Lord Temple.

THE DUELLIST.

IN THREE BOOKS.

PUBLISHED IN JANUARY, 1764.

HE production of this poem was occasioned by the following circumstances. The North Briton, in one of its numbers, had incidentally introduced some characteristic sketches of a certain government official, whom they did not mention by name; but it was generally supposed that the original of those sketches was Samuel Martin, Esq. M.P. for Camelford, Secretary to the Treasury, Treasurer to the Princess Dowager of Wales, and the hero of this poem. Mention is made in No. 37, published 12 Feb. 1763, of "the secretary of a certain board, a very apt tool of ministerial persecution, who, with a spirit worthy of a Portuguese inquisitor, is hourly looking for carrion in every office to feed the maw of the insatiable vulture. *Imo etiam in senatum venit, notat et designat unumquemque nostrum:* he marks us and all our innocent families for beggary and ruin. Neither the tenderness of age, nor the sacredness of sex is spared by the cruel Scot." And again, the 40th Number speaks "of the most treacherous, base, selfish, mean, abject, low-lived and dirty fellow that ever wriggled himself into a secretaryship."

Of these passages Mr. Martin took no notice until the day parliament met, when, in the debate* upon the proceedings taken during the recess against the persons concerned in the

---

* This debate occasioned the longest sitting which had ever taken place in the House of Commons. The Speaker was twenty hours in the chair, the House not adjourning until between seven and eight in the morning.

North Briton, he observed, with pointed expression towards
Mr. Wilkes, that the author of that paper was a malignant,
infamous scoundrel, who had stabbed him in the dark.

On the breaking up of the House, Mr. Martin received
the following letter:—

Great George Street, Westminster, Nov. 16, 1763.

SIR—You complained yesterday, before five hundred gentlemen, that you had been stabbed in the dark by the North
Briton, but I have reason to believe you was not so much in
the dark as you affected and chose to be. Was the complaint
made before so many gentlemen on purpose that they might
interpose? To cut off every pretence of ignorance as to the
author, I whisper in your ear that every passage in the
North Briton, in which you have been named or even alluded
to, was written by your humble servant,

JOHN WILKES

To this letter the following answer was returned:—

SIR—As I said in the House of Commons yesterday, that
the writer of the North Briton, who had stabbed me in the
dark, was a cowardly as well as a malignant and infamous
scoundrel; and your letter of this morning's date acknow-
ledges that every passage of the North Briton, in which I
have been named or even alluded to, was written by yourself;
I must take the liberty to repeat, that you are a malignant
and infamous scoundrel, and that I desire to give you an opportunity of shewing me whether the epithet of cowardly was
rightly applied or not.

I desire that you meet me in Hyde Park immediately with
a brace of pistols each, to determine our difference.

I shall go to the ring in Hyde Park with my pistols so concealed that nobody may see them, and I will wait in expecta-
tion of you one hour. As I shall call in my way at your
house to deliver this letter, I propose to go from thence directly
to the ring in Hyde Park, from whence we may proceed, if
it be necessary, to any more private place, and I mention
that I shall wait an hour in order to give you full time to
meet me. I am, Sir, your humble servant,

SAMUEL MARTIN.

Mr. Wilkes accordingly met Mr. Martin in Hyde Park. After the former had fired twice without effect, his antagonist, at his second shot, lodged his ball in Wilkes's belly. Mr. Martin wished to assist him, but Wilkes, who believed himself mortally wounded, insisted on his making his escape. Mr. Wilkes was carried home by some people who came up, but would not relate the circumstances of the case till he found they were already known.

The following day, Mr. Wilkes, imagining himself in the greatest danger, returned Mr. Martin his letter, that no evidence might appear against him; and compelled his relations to promise that, in case of his death, they would not molest Mr. Martin, who, he said, had behaved as a man of honour.

As the wound Mr. Wilkes had received prevented his obeying an order made by the House of Commons for his attendance, it was postponed for a week, and by a vote of the 16th of December, Dr. Heberden, and Mr. Hawkins the surgeon, were directed to attend Mr. Wilkes, observe the progress of his cure, and report it to the House. Mr. Wilkes, in a very humorous letter to Dr. Brocklesby, professed himself perfectly satisfied with his attentions, and those of Mr. Graves, his own surgeon, and declined the aid of the physicians appointed by the House. As soon as his health would permit, Mr. Wilkes withdrew to Paris, where Mr. Martin also was on a visit. They had a conciliatory interview; and Mr. Martin, in a very flattering note, declared his intention not to take any part in the proceedings of the House of Commons against Mr. Wilkes.

Mr. Martin's conduct, in this affair, appears to have been highly honourable; but the public mind was so exasperated at the danger Wilkes had been exposed to, that no credit was given to his antagonist for the spirit he had displayed.

THE DUELLIST.

BOOK I.

THE clock struck twelve; o'er half the
    globe
Darkness had spread her pitchy robe:
Morpheus, his feet with velvet shod,
Treading as if in fear he trod,
Gentle as dews at even-tide,
Distilled his poppies far and wide.
    Ambition, who, when waking, dreams
Of mighty, but fantastic schemes,
Who, when asleep, ne'er knows that rest
With which the humbler soul is blest,   10
Was building castles in the air,
Goodly to look upon and fair,
But on a bad foundation laid,
Doomed at return of morn to fade
    Pale Study, by the taper's light
Wearing away the watch of night,
Sat reading, but with o'ercharged head,
Remembered nothing that he read.
    Starving midst plenty, with a face
Which might the court of Famine grace,   20
Ragged, and filthy to behold,
Gray Avarice nodded o'er his gold.

Jealousy, his quick eye half-closed
With watchings worn, reluctant dozed;
And, mean distrust not quite forgot,
Slumbered as if he slumbered not.
  Stretched at his length on the bare ground,
His hardy offspring sleeping round,
Snored restless Labour; by his side
Lay Health, a coarse but comely bride.   30
  Virtue, without the doctor's aid,
In the soft arms of sleep was laid;
Whilst Vice, within the guilty breast,
Could not be physic'd into rest.
  Thou bloody Man! whose ruffian knife
Is drawn against thy neighbour's life,
And never scruples to descend
Into the bosom of a friend,
A firm, fast friend, by vice allied,
And to thy secret service tied: 40
In whom ten murders breed no awe,
If properly secured from law:
Thou man of Lust! whom passion fires
To foulest deeds, whose hot desires
O'er honest bars with ease make way,
Whilst idiot Beauty falls a prey,
And to indulge thy brutal flame
A Lucreece must be brought to shame;
Who dost, a brave, bold sinner, bear
Rank incest to the open air,   50
And rapes, full blown upon thy crown,
Enough to weigh a nation down:
Thou simular of Lust! vain man,
Whose restless thoughts still form the plan
Of guilt, which, withered to the root,

Thy lifeless nerves can't execute,
Whilst in thy marrowless, dry bones
Desire without enjoyment groans ;
Thou perjured Wretch ! whom falsehood clothes
E'en like a garment, who with oaths   6u
Dost trifle, as with brokers, meant
To serve thy every vile intent,
In the day's broad and searching eye
Making God witness to a lie,
Blaspheming heaven and earth for pelf,
And hanging friends to save thyself:
Thou son of Chance ! whose glorious soul,
On the four aces doomed to roll,
Was never yet with honour caught,
Nor on poor virtue lost one thought ;   70
Who dost thy wife, thy children, set,
Thy all, upon a single bet,
Risking, the desperate stake to try,
Here and hereafter on a die ;
Who, thy own private fortune lost,
Dost game on at thy country's cost,
And, grown expert in sharping rules,
First fooled thyself, now prey'st on fools :
Thou noble Gamester ! whose high place
Gives too much credit to disgrace ;   80
Who, with the motion of a die,
Dost make a mighty island fly,
The sums, I mean, of good French gold
For which a mighty island's sold ;
Who dost betray intelligence,

---

⁶⁶ Another allusion to the execution of Ayliffe, and the
popular imputations it gave rise to.   See Epistle to Hogarth,
l. 140, note.

Abuse the dearest confidence,
And, private fortune to create,
Most falsely play the game of state;
Who dost within the Alley sport
Sums, which might beggar a whole court,   90
And make us bankrupts all, if Care,
With good Earl Talbot, was not there:
Thou daring Infidel! whom pride
And sin have drawn from Reason's side;
Who, fearing his avengeful rod,
Dost wish not to believe a God;
Whose hope is founded on a plan
Which should distract the soul of man,
And make him curse his abject birth;
Whose hope is, once returned to earth,   100
There to lie down, for worms a feast,
To rot and perish like a beast;
Who dost, of punishment afraid,
And by thy crimes a coward made,
To every generous soul a curse
Than hell and all her torments worse,
When crawling to thy latter end,
Call on destruction as a friend;
Choosing to crumble into dust
Rather than rise, though rise you must: 110
Thou Hypocrite! who dost profane,
And take the patriot's name in vain;
Then most thy country's foe when most

[92] William, first Earl Talbot, Lord Steward of the King's
Household from 1761 to 1782. On his appointment to the
office, he proposed some economical reforms in the palace;
but the clamour excited among some of the retainers of the
court, together with his own want of resolution, prevented his
carrying them into execution.

Of love and loyalty you boast;
Who for the filthy love of gold
Thy friend, thy king, thy God, hast sold,
And, mocking the just claim of Hell,
Were bidders found, thyself wouldst sell.
Ye Villains! of whatever name,
Whatever rank, to whom the claim   120
Of Hell is certain; on whose lids
That worm which never dies forbids
Sweet sleep to fall, come, and behold,
Whilst envy makes your blood run cola,
Behold, by pitiless Conscience led,
So Justice wills, that holy bed
Where Peace her full dominion keeps,
And Innocence with Holland sleeps.
    Bid Terror, posting on the wind
Affray the spirits of mankind;   130
Bid Earthquakes, heaving for a vent,
Rive their concealing continent,
And, forcing an untimely birth
Through the vast bowels of the earth,

[128] Great indignation was expressed throughout the country at the gross peculations, as they were called, of Lord Holland and his associates; the City of London petitioned the
King for the redress of various grievances, the removal
of evil counsellors, particularly adverting to Lord Holland's defalcations. No notice being taken of that petition,
the Livery, at a meeting convened for the purpose, in
October, 1769, directly charged Lord Holland, in three resolutions which were adopted unanimously, as the defaulter of
" unaccounted millions;" and declared that it was the duty
of Parliament to order an investigation of his accounts, and
if the charge should prove well founded, to impeach him.
    The universal clamour thus excited induced Lord Holland to withdraw from public observation. The ministers,
who were themselves deeply implicated in similar abuses,

Endeavour, in her monstrous womb,
At once all nature to entomb;
Bid all that's horrible and dire,
All that man hates and fears, conspire
To make night hideous as they can;
Still is thy sleep, thou virtuous Man! 140
Pure as the thoughts which in thy breast
Inhabit, and insure thy rest;
Still shall thy Ayliffe, taught, though late,
Thy friendly justice in his fate,
Turned to a guardian angel, spread
Sweet dreams of comfort round thy head.

Dark was the night, by Fate decreed
For the contrivance of a deed
More black than common, which might make
This land from her foundations shake, 150
Might tear up Freedom by the root,
Destroy a Wilkes, and fix a Bute.

Deep Horror held her wide domain;
The sky in sullen drops of rain
Forewept the morn, and through the air,
Which, opening, laid its bosom bare,
Loud thunders rolled, and lightning streamed;

would not institute any prosecution against him in his life-
time, but after his death proceedings were taken against Mr.
John Powell his only acting executor, who was compelled to
pay a sum of £232,515. 4s. 8d. in discharge of some ascer-
tained balances due from Lord Holland as Paymaster General
of His Majesty's Forces. It is, however, but fair to state,
that Lord Brougham in his "Statesmen of the time of
George Third" denies that Lord Holland was dishonest; and
asserts that the imputation arose from the length of time
that elapsed between the expenditure of the public funds and
the rendering account of their disbursement. See Life of
the Duke of Bedford, in the above work.

The owl at Freedom's window screamed,
The screech-owl, prophet dire, whose breath
Brings sickness, and whose note is death;   160
The churchyard teemed, and from the tomb,
All sad and silent, through the gloom
The ghosts of men, in former times,
Whose public virtues were their crimes,
Indignant stalked; sorrow and rage
Blanked their pale cheeks; in his own age
The prop of Freedom, Hampden there
Felt after death the generous care;
Sidney, by grief, from heaven was kept,
And for his brother patriot wept: 170
All friends of Liberty, when Fate
Prepared to shorten Wilkes's date,
Heaved, deeply hurt, the heart-felt groan,
And knew that wound to be their own.
    Hail, Liberty! a glorious word,
In other countries scarcely heard,
Or heard but as a thing of course,
Without or energy or force:
Here felt, enjoyed, adored, she springs,
Far, far beyond the reach of kings;   180
Fresh blooming from our mother Earth,
With pride and joy she owns her birth
Derived from us, and in return
Bids in our breasts her genius burn;
Bids us with all those blessings live
Which Liberty alone can give,
Or nobly with that spirit die
Which makes death more than victory.
    Hail those old patriots, on whose tongue
Persuasion in the senate hung,   190

Whilst they this sacred cause maintained!
Hail those old chiefs, to honour trained,
Who spread, when other methods failed,
War's bloody banner, and prevailed!
Shall men like these unmentioned sleep
Promiscuous with the common heap,
And (Gratitude forbid the crime!)
Be carried down the stream of time
In shoals, unnoticed and forgot,
On Lethe's stream, like flags, to rot?   200
No—they shall live, and each fair name,
Recorded in the book of Fame,
Founded on honour's basis, fast
As the round earth to ages last.
Some virtues vanish with our breath;
Virtue like this lives after death.
Old Time himself, his scythe thrown by,
Himself lost in eternity,
An everlasting crown shall twine
To make a Wilkes and Sidney join.   210
    But should some slave-got villain dare
Chains for his country to prepare,
And, by his birth to slavery broke,
Make her, too, feel the galling yoke,
May he be evermore accurst,
Amongst bad men be ranked the worst;
May he be still himself, and still
Go on in vice, and perfect ill;
May his broad crimes each day increase,
Till he can't live nor die in peace;   220
May he be plunged so deep in shame,
That Satan mayn't endure his name,
And hear, scarce crawling on the earth,

His children curse him for their birth;
May Liberty, beyond the grave,
Ordain him to be still a slave,
Grant him what here he most requires
And damn him with his own desires!
    But should some villain, in support
And zeal for a despairing court,   230
Placing in craft his confidence,
And making honour a pretence
To do a deed of deepest shame,
Whilst filthy lucre is his aim;
Should such a wretch, with sword or knife
Contrive to practise 'gainst the life
Of one who, honoured through the land;
For Freedom made a glorious stand,
Whose chief, perhaps his only crime
Is, (if plain Truth at such a time   240
May dare her sentiments to tell)
That he his country loves too well;
May he—but words are all too weak
The feelings of my heart to speak—
May he—O for a noble curse
Which might his very marrow pierce—
The general contempt engage,
And be the Martin of his age.

THE DUELLIST.

BOOK II.

EEP in the bosom of a wood,
Out of the road, a temple stood;
Ancient, and much the worse for
    wear,
It called aloud for quick repair,
And, tottering from side to side,
Menaced destruction far and wide,
Nor able seemed, unless made stronger,
To hold out four or five years longer.
Four hundred pillars, from the ground
Rising in order, most unsound,   10
Some rotten to the heart, aloof,
Seem to support the tottering roof,
But to inspection nearer laid,
Instead of giving, wanted aid.
   The structure, rare and curious, made
By men most famous in their trade,
A work of years, admired by all,
Was suffered into dust to fall,
Or, just to make it hang together,
And keep off the effects of weather,   20
Was patched and patched from time to time
By wretches, whom it were a crime,

A crime, which Art would treason hold
To mention with those names of old.

Builders, who had the pile surveyed,
And those not Flitcrofts in their trade,
Doubted (the wise hand in a doubt
Merely, sometimes, to hand his out)
Whether (like churches in a brief,
Taught wisely to obtain relief   30
Through Chancery, who gives her fees
To this and other charities)
It must not, in all parts unsound,
Be ripped, and pulled down to the ground ;
Whether (though after ages ne'er
Shall raise a building to compare)
Art, if they should their art employ,
Meant to preserve, might not destroy,
As human bodies, worn away,
Battered and hasting to decay,   40
Bidding the power of Art despair,
Cannot those very medicines bear
Which, and which only, can restore,

---

[26] Henry Flitcroft, an architect of some eminence, was in
1738 appointed comptroller and afterwards Master Mason to
the Board of Works. He was one of the numerous school to
which the genius of Sir Christopher Wren gave rise, and
built the churches of St. Giles in the Fields, London, and
St. Olaves, Southwark. He died at Teddington.

[29] The system of obtaining contributions for the repair and
rebuilding of churches and colleges, and other public purposes, and occasionally for the relief of sufferers from fire,
tempest, and other casualties by reading briefs in churches,
was abolished in the year 1828 by act of 9 Geo. IV. c. 42.
When the practice commenced is uncertain; probably it was
in the reign of Queen Elizabeth. The custom is mentioned
in Cowper's *Charity*, l. 469.

And make them healthy as before.
  To Liberty, whose gracious smile
Shed peace and plenty o'er the Isle,
Our grateful ancestors, her plain
But faithful children, raised this fane.
  Full in the front, stretched out in length,
Where Nature put forth all her strength   50
In spring eternal, lay a plain
Where our brave fathers used to train
Their sons to arms, to teach the art
Of war, and steel the infant heart;
Labour, their hardy nurse, when young,
Their joints had knit, their nerves had strung;
Abstinence, foe declared to death,
Had, from the time they first drew breath,
The best of doctors, with plain food,
Kept pure the channel of their blood;   60
Health in their cheeks bade colour rise,
And Glory sparkled in their eyes.
  The instruments of husbandry,
As in contempt, were all thrown by,
And, flattering a manly pride,
War's keener tools their place supplied.
Their arrows to the head they drew;
Swift to the point their javelins flew;
They grasped the sword, they shook the spear;
Their fathers felt a pleasing fear,   70
And even Courage, standing by,
Scarcely beheld with steady eye.
Each stripling, lessoned by his sire,
Knew when to close, when to retire;
When near at hand, when from afar
To fight, and was himself a war.

Their wives, their mothers, all around,
Careless of order, on the ground,
Breathed forth to Heaven the pious vow,
And for a son's or husband's brow,   80
With eager fingers, laurel wove ;
Laurel which in the sacred grove,
Planted by Liberty, they find,
The brows of conquerors to bind,
To give them pride and spirits fit
To make a world in arms submit.
What raptures did the bosom fire
Of the young, rugged, peasant sire,
When, from the toil of mimic fight,
Returning with return of night,   90
He saw his babe resign the breast,
And, smiling, stroke those arms in jest
With which hereafter he shall make
The proudest heart in Gallia quake !
Gods ! with what joy, what honest pride,
Did each fond, wishing, rustic bride
Behold her manly swain return !
How did her love-sick bosom burn,
Though on parades he was not bred,
Nor wore the livery of red,   100
When, Pleasure heightening all her charms,
She strained her warrior in her arms,
And begged, whilst love and glory fire,
A son, a son just like his sire !
Such were the men in former times,
Ere luxury had made our crimes
Our bitter punishment, who bore
Their terrors to a foreign shore ;
Such were the men who, free from dread,

By Edwards and by Henries led,   110
Spread, like a torrent swelled with rains,
O'er haughty Gallia's trembling plains:
Such were the men, when lust of power,
To work him woe, in evil hour
Debauched the tyrant from those ways
On which a king should found his praise;
When stern Oppression, hand in hand
With Pride, stalked proudly through the land;
When weeping Justice was misled
From her fair course, and Mercy dead: 120
Such were the men, in virtue strong,
Who dared not see their country's wrong,
Who left the mattock and the spade,
And, in the robes of War arrayed,
In their rough arms, departing, took
Their helpless babes, and with a look
Stern and determined, swore to see
Those babes no more, or see them free:
Such were the men whom tyrant Pride
Could never fasten to his side   130
By threats or bribes; who, freemen born,
Chains, though of gold, behold with scorn;
Who, free from every servile awe,
Could never be divorced from law,
From that broad, general law which Sense
Made for the general defence;
Could never yield to partial ties
Which from dependant stations rise:
Could never be to slavery led,
For Property was at their head: 140
Such were the men, in days of yore,
Who, called by Liberty, before

Her temple on the sacred green,
In martial pastimes oft were seen—
Now seen no longer; in their stead,
To laziness and vermin bred,
A race who, strangers to the cause
Of Freedom, live by other laws,
On other motives fight, a prey
To interest, and slaves for pay.   150
Valour, how glorious on a plan
Of honour founded! leads their van;
Discretion, free from taint of fear,
Cool, but resolved, brings up their rear;
Discretion, Valour's better half;
Dependance holds the general's staff.
    In plain and home-spun garb arrayed,
Not for vain shew, but service, made,
In a green, flourishing old age,
Not damned yet with an equipage,   160
In rules of Porterage untaught,
Simplicity, not worth a groat,
For years had kept the temple-door;
Full on his breast a glass he wore,
Through which his bosom open lay
To every one who passed that way:
Now turned adrift—with humbler face,
But prouder heart, his vacant place
Corruption fills, and bears the key;
No entrance now without a fee.   170
    With belly round, and full fat face,
Which on the house reflected grace,
Full of good fare, and honest glee,
The steward Hospitality,
Old Welcome smiling by his side,

A good old servant, often tried
And faithful found, who kept in view
His lady's fame and interest too,
Who made each heart with joy rebound,
Yet never run her state aground,   180
Was turned off, or (which word I find
Is more in modern use) *resigned.*

Half-starved, half-starving others, bred
In beggary, with carrion fed,
Detested, and detesting all,
Made up of avarice and gall,
Boasting great thrift, yet wasting more
Than ever steward did before,
Succeeded one, who to engage
The praise of an exhausted age,   190
Assumed a name of high degree,
And called himself Economy.

Within the temple, full in sight,
Where without ceasing day and night
The workman toiled; where Labour bared
His brawny arm; where art prepared,
In regular and even rows,
Her types, a Printing press arose ;
Each workman knew his task, and each
Was honest and expert as Leach.   200

[182] The Earl of Chatham and Lord Temple resigned their
offices in 1761, and the Duke of Newcastle in 1762. The
party cry of their successors was " economy," in their zeal for
which the pension list was increased beyond precedent.

[198] Wilkes had a private printing press at his house in
Great George Street, Westminster.

[200] Dryden Leach was a printer in Crane Court, Fleet
Street : he was one of the first who introduced a taste for the
embellishments of typography. Under the celebrated general

Hence Learning struck a deeper root,
And Science brought forth riper fruit;
Hence Loyalty received support,
Even when banished from the court;
Hence Government gained strength; and hence
Religion sought and found defence;
Hence England's fairest fame arose,
And Liberty subdued her foes.

On a low, simple, turf-made throne,
Raised by Allegiance, scarcely known   210
From her attendants, glad to be
Pattern of that equality
She wished to all, so far as could
Safely consist with social good,
The goddess sat; around her head
A cheerful radiance Glory spread:
Courage, a youth of royal race,
Lovelily stern, possessed a place
On her left hand; and on her right
Sat Honour, clothed with robes of light;   220
Before her Magna Carta lay,
Which some great lawyer, of his day
The Pratt, was officed to explain

warrant, Nathan Carrington, with his King's messengers,
took Leach, his journeymen and servants, into custody; and
though it clearly appeared that the North Briton was printed
by Balfe, in the Old Bailey, Mr. Leach was detained in
confinement several days.   For this imprisonment, Leach
and his journeymen brought actions against the messengers,
and recovered damages.
[205] The first editions of his poem read, "government *was*
strength."
[223] Charles Pratt, Lord Camden, in his charge to the Jury
on the action brought by Mr. Wilkes against Mr. Wood, the
Under Secretary of State, for illegally entering his house,

And make the basis of her reign :
Peace, crowned with olive, to her breast
Two smiling, twin-born infants prest ;
At her feet couching, War was laid,
And with a brindled lion played :
Justice and Mercy, hand in hand,
Joint guardians of the happy land,   230
Together held their mighty charge,
And Truth walked all about at large ;
Health for the royal troop the feast
Prepared, and Virtue was high priest.
    Such was the fame our goddess bore,
Her temple such, in days of yore.
What changes ruthless Time presents !
Behold her ruined battlements,
Her walls decayed, her nodding spires,
Her altars broke, her dying fires,   240
Her name despised, her priests destroyed,
Her friends disgraced, her foes employed,
Herself (by ministerial arts   .
Deprived e'en of the people's hearts,
Whilst they, to work her surer woe,
Feign her to monarchy a foe)
Exiled by grief, self-doomed to dwell
With some poor hermit in a cell ;
Or, that retirement tedious grown,
If she walks forth, she walks unknown ;   250
Hooted, and pointed at with scorn
As one in some strange country born.
    Behold a rude and ruffian race,

and seizing his papers, gave his opinion against the warrant.
The Jury gave Mr. Wilkes £1,000 damages.
    [253] Carrington and his band of King's messengers; a

A band of spoilers, seize her place :
With looks, which might the heart dis-seat,
And make life sound a quick retreat ;
To rapine from the cradle bred,
A staunch old blood-hound at their head,
Who, free from virtue and from awe,
Knew none but the bad part of law,   260
They roved at large ; each on his breast
Marked with a greyhound, stood confest :
Controlment waited on their nod
High wielding persecution's rod ;
Confusion followed at their heels,
And a cast statesman held the seals ;
Those seals, for which he dear shall pay,
When awful Justice takes her day.

The Printers saw—they saw and fled ;
Science, declining, hung her head ;   270
Property in despair appeared,
And for herself destruction feared
Whilst, underfoot, the rude slaves trod
The works of men, and word of God ;
Whilst, close behind, on many a book,
In which he never deigns to look,
Which he did not, nay—could not read,
A bold, bad man (by pow'r decreed
For that bad end, who in the dark
Scorned to do mischief) set his mark   280
In the full day, the mark of Hell,
And on the Gospel stamped an L.

Liberty fled, her friends withdrew ;
Her friends, a faithful, chosen few ;

silver greyhound, the emblem of dispatch, was worn by
these men as a badge of office when on duty

Honour in grief threw up, and Shame,
Clothing herself with Honour's name,
Usurped his station ; on the throne
Which Liberty once called her own,
(Gods ! that such mighty ills should spring
Under so great, so good a king,   290
So loved, so loving, through the arts
Of statesmen, cursed with wicked hearts !)
For every darker purpose fit,
Behold in triumph State-craft sit.

THE DUELLIST.

BOOK III.

AH me! what mighty perils wait
The man who meddles with a state,
Whether to strengthen, or oppose!
False are his friends, and firm his foes:
How must his soul, once ventured in,
Plunge blindly on from sin to sin!
What toils he suffers, what disgrace,
To get, and then to keep, a place!
How often, whether wrong or right,
Must he in jest or earnest fight,   10
Risking for those both life and limb
Who would not risk one groat for him!
   Under the temple lay a cave,
Made by some guilty, coward slave,
Whose actions feared rebuke, a maze
Of intricate and winding ways,
Not to be found without a clue;
One passage only, known to few,
In paths direct led to a cell,
Where Fraud in secret loved to dwell,   20
With all her tools and slaves about her,
Nor feared lest Honesty should rout her.

In a dark corner, shunning sight
Of man, and shrinking from the light,
One dull, dim taper through the cell
Glimmering, to make more horrible
The face of darkness, she prepares,
Working unseen, all kinds of snares,
With curious, but destructive art.
Here, through the eye to catch the heart,   30
Gay stars their tinsel beams afford,
Neat artifice to trap a lord;
There, fit for all whom Folly bred,
Wave plumes of feathers for the head;
Garters the hag contrives to make,
Which, as it seems, a babe might break,
But which ambitious madmen feel
More firm and sure than chains of steel;
Which, slipped just underneath the knee,
Forbid a freeman to be free.   40
Purses she knew (did ever curse
Travel more sure than in a purse?)
Which, by some strange and magic bands,
Enslave the soul, and tie the hands.
Here Flattery, eldest born of Guile,
Weaves with rare skill the silken smile,
The courtly cringe, the supple bow,
The private squeeze, the levee vow,
With which, no strange or recent case,
Fools in, deceive fools out of place.   50
Corruption (who in former times,
Through fear or shame concealed her crimes,
And what she did, contrived to do it
So that the public might not view it)
Presumptuous grown, unfit was held

For their dark councils, and expelled;
Since in the day her business might
Be done as safe as in the night.
Her eye down bending to the ground,
Planning some dark and deadly wound,   60
Holding a dagger, on which stood,
All fresh and reeking, drops of blood;
Bearing a lanthorn, which of yore,
By Treason borrowed, Guy Fawkes bore,
By which, since they improved in trade,
Excisemen have their lanthorns made,
Assassination, her whole mind,
Blood-thirsting, on her arm reclined:
Death, grinning, at her elbow stood,
And held forth instruments of blood,   70
Vile instruments, which cowards choose,
But men of honour dare not use.
Around, his Lordship and his Grace,
Both qualified for such a place,
With many a Forbes, and many a Dun,

[75] Captain Forbes, a Scotchman of good family, in the French service, while Wilkes was at Paris, very unexpectedly challenged him in the public street for being the author of the North Briton, and for having written against Scotland. This fact coming to the knowledge of the French government, the parties were put upon their parole not to fight within the French dominions. Mr. Wilkes upon this offered to meet him in Flanders, or in any country in Europe, Asia, Africa, or America, except the dominions of France. Captain Forbes followed Wilkes to London, in order, as it was supposed, to arrange a meeting; but on receiving a hint from the government he left the kingdom. He afterwards entered the Portuguese service, in which he attained the rank of a general.

[75] Alexander Dun, a Scotchman, in December 1763 obtained admittance by his own appointment into the house of

Each a resolved, and pious son,
Wait her high bidding; each prepared
As she around her orders shared,
Proof 'gainst remorse, to run, to fly,
And bid the destined victim die,   80
Posting on Villainy's black wing,
Whether he patriot is, or king.
　　Oppression, willing to appear
An object of our love, not fear,
Or, at the most, a reverend awe
To breed, usurped the garb of Law;
A book she held, on which her eyes
Were deeply fixed, whence seemed to rise
Joy in her breast; a book of might
Most wonderful, which black to white   90
Could turn, and without help of laws,
Could make the worse the better cause.
She read, by flattering hopes deceived;
She wished, and what she wished, believed,
To make that book for ever stand
The rule of wrong through all the land;
On the back, fair and worthy note,
At large was Magna Charta wrote,
But turn your eye within, and read,
A bitter lesson, Norton's Creed.   100
Ready, e'en with a look, to run,
Fast as the coursers of the sun,
·To worry Virtue, at her hand

Mr. Wilkes; but being suspected of a design to assassinate him, was immediately seized by some gentlemen who were there on purpose to protect the demagogue. It appeared on his first examination that he was completely deranged; and he was ultimately delivered over to his friends, who undertook to confine him in a private madhouse.

Two half-starved greyhounds took their stand.
A curious model, cut in wood,
Of a most ancient castle stood
⸱ Full in her view; the gates were barr'd,
And soldiers on the watch kept guard
In the front openly, in black
Was wrote, The Tower; but on the back,   110
Marked with a Secretary's seal,
In bloody letters, The Bastile.
　　Around a table, fully bent
On mischief of most black intent,
Deeply determined, that their reign
Might longer last, to work the bane
Of one firm patriot, whose heart, tied
To honour, all their power defied,
And brought those actions into light
They wished to have concealed in night,   120
Begot, born, bred to infamy,
A privy council sat of three :
Great were their names, of high repute
And favour through the land of Bute,
　　The first (entitled to the place

---

112 This was the favourite appellation bestowed by the
partisans of Wilkes upon the Tower. Wilke's confinement
lasted six days, during which time he was debarred the use
of pen and ink; and was not permitted to see his friends.
125 The sketch of Warburton which follows is one of
Churchill's most pungent satires. William Warburton, D.D.
Bishop of Gloucester and dean of Bristol, was the son of an
attorney at Newark upon Trent, and was, in 1723, ordained
deacon in the cathedral of York, by Archbishop Dawes.
His subsequent rise in the church, he owed principally to the
high reputation his abilities had gained him in the literary
world; but it was no doubt accelerated by his friendship
with Pope, and his marriage, in 1745, with Miss Gertrude

Of honour both by gown and grace,
Who never let occasion slip
To take right hand of fellowship,
And was so proud, that should he meet
The Twelve Apostles in the street,   130
He'd turn his nose up at them all,
And shove his Saviour from the wall;
Who was so mean (Meanness and Pride
Still go together side to side)
That he would cringe, and creep, be civil,
And hold a stirrup for the devil,
If in a journey to his mind,
He'd let him mount and ride behind;
Who basely fawned through all his life,
For patrons first, then for a wife;   140
Wrote Dedications which must make
The heart of every Christian quake;
Made one man equal to, or more
Than God, then left him, as before
His God he left, and, drawn by pride,
Shifted about to t'other side;)
Was by his sire a parson made,
Merely to give the boy a trade;
But he himself was thereto drawn
By some faint omens of the lawn,   150
And on the truly Christian plan
To make himself a gentleman,

Tucker, the favourite niece of Ralph Allen, Esq. of Prior
Park, in Somersetshire, the Allworthy of Fielding's Tom
Jones. Mr. Allen rose to great wealth and consideration by
farming the cross posts, which he originated in 1720 and
put into admirable order; he died in 1764, and the bulk of
his fortune vested in the Bishop, to the prejudice of some
nearer relatives.

A title in which form arrayed him,
Though Fate ne'er thought on't when she made
    him.
  The oaths he took, 'tis very true,
But took them as all wise men do,
With an intent, if things should turn,
Rather to temporize, than burn.
Gospel and loyalty were made
To serve the purposes of trade :   160
Religion's are but paper ties,
Which bind the fool, but which the wise,
Such idle notions far above,
Draw on and off, just like a glove :
All gods, all kings, (let his great aim
Be answered) were to him the same.
  A curate first, he read and read,
And laid in, whilst he should have fed
The souls of his neglected flock,
Of reading such a mighty stock,   170
That he o'ercharged the weary brain
With more than she could well contain ;
More than she was with spirits fraught
To turn and methodize to thought,
And which, like ill-digested food,
To humours turned, and not to blood.
Brought up to London, from the plow
And pulpit, how to make a bow
He tried to learn ; he grew polite,
And was the poet's parasite.   180
With wits conversing (and wits then
Were to be found 'mongst noblemen)
He caught, or would have caught, the flame,
And would be nothing, or the same.

He drank with drunkards, lived with sinners,
Herded with infidels for dinners;
With such an emphasis and grace
Blasphemed, that Potter kept not pace:
He, in the highest reign of noon,
Bawled bawdy songs to a psalm tune;   190
Lived with men infamous and vile,
Trucked his salvation for a smile;
To catch their humour caught their plan,
And laughed at God to laugh with man;
Praised them, when living, in each breath,
And damned their memories after death.
    To prove his faith, which all admit
Is at least equal to his wit,
And make himself a man of note,
He in defence of Scripture wrote: 200
So long he wrote, and long about it,
That e'en believers 'gan to doubt it:
He wrote, too, of the inward light,
Though no one knew how he came by't,
And of that influencing grace
Which in his life ne'er found a place:
He wrote, too, of the Holy Ghost,
Of whom no more than doth a post
He knew, nor, should an angel shew him,
Would he or know, or choose to know him. 210
    Next (for he knew 'twixt every science

---

[188] Thomas Potter, Esq. M.P. for Okehampton, was in early life on very friendly terms with Mr. Allen, of Prior Park, and with Warburton; but having become intimate with Wilkes and his associates, the bishop suspected him of being the author of the notes on the "Essay on Woman." And this dissolved Mr. Potter's friendship both with Warburton and Mr. Allen.

There was a natural alliance)
He wrote, to advance his Maker's praise,
Comments on rhymes, and notes on plays,
And with an all-sufficient air
Placed himself in the critic's chair,
Usurped o'er reason full dominion,
And governed merely by opinion.
At length dethroned, and kept in awe
By one plain, simple man of law,   220

[212] The work by which Warburton first distinguished himself was "The Alliance between Church and State, or the
necessity of an established religion and a test law," 1736.

[220] Mr. Thomas Edwards, a barrister, and an accomplished
scholar and amiable man, was the author of several pleasing
sonnets in the collections of Dodsley, Pearch, and Nichols;
he also published a very ingenious work, intitled "Canons of
Criticism, by a gentleman of Lincoln's Inn," in which Warburton is severely censured.

Warburton took his revenge by introducing into his next
edition of the Dunciad, after Pope's death, a note on the
following lines in the fourth book of that poem :—

> Next bidding all draw near on bended knees,
> The queen confers her titles and degrees;
> Her children first of more distinguished sort,
> Who study Shakespeare at the inns of court.

In the note are stated the services done in the cause of
Dulness " by one Mr. Thomas Edwards, a gentleman, as he
is pleased to call himself, of Lincoln's Inn, but in reality, a
gentleman only of the Dunciad; or to speak him better in
the plain language of our honest ancestors of such mushrooms, a gentleman of the last edition."

Boswell says that soon after the "Canons of Criticism"
came out, Johnson was dining with Hayman the painter,
Tonson the bookseller, and some others, Hayman told Sir
Joshua Reynolds that the conversation having turned upon
Edwards's book, the gentlemen praised it much and Johnson allowed its merit. But when they went further and
appeared to put the author on a level with Warburton, No,
said Johnson, he has given him some smart hits, to be sure,

He armed dead friends, to vengeance true,
To abuse the man they never knew.
Examine strictly all mankind,
Most characters are mixed we find,
And vice and virtue take their turn
In the same breast to beat and burn.
Our priest was an exception here,
Nor did one spark of grace appear,
Not one dull, dim spark in his soul;
Vice, glorious vice possessed the whole,   230
And, in her service truly warm,
He was in sin most uniform.
Injurious Satire, own at least
One snivelling virtue in the priest,
One snivelling virtue, which is placed
They say, in or about the waist,
Called Chastity; the prudish dame,
Knows it at large by Virtue's name.
To this his wife, (and in these days
Wives seldom without reason praise)   240
Bears evidence—then calls her child,
And swears that Tom was vastly wild.
Ripened by a long course of years,
He great and perfect now appears.
In shape scarce of the human kind,
A man, without a manly mind;
No husband, though he's truly wed;
Though on his knees a child is bred,
No father; injured, without end

but there is no proportion between the two men; they must
not be named together. A fly, Sir, may sting a stately
horse and make him wince, but one is but an insect, and the
other is a horse still.

A foe; and though obliged, no friend;   250
A heart, which virtue ne'er disgraced;
A head, where learning runs to waste;
A gentleman well-bred, if breeding
Rests in the article of reading;
A man of this world, for the next
Was ne'er included in his text;
A judge of genius, though confessed
With not one spark of genius blessed;
Amongst the first of critics placed,
Though free from every taint of taste;   260
A Christian without faith or works,
As he would be a Turk 'mongst Turks;
A great divine, as lords agree,
Without the least divinity.
To crown all in declining age,
Inflamed with church and party rage,
Behold him, full and perfect quite,
A false saint, and true hypocrite.
   Next sat a lawyer, often tried
In perilous extremes; when Pride   270
And Power, all wild and trembling, stood,
Nor dared to tempt the raging flood,
This bold, bad man arose to view,
And gave his hand to help them through:

[266] Bishop Warburton died in 1779, having attained the great age of 81. A habitual melancholy latterly preyed upon his mind, and was aggravated by the loss of his only child, a very promising young man, who died of consumption a few years before his father.

[269] Sir Fletcher Norton, nicknamed Sir Bullface Doublefee, who was first Attorney General, then Speaker, and lastly in 1782 created Lord Grantley. He was a man of great fluency, little talent, and less principle, but not the odious character Churchill represents him.

Steeled 'gainst compassion, as they past
He saw poor Freedom breathe her last;
He saw her struggle, heard her groan;
He saw her helpless and alone,
Whelmed in that storm, which, feared, and praised
By slaves less bold, himself had raised.   280
    Bred to the law, he from the first
Of all bad lawyers was the worst.
Perfection (for bad men maintain
In ill we may perfection gain)
In others is a work of time,
And they creep on from crime to crime;
He, for a prodigy designed
To spread amazement o'er mankind,
Started full ripened all at once
A perfect knave, and perfect dunce.   290
    Who will, for him, may boast of sense,
His better guard is impudence;
His front, with tenfold plates of brass
Secured, Shame never yet could pass;
Nor on the surface of his skin
Blush for that guilt which dwelt within.
How often, in contempt of laws,
To sound the bottom of a cause,
To search out every rotten part,
And worm into its very heart,   300
Hath he ta'en briefs on false pretence,
And undertaken the defence
Of trusting fools, whom in the end
He meant to ruin, not defend!
How often, e'en in open court,
Hath the wretch made his shame his sport,
And laughed off, with a villain's case,

Throwing up briefs, and keeping fees !
Such things as, though to roguery bred,
Had struck a little villain dead.   310
Causes, whatever their import,
He undertakes, to serve a court ;
For he by heart this rule had got,—
Power can effect what law cannot.
Fools he forgives, but rogues he fears ;
If Genius, yoked with Worth, appears,
His weak soul sickens at the sight
And strives to plunge them down in night.
So loud he talks, so very loud,
He is an angel with the crowd,   320
Whilst he makes Justice hang her head,
And judges turn from pale to red.
Bid all that Nature, on a plan
Most intimate, makes dear to man,
All that with grand and general ties
Binds good and bad, the fool and wise,
Knock at his heart ; they knock in vain ;
No entrance there such suitors gain ;
Bid kneeling kings forsake the throne,
Bid at his feet his country groan ;   330
Bid Liberty stretch out her hands,
Religion plead her stronger bands ;
Bid parents, children, wife, and friends ;
If they come thwart his private ends,
Unmoved he hears the general call,
And bravely tramples on them all.
Who will, for him, may cant and whine,
And let weak Conscience with her line
Chalk out their ways; such starving rules
Are only fit for coward fools ;   340

Fellows who credit what priests tell,
And tremble at the thoughts of hell;
His spirit dares contend with Grace,
And meets Damnation face to face.

Such was our lawyer; by his side,
In all bad qualities allied,
In all bad counsels, sat a third,
By birth a lord; O sacred word!
O word most sacred, whence men get
A privilege to run in debt;   350
Whence they at large exemption claim
From Satire, and her servant Shame;
Whence they, deprived of all her force,
Forbid bold Truth to hold her course.

Consult his person, dress, and air,
He seems, which strangers well might swear,
The master, or, by courtesy,
The captain of a colliery.
Look at his visage, and agree
Half-hanged he seems, just from the tree   360
Escaped; a rope may sometimes break,
Or men be cut down by mistake.

He hath not virtue (in the school
Of Vice bred up) to live by rule;
Nor hath he sense (which none can doubt
Who know the man) to live without.
His life is a continued scene
Of all that's infamous and mean;
He knows not change, unless grown nice
And delicate, from vice to vice;   37C
Nature designed him, in a rage,
To be the Wharton of his age,

---

372 Philip Duke of Wharton who was as remarkable for

But having given all the sin,
Forgot to put the virtues in.
To run a horse, to make a match,
To revel deep, to roar a catch;
To knock a tottering watchman down,
To sweat a woman of the Town;
By fits to keep the peace, or break it,
In turn to give a pox, or take it;   380
He is, in faith, most excellent,
And, in the word's most full intent,
A true Choice Spirit we admit.
With wits a fool, with fools a wit,
Hear him but talk, and you would swear
Obscenity herself was there;
And that Profaneness had made choice,
By way of trump, to use his voice;
That, in all mean and low things great,
He had been bred at Billingsgate;   390
And that, ascending to the earth
Before the season of his birth,
Blasphemy, making way and room,
Had marked him in his mother's womb
Too honest (for the worst of men

his brilliancy as for his dissipation. He died at Tarragona,
in Spain, in a Bernardine convent, in May, 1731, without a
friend or acquaintance to close his eyes. He was no more
than 32 years of age, and as he died without issue, his duke-
dom became extinct. Previous to his death a bill of At-
tainder for High Treason, in consequence of his joining the
Pretender, had passed the House of Lords.
    [In 1845, on a claim being made to the barony of Whar-
ton, the House of Lords decided that the Duke's outlawry
was informal, and that the barony was represented by the
descendants of the daughters of his grandfather Philip, fourth
Lord Wharton.]

In forms are honest now and then)
Not to have, in the usual way,
His bills sent in; too great to pay;
Too proud to speak to, if he meets
The honest tradesman whom he cheats; 400
Too infamous to have a friend;
Too bad for bad men to commend,
Or good to name; beneath whose weight
Earth groans; who hath been spared by Fate
Only to shew, on mercy's plan,
How far and long God bears with man.
　　Such were the three who, mocking sleep,
At midnight sat, in counsel deep,
Plotting destruction 'gainst a head
Whose wisdom could not be misled; 410
Plotting destruction 'gainst a heart
Which ne'er from honour would depart.
　　" Is he not ranked amongst our foes?
Hath not his spirit dared oppose
Our dearest measures, made our name
Stand forward on the roll of shame?
Hath he not won the vulgar tribes,
By scorning menaces and bribes,
And proving, that his darling cause
Is of their liberties and laws 420
To stand the champion? In a word,
Nor need one argument be heard
Beyond this to awake our zeal,
To quicken our resolves, and steel
Our steady souls to bloody bent,
(Sure ruin to each dear intent
Each flattering hope) he, without fear,
Hath dared to make the truth appear."

They said, and, by resentment taught,
Each on revenge employed his thought;
Each, bent on mischief, racked his brain
To her full stretch, but racked in vain;
Scheme after scheme they brought to view;
All were examined; none would do:
When Fraud, with pleasure in her face,
Forth issued from her hiding place,
And at the table where they meet,
First having blest them, took her seat.
" No trifling cause, my darling Boys!
Your present thoughts and cares employs;
No common snare, no random blow,
Can work the bane of such a foe;
By Nature cautious as he's brave,
To honour only he's a slave;
In that weak part without defence,
We must to honour make pretence;
That lure shall to his ruin draw
The wretch, who stands secure in law:
Nor think that I have idly planned
This full-ripe scheme; behold at hand
With three months' training on his head,
An instrument, whom I have bred,
Born of these bowels, far from sight
Of virtue's false, but glaring light,
My youngest born, my dearest joy,
Most like myself, my darling boy:
He, never touched with vile remorse,
Resolved and crafty in his course,
Shall work our ends, complete our schemes,
Most mine, when most he Honour's seems;
Nor can be found, at home, abroad,

So firm and full a slave of Fraud."
She said, and from each envious son
A discontented murmur run
Around the table; all in place
Thought his full praise their own disgrace,
Wondering what stranger she had got,'
Who had one vice that they had not;
When straight the portals open flew,
And, clad in armour, to their view   470
Martin, the Duellist, came forth;
All knew, and all confessed his worth;
All justified, with smiles arrayed,
The happy choice their dam had made.

GOTHAM.

IN THREE BOOKS.

THE first book of this poem was published in February, 1764, and the whimsical nature of its contents gave scarcely any intimation of the shape it might in its progress assume. The publication of the third book developed the author's plan by presenting in the poet's own person, the portrait of a faultless sovereign. Notwithstanding the many beauties it contains, the plan is in itself so defective, and the vein of egotism that pervades it so undisguised, as to have prevented its acquiring the popularity of Churchill's former productions.

Gotham contains less personal satire than any other of our author's poems, and probably for that reason may now excite more interest than it did on its first appearance. The name of the author prepared his readers to expect that direct censure of individuals in which he had hitherto indulged, and the disappointment they experienced perhaps made them class this poem in a lower scale of merit than it deserved.

It is difficult to account for the title of this poem. The proverb, " As wise as the men of Gotham," is a very old one. Gotham was a village in Nottinghamshire, celebrated for the stupidity of its inhabitants, who were said to have tried to drown an eel. John Ray, in a note on the above proverb, says: " Men in all ages have made themselves merry with singling out some place and fixing the staple of stupidity and solidity there. · · · · As for Gotham,

It doth breed as wise people as any which causelessly laugh at their simplicity."

Cowper admired this poem greatly. In a letter to Mr. Unwin, he mentions a certain pitiful scribbler who had called it a catchpenny, and says: "Gotham, unless I am a greater blockhead than he, which I am far from believing, is a noble and beautiful poem, and a poem with which I make no doubt the author took as much pains as with any he ever wrote."

GOTHAM.

BOOK I.

AR off (no matter whether east or west,
A real country, or one made in jest),
Not yet by modern Mandevilles dis-
  graced,
Nor by map-jobbers wretchedly misplaced,
There lies an island, neither great nor small,
Which, for distinction sake, I Gotham call.
   The man who finds an unknown country out,
By giving it a name, acquires, no doubt,
A Gospel title, though the people there
The pious Christian thinks not worth his care;   10
Bar this pretence, and into air is hurl'd
The claim of Europe to the Western world.
   Cast by a tempest on the savage coast,
Some roving buccaneer set up a post;
A beam, in proper form transversely laid,
Of his Redeemer's cross the figure made,
Of that Redeemer, with whose laws his life,
From first to last, had been one scene of strife;

---

* Sir John Mandeville, the traveller of the 14th century.

His royal master's name thereon engraved,
Without more process, the whole race enslaved,
Cut off that charter they from Nature drew,   21
And made them slaves to men they never knew.
  Search ancient histories, consult records,
Under this title the most Christian lords
Hold (thanks to conscience) more than half the ball;
O'erthrow this title, they have none at all;
For never yet might any monarch dare,
Who lived to truth, and breathed a Christian air,
Pretend that Christ, (who came, we all agree,
To bless his people, and to set them free)   30
To make a convert ever one law gave
By which converters made him first a slave.
  Spite of the glosses of a canting priest,
Who talks of charity, but means a feast;
Who recommends it (whilst he seems to feel
The holy glowings of a real zeal)
To all his hearers, as a deed of worth,
To give them heaven, whom they have robb'd of earth,
Never shall one, one truly honest man,
Who, bless'd with Liberty, reveres her plan,   40
Allow one moment, that a savage sire
Could from his wretched race, for childish hire,
By a wild grant, their all, their freedom pass,
And sell his country for a bit of glass.
  Or grant this barbarous right, let Spain and France,
In slavery bred, as purchasers advance;
Let them, whilst conscience is at distance hurl'd,
With some gay bauble buy a golden world:
An Englishman, in charter'd freedom born,   49
Shall spurn the slavish merchandize, shall scorn
To take from others, through base private views,

What he himself would rather die, than lose.

Happy the savage of those early times,
Ere Europe's sons were known, and Europe's crimes!
Gold, cursed gold ! slept in the womb of earth,
Unfelt its mischiefs, as unknown its worth ;
In full content he found the truest wealth ;
In toil he found diversion, food, and health ;
Stranger to ease and luxury of courts,   59
His sports were labours, and his labours sports
His youth was hardy, and his old age green ;
Life's morn was vigorous, and her eve serene ;
No rules he held, but what were made for use,
No arts he learn'd, nor ills which arts produce ;
False lights he follow'd, but believed them true ;
He knew not much, but lived to what he knew.

Happy, thrice happy, now the savage race,
Since Europe took their gold, and gave them grace!
Pastors she sends to help them in their need,   69
Some who can't write, with others who can't read ;
And on sure grounds the Gospel pile to rear,
Sends missionary felons every year ;
Our vices, with more zeal than holy prayers,
She teaches them, and in return takes theirs :
Her rank oppressions give them cause to rise ;
Her want of prudence, means and arms supplies,
Whilst her brave rage, not satisfied with life,
Rising in blood, adopts the scalping-knife :
Knowledge she gives, enough to make them know

72 Punishment by transportation is unknown to the common law of England; it was first inflicted by Statute 39 Elizabeth, and it was warranted by the Habeas Corpus Act, 31 Car. II; from which period, until our colonial war, many capital offences were commuted into transportation to the plantations in America.

How abject is their state, how deep their woe; 80
The worth of freedom strongly she explains,
Whilst she bows down and loads their necks with
    chains :
Faith, too, she plants, for her own ends imprest,
To make them bear the worst and hope the best;
And whilst she teaches, on vile interest's plan,
As laws of God, the wild decrees of man,
Like Pharisees, of whom the Scriptures tell,
She makes them ten times more the sons of Hell.
    But whither do these grave reflections tend?
Are they design'd for any, or no end?   90
Briefly but this—to prove, that by no act
Which Nature made, that by no equal pact
'Twixt man and man, which might, if Justice heard,
Stand good; that by no benefits conferr'd,
Or purchase made, Europe in chains can hold
The sons of India, and her mines of gold.
Chance led her there in an accursèd hour ;
She saw, and made the country hers by power ;
Nor drawn by virtue's love from love of fame,
Shall my rash folly controvert the claim,   100
Or wish in thought that title overthrown
Which coincides with, and involves my own.
    Europe discover'd India first ; I found
My right to Gotham on the self-same ground ;
I first discover'd it, nor shall that plea
To her be granted, and denied to me ;
I plead possession, and, till one more bold
Shall drive me out will that possession hold.
With Europe's rights my kindred rights I twine ;
Hers be the Western world, be Gotham mine. 110
    Rejoice, ye happy Gothamites, rejoice ;

Lift up your voice on high, a mighty voice,
The voice of gladness ; and on every tongue,
In strains of gratitude, be praises hung,
The praises of so great and good a king ;
Shall Churchill reign, and shall not Gotham sing ?
  As on a day, a high and holy day,
Let every instrument of music play,
Ancient and modern ; those which drew their birth
(Punctilios laid aside) from Pagan earth,   120
As well as those by Christian made and Jew,
Those known to many, and those known to few ;
Those which in whim and frolic lightly float,
And those which swell the slow and solemn note;
Those which (whilst Reason stands in wonder by)
Make some complexions laugh and others cry ;
Those which, by some strange faculty of sound,
Can build walls up, and raze them to the ground ;
Those, which can tear up forests by the roots,
And make brutes dance like men, and men like
          brutes;   130
Those which, whilst Ridicule leads up the dance,
Make clowns of Monmouth ape the fops of France ;
Those which, where Lady Dulness with Lord Mayors
Presides, disdaining light and trifling airs,
Hallow the feast with psalmody, and those
Which, planted in our churches to dispose
And lift the mind to Heaven, are disgraced
With what a foppish organist calls Taste :
All, from the fiddle (on which every fool,

[120] The earliest editions of Gotham had "(Punctilios laid
wide)," for which the reading given in the text was afterwards substituted.

[132] Our author, in an excursion to Wales, resided for a
few weeks at Monmouth.

The pert son of dull sire, discharged from school,
Serves an apprenticeship in college ease,　　141
And rises through the gamut to degrees)
To those which (though less common, not less sweet)
From famed Saint Giles's, and more famed Vine-
　　street,
(Where Heaven, the utmost wish of Man to grant,
Gave me an old house, and an older aunt)
Thornton, whilst Humour pointed out the road
To her arch-cub, hath hitch'd into an ode;
All instruments, (attend, ye listening Spheres,
Attend, ye sons of men, and hear with ears)　　150
All instruments, (nor shall they seek one hand
Impress'd from modern Music's coxcomb band)
All instruments, self-acted, at my name
Shall pour forth harmony, and loud proclaim,
Loud but yet sweet, to the according globe,
My praises, whilst gay nature, in a robe,
A coxcomb doctor's robe, to the full sound
Keeps time, like Boyce, and the world dances round.
　　Rejoice, ye happy Gothamites! rejoice;
Lift up your voice on high, a mighty voice,　　160
The voice of gladness; and on every tongue,
In strains of gratitude, be praises hung,
The praises of so great and good a king:
Shall Churchill reign, and shall not Gotham sing?

---

[144] Churchill was born in Vine-street, Westminster.

[147] Alluding to a humorous burlesque "Ode on St. Cecilia's
Day," written by Bonnell Thornton, and adapted to the ancient British music, viz. the salt box, the Jew's harp, the
marrow bones and cleavers, the hum strum or hurdy gurdy,
&c. as it was performed at Ranelagh, on June 10, 1763.

[158] William Boyce, a celebrated musician, was born in
1710. He was, whilst a young man, seized with an incurable

Infancy, straining backward from the breast
Tetchy and wayward, what he loveth best
Refusing in his fits, whilst all the while
The mother eyes the wrangler with a smile,
And the fond father sits on t'other side,   169
Laughs at his moods, and views his spleen with pride,
Shall murmur forth my name, whilst at his hand
Nurse stands interpreter through Gotham's land.

Childhood, who like an April morn appears,
Sunshine and rain, hopes clouded o'er with fears,
Pleased and displeased by starts, in passion warm,
In reason weak; who wrought into a storm,
Like to the fretful billows of the deep,
Soon spends his rage, and cries himself asleep;
Who, with a feverish appetite oppress'd,
For trifles sighs, but hates them when possess'd,
His trembling lash suspended in the air,   181
Half-bent, and stroking back his long, lank hair,
Shall to his mates look up with eager glee,
And let his top go down to prate of me.

Youth, who, fierce, fickle, insolent and vain,
Impatient urges on to Manhood's reign,
Impatient urges on, yet, with a cast
Of dear regard, looks back on Childhood past,
In the mid-chase, when the hot blood runs high,
And the quick spirits mount into his eye;   190

deafness. Notwithstanding this defect, he continued his
studies with surprising perseverance, and in 1749, received
from the university of Cambridge the degree of Mus. D. In
1757 he was appointed master of the king's band, and
organist and composer to his majesty. He died in 1779,
and was interred in St. Paul's cathedral. In the English
school of composition he ranks with Dr. Arne, and is inferior
only to Purcell.

When pleasure, which he deems his greatest wealth,
Beats in his heart, and paints his cheeks with health;
When the chafed steed tugs proudly at the rein,
And, ere he starts, hath run o'er half the plain;
When, wing'd with fear, the stag flies full in view,
And in full cry the eager hounds pursue,
Shall shout my praise to hills which shout again,
And e'en the huntsman stop to cry Amen.
  Manhood, of form erect, who would not bow
Though worlds should crack around him; on his
     brow   200
Wisdom serene, to passion giving law,
Bespeaking love, and yet commanding awe;
Dignity into grace by mildness wrought;
Courage attemper'd, and refined by thought:
Virtue supreme enthroned, within his breast
The image of his Maker deep imprest;
Lord of this earth, which trembles at his nod,
With reason bless'd, and only less than God;
Manhood, though weeping Beauty kneels for aid,
Though Honour calls, in Danger's form array'd,
Though clothed with sackcloth, Justice in the
     gates,   211
By wicked elders chain'd, Redemption waits,
Manhood shall steal an hour, a little hour,
(Is't not a little one?) to hail my power.
  Old Age, a second child, by Nature curst
With more and greater evils than the first:
Weak, sickly, full of pains, in every breath
Railing at life, and yet afraid of death;
Putting things off, with sage and solemn air,
From day to day, without one day to spare; 220
Without enjoyment covetous of pelf,

Tiresome to friends, and tiresome to himself;
His faculties impair'd, his temper sour'd,
His memory of recent things devour'd
E'en with the acting, on his shatter'd brain,
Though the false registers of youth remain;
From morn to evening babbling forth vain praise
Of those rare men, who lived in those rare days,
When he, the hero of his tale, was young;
Dull repetitions faltering on his tongue;   230
Praising gray hairs, sure mark of Wisdom's sway,
E'en whilst he curses Time, which made him gray;
Scoffing at youth, e'en whilst he would afford
All but his gold to have his youth restored,
Shall for a moment, from himself set free,
Lean on his crutch, and pipe forth praise to me.

    Rejoice, ye happy Gothamites! rejoice;
Lift up your voice on high, a mighty voice,
The voice of gladness; and on every tongue,
In strains of gratitude, be praises hung,   240
The praises of so great and good a king;
Shall Churchill reign, and shall not Gotham sing?

    Things without life shall in this chorus join,
And, dumb to others' praise, be loud in mine.

    The snow-drop, who in habit white and plain,
Comes on, the herald of fair Flora's train;
The coxcomb crocus, flower of simple note,
Who, by her side struts in a herald's coat;
The tulip, idly glaring to the view,   249
Who, though no clown, his birth from Holland drew;

---

²²⁶ The reading given in the text is that of the later edition; the first edition has " stale register."
²⁵⁰ The mania that raged in Holland, and particularly among the inhabitants of Haerlem, for the cultivation of tulips in 1634 and the three following years, would scarcely

Who, once full-dress'd, fears from his place to stir,
The fop of flowers, the More of a parterre;
The woodbine, who her elm in marriage meets,
And brings her dowry in surrounding sweets;
The lily, silver mistress of the vale,
The rose of Sharon, which perfumes the gale;
The jessamine, with which the queen of flowers
To charm her god adorns his favourite bowers,
Which brides, by the plain hand of Neatness drest,
Unenvied rival, wear upon their breast,   260
Sweet as the incense of the morn, and chaste
As the pure zone which circles Dian's waist;
All flowers of various names, and various forms,
Which the sun into strength and beauty warms,
From the dwarf daisy, which, like infants, clings,
And fears to leave the earth from whence it springs,
To the proud giant of the garden race,
Who, madly rushing to the sun's embrace,
O'ertops her fellows with aspiring aim,
Demands his wedded love, and bears his name;
All, one and all, shall in this chorus join,   271
And, dumb to others' praise, be loud in mine.

be credited, was it not authenticated by the incontrovertible
testimony of contemporary historians. The price of tulips
rose to an extravagant height. Several merchants and
tradesmen quitted their counting houses and shops, to devote
themselves to the culture of these flowers; and it is related
that in the city of Haerlem alone, they had during these
three years traded in tulips to the amount of a million sterling. In 1637, one collection of tulips belonging to Wouters
Brockholmeister fetched at a public sale above £9,000. In
a three days' sale, the Viceroy was sold for £250, Admiral
Tiefkins £440, Admiral Van Eyk £160, Grebber £148,
Schiller £100, Semper Augustus £550. One person afterwards sold three Semper Augustuses for £1000 each.

Rejoice, yo happy Gothamites! rejoice;
Lift up your voice on high, a mighty voice,
The voice of gladness; and on every tongue,
In strains of gratitude, be praises hung,
The praises of so great and good a king;
Shall Churchill reign, and shall not Gotham sing?
    Forming a gloom, through which, to spleen-
        struck minds,
Religion, horror stamp'd, a passage finds,   280
The ivy crawling o'er the hallow'd cell
Where some old hermit's wont his beads to tell
By day, by night; the myrtle ever green,
Beneath whose shade Love holds his rites unseen;
The willow, weeping o'er the fatal wave
Where many a lover finds a watery grave;
The cypress, sacred held when lovers mourn
Their true love snatch'd away; the laurel worn
By poets in old time, but destined now,
In grief to wither on a Whitehead's brow;   290
The fig, which, large as what in India grows,
Itself a grove, gave our first parents clothes;
The vine, which, like a blushing, new-made bride,
Clustering, empurples all the mountain's side;
The yew, which in the place of sculptured stone,
Marks out the resting-place of men unknown;
The hedge-row elm, the pine, of mountain race;
The fir, the Scotch fir, never out of place;
The cedar, whose top mates the highest cloud,
Whilst his old father Lebanon grows proud   300
Of such a child, and his vast body laid
Out many a mile, enjoys the filial shade;

---

280 Poet Laureate: see *Prophecy of Famine*, l. 256, note.

The oak, when living, monarch of the wood ;
The English oak, which, dead, commands the flood ;
All, one and all, shall in this chorus join,
And dumb to others' praise, be loud in mine.
  Rejoice, ye happy Gothamites ! rejoice ;
Lift up your voice on high, a mighty voice,
The voice of gladness ; and on every tongue,
In strains of gratitude, be praises hung,   310
The praises of so great and good a king ;
Shall Churchill reign, and shall not Gotham sing ?
  The showers, which make the young hills, like
              young lambs,
Bound and rebound ; the old hills, like old rams,
Unwieldy, jump for joy; the streams, which glide,
Whilst Plenty marches smiling by their side,
And from their bosom rising Commerce springs ;
The winds, which rise with healing on their wings,
Before whose cleansing breath Contagion flies ;
The sun, who, travelling in eastern skies,   320
Fresh, full of strength, just risen from his bed,
Though in Jove's pastures they were born and bred,
With voice and whip can scarce make his steeds stir,
Step by step, up the perpendicular ;
Who, at the hour of eve, panting for rest,
Rolls on amain, and gallops down the west
As fast as Jehu, oil'd for Ahab's sin,
Drove for a crown, or postboys for an inn ;
The moon, who holds o'er night her silver reign,
Regent of tides, and mistress of the brain ;   330
Who to her sons, those sons who own her power
And do her homage at the midnight hour,
Gives madness as a blessing, but dispenses
Wisdom to fools, and damns them with their senses;

The stars, who, by I know not what strange right,
Preside o'er mortals in their own despite,
Who, without reason, govern those who most
(How truly, judge from thence!) of reason boast,
And, by some mighty magic yet unknown,
Our actions guide, yet cannot guide their own; 340
All, one and all, shall in this chorus join,
And, dumb to others' praise, be loud in mine.
   Rejoice, ye happy Gothamites! rejoice;
Lift up your voice on high, a mighty voice,
The voice of gladness; and on every tongue,
In strains of gratitude, be praises hung,
The praises of so great and good a king;
Shall Churchill reign, and shall not Gotham sing?
   The moment, minute, hour, day, week, month,
      year,
Morning and eve, as they in turn appear;   350
Moments and minutes, which, without a crime,
Can't be omitted in accounts of time,
Or, if omitted, (proof we might afford)
Worthy by parliaments to be restored;
The hours, which, dress'd by turns in black and
      white,
Ordain'd as handmaids, wait on day and night;
The day, those hours, I mean, when light presides,
And Business in a cart with Prudence rides;
The night, those hours, I mean, with darkness hung,
When Sense speaks free, and Folly holds her tongue;
The morn, when Nature, rousing from her strife
With death-like sleep, awakes to second life;   362
The eve, when, as unequal to the task,
She mercy from her foe descends to ask;
The week, in which six days are kindly given

To think of earth, and one to think of heaven;
The months, twelve sisters, all of different hue,
Though there appears in all a likeness too;
Not such a likeness as, through Hayman's works,
Dull Mannerist! in Christians, Jews, and Turks,
Cloys with a sameness in each female face;   371
But a strange something, born of Art and Grace,
Which speaks them all, to vary and adorn,
At different times of the same parents born;
All, one and all, shall in this chorus join,
And, dumb to others' praise, be loud in mine.

   Rejoice, ye happy Gothamites! rejoice;
Lift up your voice on high, a mighty voice,
The voice of gladness; and on every tongue,
In strains of gratitude, be praises hung,   380
The praises of so great and good a king;
Shall Churchill reign, and shall not Gotham sing?

   Frore January, leader of the year,
Minced-pies in van and calves' heads in the rear;
Dull February, in whose leaden reign
My mother bore a bard without a brain;
March, various, fierce, and wild, with wind-crack'd
      cheeks,
By wilder Welshmen led, and crown'd with leeks;

---

369 Francis Hayman was more distinguished as a choice
spirit than as an artist. He was a member of the Beef
Steak, the Spiller's Head, Old Slaughters, and other clubs
of note. Among his best paintings are those of Henry IV.
and of the Archer at Vauxhall. The want of imaginative
power, to which Churchill refers, prevented Hayman from
attaining eminence in his profession.

383 Frore, *frozen.*

384 It is said that the Roundheads used to celebrate the
anniversary of Charles the First's execution by having a
calf's head on table.

April, with fools, and May, with bastards blest;
June, with White Roses on her rebel breast;   390
July, to whom, the Dog-star in her train,
Saint James gives oysters, and Saint Swithin rain;
August, who, banish'd from her Smithfield stand,
To Chelsea flies, with Doggett in her hand;
September, when by custom (right divine)
Geese are ordain'd to bleed at Michael's shrine,
Whilst the priest, not so full of grace as wit,
Falls to unbless'd, nor gives the saint a bit;
October, who the cause of freedom join'd,
And gave a second George to bless mankind;   400
November, who, at once to grace our earth,
Saint Andrew boasts, and our Augusta's birth;
December, last of months, but best, who gave
A Christ to man, a Saviour to the slave,
Whilst, falsely grateful, man, at the full feast,
To do God honour makes himself a beast;

---

[393] Alluding to the shortening of Bartholomew fair, and
to the annual rowing match for a waterman's coat and silver
badge on the 1st of August, the anniversary of the accession
of King George the First. This ceremony was instituted by
Thomas Doggett, an actor, manager, and poet, who flourished
in the early part of the last century.

[400] George the Second was born the 30th of October, 1683.
His accession was hailed with delight by all parties; and
Mr. Hallam, in his Constitutional History, describes his
reign as the most prosperous period England had known.

[402] Augusta, daughter of Frederic, Duke of Saxe-Gotha,
was born November 30, 1719, and was married April 27,
1736, to Frederic, Prince of Wales, whom she survived. As
Princess Dowager she was thought to have an injurious influence over her son, George III, in the earlier part of his
reign; and she incurred some scandal on account of the un-
qualified public support and private friendship she gave to
the Earl of Bute. She died 8th Jan. 1772.

All, one and all, shall in this chorus join,
And, dumb to others' praise, be loud in mine.
  Rejoice, ye happy Gothamites! rejoice;
Lift up your voice on high, a mighty voice,   410
The voice of gladness; and on every tongue,
In strains of gratitude, be praises hung,
The praises of so great and good a king;
Shall Churchill reign, and shall not Gotham sing?
  The seasons as they roll; Spring, by her side
Lechery and Lent, lay-folly and church-pride,
By a rank monk to copulation led,
A tub of sainted salt-fish on her head;
Summer, in light, transparent gauze array'd,
Like maids of honour at a masquerade,   420
In bawdry gauze, for which our daughters leave
The fig, more modest, first brought up by Eve,
Panting for breath, inflamed with lustful fires,
Yet wanting strength to perfect her desires,
Leaning on Sloth, who, fainting with the heat,
Stops at each step, and slumbers on his feet;
Autumn, when Nature, who with sorrow feels
Her dread foe Winter treading on her heels,
Makes up in value what she wants in length,
Exerts her powers, and puts forth all her strength,
Bids corn and fruits in full perfection rise,   431
Corn fairly tax'd, and fruits without excise;
Winter, benumb'd with cold, no longer known

---

[420] The notorious Duchess of Kingston, when Miss Chudleigh, and a maid of honour to her majesty, appeared at a masquerade in a dress of gauze, which was so transparent as to display at once the graces of her person and of her mind.

[432] The budget of ways and means for the year 1763, contained an excise upon cyder and perry. This duty

By robes of fur, since furs became our own;
A hag, who, loathing all, by all is loath'd,
With weekly, daily, hourly, libels clothed,
Vile Faction at her heels, who, mighty grown,
Would rule the ruler, and foreclose the throne,
Would turn all state affairs into a trade,
Make laws one day, the next to be unmade,   440
Beggar at home a people fear'd abroad,
And, force defeated, make them slaves by fraud;
All, one and all, shall in this chorus join,
And, dumb to others' praise, be loud in mine.
     Rejoice, ye happy Gothamites! rejoice;
Lift up your voice on high, a mighty voice,
The voice of gladness; and on every tongue,
In strains of gratitude, be praises hung,
The praises of so great and good a king;   449
Shall Churchill reign, and shall not Gotham sing?
     The year, grand circle! in whose ample round
The seasons regular and fix'd are bound,
Who, in his course repeated o'er and o'er,
Sees the same things which he had seen before;
(The same stars keep their watch, and the same sun
Runs in the track where he from first hath run;
The same moon rules the night; tides ebb and flow,
Man is a puppet and this world a show;
Their old, dull follies, old, dull fools pursue,
And vice in nothing, but in mode, is new;   460
He, —————— a lord (now fair befal that pride,

being partial and oppressive, met with much opposition;
the tax however was retained until the year 1766, when it
had become so universally obnoxious as to compel its repeal.
     434 Probably alluding to the recent acquisition of Canada,
and the disappointment experienced by the first adventurers
in the fur trade.

He lived a villain, but a lord he died)
Dashwood is pious, Berkeley fix'd as Fate,
Sandwich (thank Heaven!) first Minister of State,
And, though by fools despised, by saints unbless'd,
By friends neglected, and by foes oppress'd,
Scorning the servile arts of each court elf,
Founded on honour, Wilkes is still himself)
The year, encircled with the various train
Which waits, and fills the glories of his reign,   470
Shall, taking up this theme, in chorus join,
And, dumb to others' praise, be loud in mine.

Rejoice, ye happy Gothamites! rejoice;
Lift up your voice on high, a mighty voice,
The voice of gladness; and on every tongue,
In strains of gratitude, be praises hung,
The praises of so great and good a king; ·
Shall Churchill reign, and shall not Gotham sing?

Thus far in sport—nor let our critics hence,
Who sell out Monthly trash, and call it Sense,   480

⁴⁶³ Sir Francis Dashwood founded Medmenham Abbey referred to in the Candidate (l. 696). He also erected a church at the top of a very steep hill, for the convenience of a town situated at the foot.

⁴⁶³ Colonel Norborne Berkeley, in whose favour the extinct barony of Bottetourt was revived. This mode of giving precedence, which was also adopted in favour of Sir Francis Dashwood, who thus obtained the barony of Le Despencer, gave much offence to the ancient nobility. The words in the text allude to an expression contained in a letter addressed by the Colonel to the Freeholders of Gloucestershire.

⁴⁶⁴ Lord Sandwich was never First Minister. In April, 1763, he succeeded Mr. Grenville, who became Prime Minister, as First Lord of the Admiralty. In September he was appointed Secretary of State, and held that office at the time Gotham was published. In 1771 Lord Sandwich was again appointed First Lord of the Admiralty, in Lord North's Cabinet.

Too lightly of our present labours deem,
Or judge at random of so high a theme;
High is our theme, and worthy are the men
To feel the sharpest stroke of Satire's pen;
But when kind Time a proper season brings,
In serious mood to treat of serious things,
Then shall they find, disdaining idle play,
That I can be as grave and dull as they.

   Thus far in sport—nor let half patriots, (those
Who shrink from every blast of Power which blows,
Who, with tame cowardice familiar grown,   491
Would hear my thoughts, but fear to speak their own;
Who, lest bold truths, to do sage Prudence spite,
Should burst the portals of their lips by night,
Tremble to trust themselves one hour in sleep)
Condemn our course, and hold our caution cheap;
When brave Occasion bids, for some great end,
When Honour calls the poet as a friend,
Then shall they find that, e'en on danger's brink,
He dares to speak what they scarce dare to think.

GOTHAM.

BOOK II.

OW much mistaken are the men who think
That all who will without restraint may
    drink;
May largely drink, e'en till their bowels
    burst,
Pleading no right but merely that of thirst,
At the pure waters of the living well,
Beside whose streams the Muses love to dwell!
Verse is with them a knack, an idle toy,
A rattle gilded o'er, on which a boy
May play untaught; whilst, without art or force,
Make it but jingle, music comes of course.   10
   Little do such men know the toil, the pains,
The daily, nightly racking of the brains,
To range the thoughts, the matter to digest,
To cull fit phrases, and reject the rest;
To know the times when Humour on the cheek
Of Mirth may hold her sports; when Wit should
    speak,
And when be silent; when to use the powers
Of ornament, and how to place the flowers,
So that they neither give a tawdry glare,
" Nor waste their sweetness in the desert air;"   20

To form, (which few can do, and scarcely one,
One critic in an age, can find when done)
To form a plan, to strike a grand outline,
To fill it up, and make the picture shine
A full and perfect piece ; to make coy Rhyme
Renounce her follies, and with Sense keep time ;
To make proud Sense against her nature bend,
And wear the chains of Rhyme, yet call her friend.

   Some fops there are, amongst the scribbling tribe,
Who make it all their business to describe,   30
No matter whether in or out of place ;
Studious of finery, and fond of lace,
Alike they trim, as coxcomb fancy brings,
The rags of beggars, and the robes of kings.
Let dull Propriety in state preside
O'er her dull children ; Nature is their guide,
Wild Nature, who at random breaks the fence
Of those tame drudges, Judgment, Taste, and Sense,
Nor would forgive herself the mighty crime
Of keeping terms with person, place, and time. 40

   Let liquid gold emblaze the sun at noon,
With borrow'd beams let silver pale the moon ;
Let surges hoarse lash the resounding shore,
Let streams meander, and let torrents roar ;
Let them breed up the melancholy breeze
To sigh with sighing, sob with sobbing trees ;
Let vales embroidery wear ; let flowers be tinged
With various tints ; let clouds be laced or fringed,
They have their wish ; like idle monarch boys,
Neglecting things of weight, they sigh for toys ; 50
Give them the crown, the sceptre, and the robe,
Who will may take the power, and rule the globe.

   Others there are who, in one solemn pace,

With as much zeal as Quakers rail at lace,
Railing at needful ornament, depend
On sense to bring them to their journey's end :
They would not (Heaven forbid!) their course delay,
Nor for a moment step out of the way,
To make the barren road those graces wear.   59
Which Nature would, if pleased, have planted there.

Vain Men ! who blindly thwarting Nature's plan,
Ne'er find a passage to the heart of man ;
Who, bred 'mongst fogs in academic land,
Scorn every thing they do not understand ;
Who, destitute of humour, wit, and taste,
Let all their little knowledge run to waste,
And frustrate each good purpose, whilst they wear
The robes of Learning with a sloven's air.
Though solid Reasoning arms each sterling line, 69
Though Truth declares aloud, " This work is mine,"
Vice, whilst from page to page dull morals creep,
Throws by the book, and Virtue falls asleep.

Sense, mere dull, formal Sense, in this gay town,
Must have some vehicle to pass her down ;
Nor can she for an hour insure her reign,
Unless she brings fair Pleasure in her train.
Let her from day to day, from year to year,
In all her grave solemnities appear,
And, with the voice of trumpets, through the
        streets,
Deal lectures out to every one she meets ;   80
Half who pass by are deaf, and t'other half
Can hear indeed, but only hear to laugh.

Quit then, ye graver sons of letter'd Pride,
Taking for once Experience as a guide,
Quit this grand error, this dull college mode ;

Be your pursuits the same, but change the road ;
Write, or at least appear to write, with ease,
" And if you mean to profit, learn to please."
In vain for such mistakes they pardon claim,
Because they wield the pen in Virtue's name :   90
Thrice sacred is that name, thrice bless'd the man
Who thinks, speaks, writes, and lives on such a plan!
This, in himself, himself of course must bless,
But cannot with the world promote success.
He may be strong, but, with effect to speak,
Should recollect his readers may be weak :
Plain rigid truths, which saints with comfort bear,
Will make the sinner tremble and despair.
True Virtue acts from love, and the great end
At which she nobly aims, is to amend ;   100
How then do those mistake, who arm her laws
With rigour not their own, and hurt the cause
They mean to help, whilst with a zealot rage
They make that goddess, whom they'd have engage
Our dearest love, in hideous terror rise !
Such may be honest, but they can't be wise.
    In her own full and perfect blaze of light
Virtue breaks forth too strong for human sight ;
The dazzled eye, that nice but weaker sense,
Shuts herself up in darkness for defence :   110
But to make strong conviction deeper sink,
To make the callous feel, the thoughtless think,
Like God made man, she lays her glory by,
And beams mild comfort on the ravish'd eye :
In earnest most when most she seems in jest,
She worms into, and winds around, the breast ;
To conquer vice, of vice appears the friend,
And seems unlike herself to gain her end.

The sons of Sin, to while away the time
Which lingers on their hands, of each black crime
To hush the painful memory, and keep   121
The tyrant Conscience in delusive sleep,
Read on at random, nor suspect the dart
Until they find it rooted in their heart.
'Gainst vice they give their vote, nor know at first
That, cursing that, themselves too they have curst;
They see not till they fall into the snares—
Deluded into virtue unawares.
Thus the shrewd doctor, in the spleen-struck mind
When pregnant horror sits and broods o'er wind,
Discarding drugs, and striving how to please,   131
Lures on insensibly, by slow degrees,
The patient to those manly sports which bind
The slacken'd sinews, and relieve the mind;
The patient feels a change as wrought by stealth,
And wonders on demand to find it health.

   Some few—whom Fate ordain'd to deal in rhymes
In other lands, and here, in other times;
Whom, waiting at their birth, the midwife Muse
Sprinkled all over with Castalian dews;   140
To whom true Genius gave his magic pen,
Whom Art by just degrees led up to men—
Some few, extremes well shunn'd, have steer'd
      between
These dangerous rocks, and held the golden mean:
Sense in their works maintains her proper state,
But never sleeps, or labours with her weight;
Grace makes the whole look elegant and gay,
But never dares from Sense to run astray:
So nice the master's touch, so great his care,
The colours boldly glow, not idly glare;   150

Mutually giving, and receiving aid,
They set each other off like light and shade,
And, as by stealth, with so much softness blend,
'Tis hard to say where they begin or end.
Both give us charms, and neither gives offence ;
Sense perfects grace, and grace enlivens sense.

Peace to the men who these high honours claim,
Health to their souls, and to their memories fame :
Be it my task, and no mean task, to teach
A reverence for that worth I cannot reach :   160
Let me at distance, with a steady eye,
Observe and mark their passage to the sky ;
From envy free, applaud such rising worth,
And praise their heaven though pinion'd down to
        earth.
Had I the power I could not have the time,
Whilst spirits flow, and life is in her prime,
Without a sin 'gainst pleasure, to design
A plan, to methodize each thought, each line,
Highly to finish, and make every grace,
In itself charming, take new charms from place.
Nothing of books, and little known of men,   171
When the mad fit comes on, I seize the pen,
Rough as they run, the rapid thoughts set down,
Rough as they run, discharge them on the town ;
Hence rude, unfinish'd brats, before their time,
Are born into this idle world of Rhyme,
And the poor slattern Muse is brought to bed
" With all her imperfections on her head."
Some, as no life appears, no pulses play

---

[171] Churchill's knowledge was general and extensive
What Prior said of the Duke of Dorset is equally true of the
poet : " Contemnebat literas potius quam nesciebat."

Through the dull dubious mass; no breath makes
    way,   180
Doubt, greatly doubt, till for a glass they call,
Whether the child can be baptized at all.
Others, on other grounds objections frame,
And, granting that the child may have a name,
Doubt, as the sex might well a midwife pose,
Whether they should baptize it Verse or Prose.
    E'en what my masters please; bards, mild,
        meek men,
In love to critics stumble now and then.
Something I do myself, and something too,
If they can do it, leave for them to do.   190
In the small compass of my careless page
Critics may find employment for an age:
Without my blunders they were all undone;
I twenty feed where Mason can feed one.
    When Satire stoops, unmindful of her state,
To praise the man I love, curse him I hate;
When sense, in tides of passion borne along,
Sinking to prose, degrades the name of song,
The censor smiles, and whilst my credit bleeds,
With as high relish on the carrion feeds   200
As the proud Earl fed at a turtle feast,
Who turn'd by gluttony to worse than beast,
Ate till his bowels gush'd upon the floor,
Yet still ate on, and dying call'd for more.
    When loose Digression, like a colt unbroke,
Spurning connexion and her formal yoke,

[205] Churchill wrote with great rapidity, and generally published his compositions directly they were finished. This may account for the involved sentences and lengthy parentheses, which are the most obvious, if not the worst, blemishes of his style.

Bounds through the forest, wanders far astray
From the known path, and loves to lose her way,
'Tis a full feast to all the mongrel pack
To run the rambler down and bring her back. 210
   When gay Description, Fancy's fairy child,
Wild without art, and yet with pleasure wild,
Waking with Nature at the morning hour
To the lark's call, walks o'er the opening flower
Which largely drank all night of heaven's fresh dew,
And, like a mountain nymph of Dian's crew,
So lightly walks she not one mark imprints,
Nor brushes off the dews, nor soils the tints;
When thus Description sports, even at the time
That drums should beat and cannons roar in rhyme,
Critics can live on such a fault as that   221
From one month to the other and grow fat.
   Ye mighty Monthly Judges! in a dearth
Of letter'd blockheads, conscious of the worth
Of my materials, which against your will
Oft you've confess'd, and shall confess it still;
Materials rich, though rude, inflamed with thought,
Though more by fancy than by judgment wrought;
Take, use them as your own, a work begin,
Which suits your genius well, and weave them in,
Framed for the critic loom with critic art,   231
Till thread on thread depending, part on part,
Colour with colour mingling, light with shade,
To your dull taste a formal work is made,
And, having wrought them into one grand piece,
Swear it surpasses Rome, and rivals Greece.
   Nor think this much, for at one single word,
Soon as the mighty critic fiat's heard,
Science attends their call; their power is own'd;

Order takes place, and Genius is dethroned; 240
Letters dance into books, defiance hurl'd
At means, as atoms danced into a world.
Me higher business calls, a greater plan,
Worthy man's whole employ, the good of man,
The good of man committed to my charge;
If idle Fancy rambles forth at large,
Careless of such a trust, these harmless lays
May Friendship envy, and may Folly praise;
The crown of Gotham may some Scot assume,
And vagrant Stuarts reign in Churchill's room. 250
O my poor People! O thou wretched Earth!
To whose dear love, though not engaged by birth,
My heart is fix'd, my service deeply sworn,
How, (by thy father can that thought be borne?
For monarchs, would they all but think like me,
Are only fathers in the best degree)
How must thy glories fade, in every land
Thy name be laugh'd to scorn, thy mighty hand
Be shorten'd, and thy zeal, by foes confess'd, 259
Bless'd in thyself, to make thy neighbours bless'd,
Be robb'd of vigour; how must Freedom's pile,
The boast of ages, which adorns the Isle,
And makes it great and glorious, fear'd abroad,
Happy at home, secure from force and fraud;
How must that pile, by ancient Wisdom raised
On a firm rock, by friends admired and praised,
Envied by foes, and wonder'd at by all,
In one short moment into ruins fall,
Should any slip of Stuart's tyrant race,
Or bastard or legitimate, disgrace 270
Thy royal seat of empire! but what care,
What sorrow, must be mine, what deep despair

And self-reproaches, should that hated line
Admittance gain through any fault of mine!
Cursed be the cause whence Gotham's evils spring,
Though that cursed cause be found in Gotham's king.
Let War, with all his needy ruffian band,
In pomp of horror stalk through Gotham's land
Knee-deep in blood; let all her stately towers
Sink in the dust; that court which now is ours
Become a den, where beasts may, if they can,   281
A lodging find, nor fear rebuke from man;
Where yellow harvests rise be brambles found;
Where vines now creep let thistles curse the
        ground;
Dry in her thousand valleys be the rills;
Barren the cattle on her thousand hills:
Where Power is placed let tigers prowl for prey;
Where Justice lodges let wild asses bray;
Let cormorants in churches make their nest,
And on the sails of commerce bitterns rest;   290
Be all, though princes in the earth before,
Her merchants bankrupts, and her marts no more;
Much rather would I, might the will of Fate
Give me to choose, see Gotham's ruin'd state,
By ills on ills thus to the earth weigh'd down,
Than live to see a Stuart wear her crown.
Let Heaven in vengeance arm all Nature's host,
Those servants who their Maker know, who boast
Obedience as their glory, and fulfil,   299
Unquestion'd, their great Master's sacred will;
Let raging winds root up the boiling deep,
And, with destruction big, o'er Gotham sweep;
Let rains rush down, till Faith, with doubtful eye,
Looks for the sign of mercy in the sky;   ·

Let Pestilence in all her horrors rise;
Where'er I turn, let Famine blast my eyes;
Let the earth yawn, and, ere they're time to think,
In the deep gulf let all my subjects sink
Before my eyes, whilst on the verge I reel;
Feeling, but as a monarch ought to feel,   310
Not for myself, but them,—I'll kiss the rod,
And, having own'd the justice of my God,
Myself with firmness to the ruin give,
And die with those for whom I wish to live.
   This, (but may Heaven's more merciful decrees
Ne'er tempt his servant with such ills as these)
This, or my soul deceives me, I could bear;
But that the Stuart race my crown should wear,
That crown, where, highly cherish'd, Freedom shone
Bright as the glories of the mid-day sun;   320
Born and bred slaves, that they, with proud misrule,
Should make brave, freeborn men, like boys at
      school,
To the whip crouch and tremble—O, that thought!
The labouring brain is e'en to madness brought
By the dread vision; at the mere surmise
The thronging spirits, as in tumult, rise;
My heart as for a passage, loudly beats,
And turn me where I will, distraction meets.
   O, my brave fellows! great in arts and arms,
The wonder of the earth, whom glory warms   330
To high achievements; can your spirits bend,
Through base control (ye never can descend
So low by choice) to wear a tyrant's chain,
Or let in Freedom's seat a Stuart reign?
If Fame, who hath for ages, far and wide,
Spread in all realms the cowardice, the pride,

The tyranny and falsehood of those lords,
Contents you not, search England's fair records;
England, where first the breath of life I drew,
Where next to Gotham, my best love is due;   340
There once they ruled; though crush'd by William's
    hand,
They rule no more to curse that happy land.
    The first, who, from his native soil removed,
Held England's sceptre, a tame tyrant proved:
Virtue he lack'd, cursed with those thoughts which
    spring
In souls of vulgar stamp, to be a king:
Spirit he had not, though he laugh'd at laws,
To play the bold-faced tyrant with applause;
On practices most mean he raised his pride,
And Craft oft gave what Wisdom oft denied.   350
    Ne'er could he feel how truly man is blest
In blessing those around him; in his breast,
Crowded with follies, Honour found no room;
Mark'd for a coward in his mother's womb,
He was too proud without affronts to live,
Too timorous to punish or forgive.
    To gain a crown, which had in course of time,
By fair descent been his without a crime,
He bore a mother's exile; to secure
A greater crown, he basely could endure   360
The spilling of her blood by foreign knife;
Nor dared revenge her death, who gave him life;
Nay, by fond Fear, and fond Ambition led,
Struck hands with those by whom her blood was
    shed.
    Call'd up to power, scarce warm on England's
    throne,

He fill'd her court with beggars from his own:
Turn where you would the eye with Scots was
    caught,
Or English knaves, who would be Scotsmen thought.
To vain expense unbounded loose he gave,
The dupe of minions, and of slaves the slave; 370
On false pretences mighty sums he raised,
And damn'd those senates rich, whom poor he
    praised:
From empire thrown, and doom'd to beg her bread,
On foreign bounty whilst a daughter fed,
He lavish'd sums, for her received, on men
Whose names would fix dishonour on my pen.
    Lies were his playthings, parliaments his sport;
Book-worms and catamites engross'd the court:
Vain of the scholar, like all Scotsmen since
The pedant scholar, he forgot the prince; 380
And having with some trifles stored his brain,
Ne'er learn'd, nor wish'd to learn, the arts to reign.
Enough he knew to make him vain and proud,
Mock'd by the wise, the wonder of the crowd;
False friend, false son, false father, and false king,
False wit, false statesman, and false everything:
When he should act he idly chose to prate,
And pamphlets wrote when he should save the state.
    Religious, if religion holds in whim
To talk with all, he let all talk with him; 390
Not on God's honour, but his own intent,
Not for religion's sake, but argument;
More vain if some sly, artful, High-Dutch slave,
Or, from the Jesuit school, some precious knave
Conviction feign'd, than if, to peace restored
By his full soldiership, worlds hail'd him Lord.

Power was his wish, unbounded as his will,
The power, without control, of doing ill;
But what he wish'd, what he made bishops preach,
And statesmen warrant, hung within his reach,
He dared not seize; fear gave, to gall his pride,
That freedom to the realm his will denied.   402

Of treaties fond, o'erweening of his parts,
In every treaty, of his own mean arts
He fell the dupe: peace was his coward care,
E'en at a time when justice call'd for war:
His pen he'd draw to prove his lack of wit,
But rather than unsheath the sword, submit.
Truth fairly must record; and, pleased to live
In league with mercy, justice may forgive   410
Kingdoms betray'd, and worlds resign'd to Spain,
But never can forgive a Raleigh slain.

At length, (with white let Freedom mark that
        year)
Nor fear'd by those whom most he wish'd to fear,
Not loved by those whom most he wish'd to love,
He went to answer for his faults above,
To answer to that God from whom alone
He claim'd to hold and to abuse the throne,
Leaving behind, a curse to all his line,
The bloody legacy of Right Divine.   420

With many virtues which a radiance fling
Round private men; with few which grace a king,
And speak the monarch, at that time of life
When passion holds with reason doubtful strife,
Succeeded Charles, by a mean sire undone,

---

420 The misfortunes and death of Charles I. may all be attributed to the implicit belief in the Divine Right of Kings, in which he was educated.

Who envied virtue even in a son.

His youth was froward, turbulent, and wild;
He took the man up ere he left the child;
His soul was eager for imperial sway
Ere he had learn'd the lesson to obey.   430
Surrounded by a fawning, flattering throng,
Judgment each day grew weak, and humour strong;
Wisdom was treated as a noisome weed,
And all his follies let to run to seed.

What ills from such beginnings needs must spring!
What ills to such a land from such a king!
What could she hope! what had she not to fear!
Base Buckingham possess'd his youthful ear;
Strafford and Laud, when mounted on the throne,
Engross'd his love, and made him all their own;
Strafford and Laud, who boldly dared avow   441
The traitorous doctrine taught by Tories now;
Each strove t' undo him in his turn and hour,
The first with pleasure, and the last with power.

Thinking (vain thought, disgraceful to the
          throne!)
That all mankind were made for kings alone,
That subjects were but slaves, and what was whim,
Or worse, in common men, was law in him;

[438] George Villiers, Duke of Buckingham, assassinated in 1629.

The following lines, written by our author, were engraved on a cup of £500 value, presented by a Mr. Stephenson of Ludgate Hill to Mr. Wilkes:

Proud Buckingham, for law too mighty grown,
A patriot dagger probed, and from the throne
Sever'd its minion. In succeeding times
May all those favourites who adopt his crimes,
Partake his fate, and every Villiers feel
The keen, deep searchings of a Felton's steel.

Drunk with Prerogative, which Fate decreed
To guard good kings, and tyrants to mislead,   450
Which in a fair proportion to deny
Allegiance dares not, which to hold too high
No good can wish, no coward king can dare,
And held too high no English subject bear ;
Besieged by men of deep and subtle arts,
Men void of principle, and damn'd with parts,
Who saw his weakness, made their king their tool,
Then most a slave when most he seem'd to rule ;
Taking all public steps for private ends,
Deceived by favourites, whom he call'd friends,
He had not strength enough of soul to find   461
That monarchs, meant as blessings to mankind,
Sink their great state, and stamp their fame undone,
When what was meant for all, they give to one.
Listening uxorious whilst a woman's prate
Modell'd the church and parcell'd out the state,
Whilst (in the state not more than women read)
High-churchmen preach'd, and turn'd his pious
            head ;
Tutor'd to see with ministerial eyes ;
Forbid to hear a loyal nation's cries ;   470
Made to believe (what can't a favourite do ?)
He heard a nation, hearing one or two ;
Taught by state-quacks himself secure to think,
And out of danger e'en on danger's brink ;
Whilst power was daily crumbling from his hand,
Whilst murmurs ran through an insulted land,
As if to sanction tyrants Heaven was bound,

465 The intriguing character and religious prejudices of
Henrietta contributed in no small degree to the melancholy
fate of her husband.

He proudly sought the ruin which he found.
Twelve years, twelve tedious and inglorious years,
Did England, crush'd by power, and awed by fears,
Whilst proud Oppression struck at Freedom's root,
Lament her senates lost, her Hampden mute : 482
Illegal taxes and oppressive loans,
In spite of all her pride, call'd forth her groans ;
Patience was heard her griefs aloud to tell,
And Loyalty was tempted to rebel.
Each day new acts of outrage shook the state,
New courts were raised to give new doctrines weight ;
State-Inquisitions kept the realm in awe, 489
And cursed Star-Chambers made or ruled the law;
Juries were pack'd, and judges were unsound ;
Through the whole kingdom not one Pratt was found.
From the first moments of his giddy youth
He hated senates, for they told him truth :
At length against his will compell'd to treat,
Those whom he could not fright he strove to cheat ;
With base dissembling every grievance heard,
And often giving, often broke his word.
Oh where shall hapless Truth for refuge fly,
If kings, who should protect her, dare to lie ? 500
Those who, the general good their real aim,
Sought in their country's good their monarch's fame ;
Those who were anxious for his safety ; those
Who were induced by duty to oppose,
Their truth suspected, and their worth unknown,
He held as foes and traitors to his throne,
Nor found his fatal error till the hour
Of saving him was gone and past ; till power
Had shifted hands, to blast his hapless reign,

479 No Parliament sat from March 1628 to April 1640.

Making their faith and his repentance vain.   510
   Hence (be that curse confined to Gotham's foes)
War, dread to mention, civil war arose ;
All acts of outrage and all acts of shame
Stalk'd forth at large, disguised with honour's name ;
Rebellion, raising high her bloody hand,
Spread universal havoc through the land ;
With zeal for party, and with passion drunk,
In public rage all private love was sunk ;
Friend against friend, brother 'gainst brother stood,
And the son's weapon drank the father's blood ;
Nature, aghast, and fearful lest her reign   521
Should last no longer, bled in every vein.

   Unhappy Stuart ! harshly though that name
Grates on my ear, I should have died with shame
To see my king before his subjects stand,
And at their bar hold up his royal hand ;
At their commands to hear the monarch plead.
By their decrees to see that monarch bleed.
What though thy faults were many and were great?
What though they shook the basis of the state ?
In royalty secure thy person stood,   531
And sacred was the fountain of thy blood.
Vile ministers, who dared abuse their trust,
Who dared seduce a king to be unjust,
Vengeance, with justice leagued, with power made
      strong,
Had nobly crush'd ; " The king could do no wrong."
   Yet grieve not, Charles, nor thy hard fortunes
      blame ;
They took thy life, but they secured thy fame.
Their greater crimes made thine like specks appear,
From which the sun in glory is not clear.   540

Hadst thou in peace and years resign'd thy breath
At Nature's call; hadst thou laid down in death
As in a sleep, thy name by Justice borne
On the four winds, had been in pieces torn.
Pity, the virtue of a generous soul,
Sometimes the vice, hath made thy memory whole.
Misfortunes gave what virtue could not give,
And bade, the tyrant slain, the martyr live.

 Ye Princes of the earth! ye mighty few!   549
Who worlds subduing, can't yourselves subdue;
Who, goodness scorn'd, wish only to be great,
Whose breath is blasting, and whose voice is fate;
Who own no law, no reason, but your will,
And scorn restraint, though 'tis from doing ill;
Who of all passions groan beneath the worst,
Then only bless'd when they make others curst;
Think not, for wrongs like these, unscourged to live;
Long may ye sin, and long may Heaven forgive;
But when ye least expect, in sorrow's day,
Vengeance shall fall more heavy for delay;   560
Nor think, that vengeance heap'd on you alone
Shall (poor amends) for injured worlds atone;
No, like some base distemper, which remains,
Transmitted from the tainted father's veins
In the son's blood, such broad and general crimes
Shall call down vengeance e'en to latest times,
Call vengeance down on all who bear your name,
And make their portion bitterness and shame.

 From land to land for years compell'd to roam,
Whilst Usurpation lorded it at home;   570
Of majesty unmindful, forced to fly,
Not daring, like a king, to reign or die;
Recall'd to repossess his lawful throne

More at his people's seeking than his own,
Another Charles succeeded.   In the school
Of travel he had learn'd to play the fool,
And like pert pupils with dull tutors sent
To shame their country on the Continent,
From love of England by long absence wean'd,
From every court he every folly glean'd,   580
And was, so close do evil habits cling,
Till crown'd a beggar, and when crown'd, no king.
   Those grand and general powers which Heaven
      design'd
An instance of his mercy to mankind
Were lost, in storms of dissipation hurl'd,
Nor would he give one hour to bless a world
Lighter than Levity which strides the blast,
And of the present fond, forgets the past,
He changed and changed, but, every hope to curse,
Changed only from one folly to a worse: 590
State he resigned to those whom state could please;
Careless of majesty, his wish was ease;
Pleasure, and pleasure only, was his aim;
Kings of less wit might hunt the bubble fame;
Dignity through his reign was made a sport,
Nor dared Decorum shew her face at court:
Morality, was held a standing jest,
And faith, a necessary fraud at best:
Courtiers, their monarch ever in their view,
Possess'd great talents, and abused them too: 600
Whate'er was light, impertinent, and vain,
Whate'er was loose, indecent, and profane,
(So ripe was folly, folly to acquit)
Stood all absolved in that poor bauble, wit.
   In gratitude, alas! but little read,

He let his father's servants beg their bread,
His father's faithful servants and his own,
To place the foes of both around his throne.
Bad counsels he embraced through indolence,
Through love of ease, and not through want of
    sense; 610
He saw them wrong, but rather let them go
As right, than take the pains to make them so.
Women ruled all, and ministers of state
Were for commands at toilets forced to wait:
Women, who have as monarchs graced the land,
But never govern'd well at second hand.
To make all other errors slight appear,
In memory fix'd stand Dunkirk and Tangier;
In memory fix'd so deep, that time in vain 619
Shall strive to wipe those records from the brain,
Amboyna stands—Gods! that a king could hold
In such high estimate vile, paltry gold,
And of his duty be so careless found,
That when the blood of subjects from the ground
For vengeance call'd, he should reject their cry,
And, bribed from honour, lay his thunders by,

[613] " They (the House of Commons) have signed and sealed
£10,000 a-year more to the Duchess of Cleveland. . . . . .
All promotions, spiritual and temporal, pass under her cogni-
zance."—ANDREW MARVELL.

[618] Dunkirk surrendered to Cromwell in 1658, and was, in
1662, sold by Charles II. to Louis XIV. for about £500,000.

[618] Tangier, in Africa, formed a part of the dowry brought
by Catherine of Portugal to Charles II. The place was dis-
mantled and deserted in 1683, to avoid the expense of
holding it.

[621] Churchill is here guilty of an anachronism. The mas-
sacre of the British settlers in Amboyna, one of the Molucca
Islands, by the Dutch residents, took place in 1623, during
the reign of James I, and before Charles II. was born.

Give Holland peace, whilst English victims groan'd,
And butcher'd subjects wander'd unatoned!
O dear, deep injury to England's fame,
To them, to us, to all! to him deep shame!   630
Of all the passions which from frailty spring,
Avarice is that which least becomes a king.

To crown the whole, scorning the public good,
Which through his reign he little understood
Or little heeded, with too narrow aim
He reassumed a bigot brother's claim,
And having made time-serving senates bow,
Suddenly died, that brother best knew how.

No matter how—he slept amongst the dead,
And James his brother reignéd in his stead: 640
But such a reign—so glaring an offence
'In every step 'gainst freedom, law, and sense,
'Gainst all the rights of Nature's general plan,
'Gainst all which constitutes an Englishman.
That the relation would mere fiction seem,
The mock creation of a poet's dream;
And the poor bard's would, in this sceptic age,
Appear as false as *their* historian's page.

Ambitious folly seized the seat of wit,
Christians were forced by bigots to submit;   650
Pride without sense, without religion zeal
Made daring inroads on the commonweal;
Stern Persecution raised her iron rod,

---

[636] The first edition has 'reassured' for 'reassumed.'

[638] This line appears to imply that Charles was poisoned by his brother; his death was certainly sudden, attended with some suspicious appearances, and happened at a critical period; but Burnet, who cannot be accused of partiality to James, admits that he never heard any one suspect him of being accessory to his brother's death.

And call'd the pride of kings the power of God;
Conscience and fame were sacrificed to Rome,
And England wept at Freedom's sacred tomb.

Her laws despised, her constitution wrench'd
From its due, natural frame, her rights retrench'd
Beyond a coward's sufferance; conscience forced,
And healing justice from the crown divorced; 66c
Each moment pregnant with vile acts of power;
Her patriot Bishops sentenced to the Tower;
Her Oxford (who yet loves the Stuart name)
Branded with arbitrary marks of shame,
She wept—but wept not long; to arms she flew,
At Honour's call the avenging sword she drew,
Turn'd all her terrors on the tyrant's head,
And sent him in despair to beg his bread;
Whilst she, (may every state in such distress
Dare with such zeal, and meet with such success)
Whilst she, (may Gotham, should my abject mind
Choose to enslave rather than free mankind, 672
Pursue her steps, tear the proud tyrant down,
Nor let me wear if I abuse the crown)
Whilst she, (through every age in every land,
Written in gold, let Revolution stand)
Whilst she, secured in liberty and law,
Found what she sought, a saviour in Nassau.

66² Alluding to the committal to the Tower, trial, and
acquittal in 1688 of Dr. Sancroft, Archbishop of Canterbury,
Dr. Lloyd, Bishop of St. Asaph, Dr. Ken, Bishop of Bath
and Wells, Dr. Turner, Bishop of Ely, Dr. Lake, Bishop of
Chichester, Dr. White, Bishop of Peterborough, and Sir
Jonathan Trelawney, Bishop of Bristol, for refusing to publish
in the churches of their dioceses a proclamation of liberty of
conscience issued, on his own authority, by James II, which
practically nullified the Act of Uniformity.

GOTHAM.

BOOK III.

AN the fond mother from herself de-
    part?
Can she forget the darling of her heart,
The little darling whom she bore and
    bred,
Nursed on her knees, and at her bosom fed,
To whom she seem'd her every thought to give,
And in whose life alone she seem'd to live?
Yes, from herself the mother may depart,
She may forget the darling of her heart,
The little darling whom she bore and bred,
Nursed on her knees, and at her bosom fed,   10
To whom she seem'd her every thought to give,
And in whose life alone she seem'd to live;
But I cannot forget, whilst life remains,
And pours her current through these swelling veins,
Whilst Memory offers up at Reason's shrine;
But I cannot forget that Gotham's mine.

    Can the stern mother, than the brutes more wild,
From her disnatured breast tear her young child,

Flesh of her flesh, and of her bone the bone,
And dash the smiling babe against a stone ? 20
Yes, the stern mother, than the brutes more wild,
From her disnatured breast may tear her child,
Flesh of her flesh, and of her bone the bone,
And dash the smiling babe against a stone ;
But I, (forbid it, Heav'n !) but I can ne'er
The love of Gotham from this bosom tear ;
Can ne'er so far true royalty pervert
From its fair course, to do my people hurt.

 With how much ease, with how much confidence,
As if, superior to each grosser sense 30
Reason had only, in full power array'd,
To manifest her will, and be obey'd,
Men make resolves, and pass into decrees
The motions of the mind ! with how much ease,
In such resolves, doth passion make a flaw,
And bring to nothing what was raised to law !

 In empire young, scarce warm on Gotham's throne,
The dangers and the sweets of power unknown,
Pleased, though I scarce know why, like some
   young child,
Whose little senses each new toy turns wild, 40
How do I hold sweet dalliance with my crown,
And wanton with dominion ; how lay down,
Without the sanction of a precedent,
Rules of most large and absolute extent ;
Rules, which from sense of public virtue spring,
And all at once commence a patriot king !

 But, for the day of trial is at hand,
And the whole fortunes of a mighty land
Are staked on me, and all their weal or woe
Must from my good or evil conduct flow, 50

Will I, or can I, on a fair review,
As I assume that name, deserve it too?
Have I well weigh'd the great, the noble part
I'm now to play? have I explored my heart,
That labyrinth of fraud, that deep, dark cell,
Where, unsuspected, e'en by me, may dwell
Ten thousand follies? have I found out there
What I am fit to do, and what to bear?
Have I traced every passion to its rise,   59
Nor spared one lurking seed of treach'rous vice?
Have I familiar with my nature grown?
And am I fairly to myself made known?

 A patriot king—why, 'tis a name which bears
The more immediate stamp of Heaven; which wears
The nearest, best resemblance we can shew
Of God above, through all his works below.
 To still the voice of discord in the land,
To make weak Faction's discontented band,
Detected, weak, and crumbling to decay,   69
With hunger pinch'd, on their own vitals prey;
Like brethren, in the selfsame interests warm'd,
Like different bodies with one soul inform'd;
To make a nation, nobly raised above
All meaner thought, grow up in common love;
To give the laws due vigour, and to hold
That secret balance, temperate, yet bold,
With such an equal hand, that those who fear
May yet approve, and own my justice clear;
To be a common father, to secure
The weak from violence, from pride the poor;   80
Vice and her sons to banish in disgrace,
To make Corruption dread to shew her face;
To bid afflicted Virtue take new state

And be, at last, acquainted with the great;
Of all religions to elect the best,
Nor let her priests be made a standing jest;
Rewards for worth with liberal hand to carve,
To love the arts, nor let the artists starve;
To make fair plenty through the realm increase,
Give fame in war, and happiness in peace; 90
To see my people virtuous, great and free,
And know that all those blessings flow from me;
O! 'tis a joy too exquisite, a thought
Which flatters Nature more than flattery ought;
'Tis a great, glorious task, for man too hard,
But no less great, less glorious, the reward;
The best reward which here to man is given,
'Tis more than earth, and little short of heaven;
A task (if such comparison may be)
The same in nature, differing in degree, 100
Like that which God, on whom for aid I call,
Performs with ease, and yet performs to all.
How much do they mistake, how little know
Of kings, of kingdoms, and the pains which flow
From royalty, who fancy that a crown,
Because it glistens, must be lined with down!
With outside shew, and vain appearance caught,
They look no farther, and, by Folly taught,
Prize high the toys of thrones, but never find
One of the many cares which lurk behind. 110
The gem they worship which a crown adorns,
Nor once suspect that crown is lined with thorns.
Oh, might reflection folly's place supply!
Would we one moment use her piercing eye,
Then should we find what woe from grandeur
          springs,

And learn to pity, not to envy kings.

The villager, born humbly and bred hard,
Content his wealth, and Poverty his guard,
In action simply just, in conscience clear,
By guilt untainted, undisturb'd by fear,   120
His means but scanty, and his wants but few,
Labour his business, and his pleasure too,
Enjoys more comforts in a single hour
Than ages give the wretch condemn'd to power.

Call'd up by health he rises with the day,
And goes to work, as if he went to play,
Whistling off toils, one half of which might make
The stoutest Atlas of a palace quake ;
'Gainst heat and cold, which make us cowards faint,
Harden'd by constant use, without complaint   130
He bears what we should think it death to bear :
Short are his meals, and homely is his fare ;
His thirst he slakes at some pure neighbouring
          brook,
Nor asks for sauce where Appetite stands cook.
When the dews fall, and when the sun retires
Behind the mountains, when the village fires,
Which, waken'd all at once, speak supper nigh,
At distance catch, and fix his longing eye,
Homeward he hies, and with his manly brood   139
Of raw-boned cubs enjoys that clean, coarse food
Which, season'd with good humour, his fond bride
'Gainst his return is happy to provide.
Then, free from care, and free from thought, he
          creeps
Into his straw, and till the morning sleeps.

Not so the king—with anxious cares opprest
His bosom labours, and admits not rest :

A glorious wretch, he sweats beneath the weight
Of majesty, and gives up ease for state :
E'en when his smiles, which by the fools of pride
Are treasured and preserved, from side to side 150
Fly round the court, e'en when compell'd by form,
He seems most calm, his soul is in a storm ;
Care, like a spectre seen by him alone,
With all her nest of vipers, round his throne
By day crawls full in view ; when night bids sleep,
Sweet nurse of Nature, o'er the senses creep ;
When Misery herself no more complains,
And slaves, if possible, forget their chains,
Though his sense weakens, though his eyes grow dim
That rest, which comes to all, comes not to him.
E'en at that hour, Care, tyrant Care, forbids 161
The dew of sleep to fall upon his lids ;
From night to night she watches at his bed ;
Now, as one moped, sits brooding e'er his head ;
Anon she starts, and, borne on raven's wings,
Croaks forth aloud—Sleep was not made for kings.

   Thrice hath the moon, who governs this vast ball,
Who rules most absolute o'er me and all ;
To whom, by full conviction taught to bow,
At new, at full, I pay the duteous vow ; 170
Thrice hath the moon her wonted course pursued,
Thrice hath she lost her form, and thrice renew'd,
Since, (blessed be that season, for before
I was a mere, mere mortal, and no more,
One of the herd, a lump of common clay,
Inform'd with life, to die and pass away)
Since I became a king, and Gotham's throne,
With full and ample power, became my own ;
Thrice hath the moon her wonted course pursued,

Thrice hath she lost her form, and thrice renew'd,
Since sleep, kind sleep, who like a friend supplies
New vigour for new toil, hath closed these eyes:
Nor, if my toils are answer'd with success,
And I am made an instrument to bless
The people whom I love, shall I repine;
Theirs be the benefit, the labour mine.

Mindful of that high rank in which I stand,
Of millions lord, sole ruler in the land,
Let me, and Reason shall her aid afford,
Rule my own spirit, of myself be lord.   190
With an ill grace that monarch wears his crown,
Who, stern and hard of nature, wears a frown
'Gainst faults in other men, yet all the while
Meets his own vices with a partial smile.
How can a king (yet on record we find
Such kings have been, such curses of mankind)
Enforce that law 'gainst some poor subject elf
Which Conscience tells him he hath broke himself?
Can he some petty rogue to justice call
For robbing one, when he himself robs all?   200
Must not, unless extinguish'd, conscience fly
Into his cheek, and blast his fading eye,
To scourge the oppressor, when the state, distress'd
And sunk to ruin, is by him oppress'd?
Against himself doth he not sentence give?
If one must die, t' other's not fit to live.

Weak is that throne, and in itself unsound,
Which takes not solid virtue for its ground.
All envy power in others, and complain
Of that which they would perish to obtain.   210
Nor can those spirits, turbulent and bold,
Not to be awed by threats, nor bought with gold,

Be hush'd to peace but when fair, legal sway
Makes it their real interest to obey,
When kings,—and none but fools can then rebel,—
Not less in virtue, than in power, excel.

 Be that my object, that my constant care,
And may my soul's best wishes centre there;
Be it my task to seek, nor seek in vain,
Not only how to live, but how to reign, 220
And to those virtues which from reason spring,
And grace the man, join those which grace the king.

 First, (for strict duty bids my care extend
And reach to all, who on that care depend;
Bids me with servants keep a steady hand,
And watch o'er all my proxies in the land)
First, (and that method reason shall support)
Before I look into and purge my court,
Before I cleanse the stable of the state
Let me fix things which to myself relate: 23c
That done, and all accounts well settled here,
In resolution firm, in honour clear,
Tremble, ye slaves! who dare abuse your trust,
Who dare be villains when your king is just.

 Are there, amongst those officers of state
To whom our sacred power we delegate,
Who hold our place and office in the realm,
Who, in our name commissioned, guide the helm;
Are there who, trusting to our love of ease,
Oppress our subjects, wrest our just decrees, 210
And make the laws, warped from their fair intent,
To speak a language which they never meant;
Are there such men, and can the fools depend
On holding out in safety to their end?
Can they so much, from thoughts of danger free,

Deceive themselves, so much misdeem of me,
To think that I will prove a statesman's tool,
And live a stranger where I ought to rule ?
What ! to myself and to my state unjust,
Shall I from ministers take things on trust,   250
And, sinking low the credit of my throne,
Depend upon dependents of my own ?
Shall I, most certain source of future cares,
Not use my judgment, but depend on theirs ?
Shall I, true puppet-like, be mocked with state,
Have nothing but the name of being great ;
Attend at councils which I must not weigh,
Do what they bid, and what they dictate, say,
Enrobed, and hoisted up into my chair,
Only to be a royal cipher there ?   260
Perish the thought—'tis treason to my throne—
And who but thinks it, could his thoughts be known,
Insults me more than he, who leagued with Hell,
Shall rise in arms, and 'gainst my crown rebel.
    The wicked statesman, whose false heart pursues
A train of guilt, who acts with double views,
And wears a double face ; whose base designs
Strike at his monarch's throne ; who undermines
E'en whilst he seems his wishes to support ;
Who seizes all departments ; packs a court ;   270
Maintains an agent on the judgment-seat
To screen his crimes, and make his frauds complete ;
New-models armies, and around the throne
Will suffer none but creatures of his own,
Conscious of such his baseness, well may try
Against the light to shut his master's eye,
To keep him coop'd, and far removed from those
Who, brave and honest, dare his crimes disclose,

Nor ever let him in one place appear,   279
Where truth, unwelcome truth, may wound his ear.
  Attempts like these, well-weigh'd, themselves
          proclaim,
And, whilst they publish, baulk their author's aim.
Kings must be blind into such snares to run,
Or, worse, with open eyes must be undone.
The minister of honesty and worth
Demands the day to bring his actions forth;
Calls on the sun to shine with fiercer rays,
And braves that trial which must end in praise.
None fly the day, and seek the shades of night,
But those whose actions cannot bear the light;
None wish their king in ignorance to hold   291
But those who feel that knowledge must unfold
Their hidden guilt; and, that dark mist dispell'd
By which their places and their lives are held,
Confusion wait them, and, by justice led,
In vengeance fall on every traitor's head.
  Aware of this, and caution'd 'gainst the pit
Where kings have oft been lost, shall I submit,
And rust in chains like these? Shall I give way,
And whilst my helpless subjects fall a prey   300
To power abused, in ignorance sit down,
Nor dare assert the honour of my crown?
When stern Rebellion, (if that odious name
Justly belongs to those whose only aim,
Is to preserve their country; who oppose,
In honour leagued, none but their country's foes;
Who only seek their own, and found their cause
In due regard for violated laws)
When stern Rebellion, who no longer feels
Nor fears rebuke, a nation at her heels,   310

A nation up in arms, though strong not proud,
Knocks at the palace gate, and, calling loud
For due redress, presents, from Truth's fair pen,
A list of wrongs, not to be borne by men :
How must that king be humbled, how disgrace
All that is royal in his name and place,
Who, thus call'd forth to answer, can advance
No other plea but that of ignorance !
A vile defence, which, was his all at stake,
The meanest subject well might blush to make ;   320
A filthy source from whence shame ever springs ;
A stain to all, but most a stain to kings.
The soul, with great and manly feelings warm'd,
Panting for knowledge, rests not till inform'd ;
And shall not I, fired with the glorious zeal,
Feel those brave passions which my subjects feel?
Or can a just excuse from ignorance flow
To me, whose first great duty is—to know ?

Hence, Ignorance :—thy settled, dull, blank eye,
Would hurt me, though I knew no reason why—
Hence, Ignorance !—thy slavish shackles bind   331
The free-born soul, and lethargise the mind—
Of thee, begot by Pride, who look'd with scorn
On every meaner match, of thee was born
That grave inflexibility of soul
Which Reason can't convince, nor fear control ;
Which neither arguments, nor prayers can reach,
And nothing less than utter ruin teach—
Hence, Ignorance !—hence to that depth of night
Where thou wast born, where not one gleam of
                    light   340
May wound thine eye—hence to some dreary cell
Where monks with superstition love to dwell ;

Or in some college soothe thy lazy pride,
And with the heads of colleges reside;
Fit mate for Royalty thou canst not be,
And if no mate for kings, no mate for me.
   Come, Study! like a torrent swell'd with rains,
Which, rushing down the mountains, o'er the plains
Spreads horror wide, and yet, in horror kind,
Leaves seeds of future fruitfulness behind;   350
Come, Study!—painful though thy course, and
     slow,
Thy real worth by thy effects we know—   ·
Parent of Knowledge, come—not thee I call   ·
Who, grave and dull, in college or in hall
Dost sit, all solemn sad, and moping, weigh
Things which, when found, thy labours can't re-
     pay—
Nor, in one hand, fit emblem of thy trade,
A rod, in t' other, gaudily array'd,
A hornbook, gilt and letter'd, call I thee,
Who dost in form preside o'er A, B, C—   360
Nor (Siren though thou art, and thy strange charms,
As 'twere by magic, lure men to thine arms)
Do I call thee, who, through a winding maze,
A labyrinth of puzzling, pleasing ways,
Dost lead us at the last to those rich plains,
Where, in full glory, real Science reigns;
   Fair though thou art, and lovely to mine eye,
Though full rewards in thy possession lie
To crown man's wish, and do thy favourites grace,
Though, (was I station'd in an humbler place) 370
I could be ever happy in thy sight,
Toil with thee all the day, and through the night
Toil on from watch to watch, bidding my eye,

Fast rivetted on science, sleep defy;
Yet (such the hardships which from empire flow)
Must I thy sweet society forego,
And to some happy rival's arms resign
Those charms which can, alas! no more be mine.
    No more from hour to hour, from day to day,
Shall I pursue thy steps, and urge my way   380
Where eager love of Science calls; no more
Attempt those paths which man ne'er trod before;
No more the mountain scaled, the desert cross'd
Losing myself, nor knowing I was lost,
Travel through woods, through wilds, from morn
    to night,
From night to morn, yet travel with delight,
And having found thee, lay me down content,
Own all my toil well paid, my time well spent.
    Farewell, ye Muses too,—for such mean things
Must not presume to dwell with mighty kings—
Farewell, ye Muses! though it cuts my heart, 391
E'en to the quick, we must for ever part.
    When the fresh morn bade lusty Nature wake;
When the birds, sweetly twittering through the
    brake,
Tune their soft pipes; when from the neighbouring
    bloom
Sipping the dew, each zephyr stole perfume;
When all things with new vigour were inspired,
And seem'd to say they never could be tired,
How often have we stray'd, whilst sportive rhyme
Deceived the way, and clipp'd the wings of Time,
O'er hill, o'er dale, how often laugh'd to see 401
Yourselves made visible to none but me,
The clown, his work suspended, gape and stare,

And seem'd to think that I conversed with air.
When the sun, beating on the parchèd soil,
Seem'd to proclaim an interval of toil;
When a faint languor crept through every breast,
And things most used to labour wish'd for rest,
How often, underneath a reverend oak,
Where safe and fearless of the impious stroke, 410
Some sacred Dryad lived: or in some grove
Where, with capricious fingers, Fancy wove
Her fairy bower, whilst Nature all the while
Look'd on, and view'd her mockeries with a smile,
Have we held converse sweet! how often laid,
Fast by the Thames, in Ham's inspiring shade,
Amongst those poets which make up your train,
And, after death, pour forth the sacred strain,
Have I, at your command, in verse grown grey,
But not impair'd, heard Dryden tune that lay 420
Which might have drawn an angel from his sphere,
And kept him from his office listening here.
When dreary Night, with Morpheus in her train,
Led on by Silence to resume her reign,
With darkness covering, as with a robe,
The scene of levity, blank'd half the globe.
How oft, enchanted with your heavenly strains,
Which stole me from myself; which in soft chains
Of music bound my soul; how oft have I,
Sounds more than human floating through the sky,
Attentive sat, whilst Night, against her will, 431
Transported with the harmony, stood still!

---

[422] The two following lines were intended to close this
sentence, but Churchill did not print them:
    Whilst Pope with envy stung, inflamed with pride,
    Piped to the vacant air on t' other side.

How oft in raptures, which man scarce could bear,
Have I, when gone, still thought the Muses there,
Still heard their music, and, as mute as death,
Sat all attention, drew in every breath,
Lest, breathing all too rudely, I should wound
And mar that magic excellence of sound ;
Then, Sense returning with return of day,
Have chid the night, which fled so fast away. 440
    Such my pursuits, and such my joys of yore ;
Such were my mates, but now my mates no more.
Placed out of Envy's walk, (for Envy, sure,
Would never haunt the cottage of the poor,
Would never stoop to wound my homespun lays)
With some few friends, and some small share of
        praise,
Beneath oppression, undisturb'd by strife,
In peace I trod the humble vale of life.
Farewell, these scenes of ease, this tranquil state;
Welcome the troubles which on empire wait : 450
Light toys from this day forth I disavow ;
They pleased me once, but cannot suit me now :
To common men all common things are free ;
What honours them might fix disgrace on me.
Call'd to a throne, and o'er a mighty land
Ordain'd to rule, my head, my heart, my hand
Are all engross'd, each private view withstood,
And task'd to labour for the public good :
Be this my study ; to this one great end
May every thought, may every action tend.   460
    Let me the page of history turn o'er,
The instructive page, and heedfully explore
What faithful pens of former times have wrote
Of former kings ; what they did worthy note,

What worthy blame; and from the sacred tomb
Where righteous monarchs sleep, where laurels
    bloom
Unhurt by time, let me a garland twine
Which, robbing not their fame, may add to mine.
   Nor let me with a vain and idle eye
Glance o'er those scenes, and in a hurry fly   470
Quick as a post which travels day and night;
Nor let me dwell there, lured by false delight;
And, into barren theory betray'd,
Forget that monarchs are for action made.
When amorous Spring, repairing all his charms,
Calls Nature forth from hoary Winter's arms,
Where, like a virgin to some lecher sold,
Three wretched months, she lay benumb'd, and cold;
When the weak flower, which, shrinking from the
    breath
Of the rude North, and timorous of death,   480
To its kind mother earth for shelter fled,
And on her bosom hid its tender head,
Peeps forth afresh, and, cheer'd by milder skies,
Bids in full splendour all her beauties rise,
The hive is up in arms—expert to teach,
Nor, proudly, to be taught unwilling, each
Seems from her fellow a new zeal to catch;
Strength in her limbs. and on her wings dispatch,
The bee goes forth; from herb to herb she flies,
From flower to flower, and loads her lab'ring thighs
With treasured sweets, robbing those flowers,
    which, left,   491
Find not themselves made poorer by the theft,
Their scents as lively, and their looks as fair,
As if the pillager had not been there.

Ne'er doth she flit on Pleasure's silken wing;
Ne'er doth she, loitering, let the bloom of Spring
Unrifled pass, and on the downy breast
Of some fair flower indulge untimely rest:
Ne'er doth she, drinking deep of those rich dews
Which chymist Night prepared, that faith abuse
Due to the hive, and, selfish in her toils,   501
To her own private use convert the spoils:
Love of the stock first call'd her forth to roam,
And to the stock she brings her booty home.
    Be this my pattern—as becomes a king,
Let me fly all abroad on Reason's wing:
Let mine eye, like the lightning, through the earth
Run to and fro, nor let one deed of worth,
In any place and time, nor let one man,
Whose actions may enrich dominion's plan,   510
Escape my note: be all, from the first day
Of Nature to this hour, be all my prey.
From those whom Time, at the desire of Fame.
Hath spared, let Virtue catch an equal flame:
From those who, not in mercy, but in rage,
Time hath reprieved to damn from age to age,
Let me take warning, lesson'd to distil,
And, imitating Heaven, draw good from ill:
Nor let these great researches in my breast
A monument of useless labour rest;   520
No—let them spread—the effects let Gotham share,
And reap the harvest of their monarch's care:
Be other times, and other countries known,
Only to give fresh blessings to my own.
    Let me, (and may that God to whom I fly,
On whom for needful succour I rely
In this great hour, that glorious God of truth,

Through whom I reign, in mercy to my youth,
Assist my weakness, and direct me right;
From every speck which hangs upon the sight 530
Purge my mind's eye, nor let one cloud remain
To spread the shades of error o'er my brain),
Let me, impartial, with unwearied thought,
Try men and things; let me, as monarchs ought,
Examine well on what my power depends;
What are the general principles, and ends
Of government; how empire first began;
And wherefore man was raised to reign o'er man.
Let me consider, as from one great source
We see a thousand rivers take their course, 540
Dispersed, and into different channels led,
Yet by their parent still supplied and fed,
That government, (though branch'd out far and wide,
In various modes to various lands applied)
Howe'er it differs in its outward frame,
In the main ground-work's every where the same;
The same her view, though different her plan,
Her grand and general view—the good of man.
Let me find out, by reason's sacred beams,
What system in itself most perfect seems, 550
Most worthy man, most likely to conduce
To all the purposes of general use;
Let me find, too, where, by fair reason tried,
It fails, when to particulars applied;
Why in that mode all nations do not join,
And, chiefly, why it cannot suit with mine.
Let me the gradual rise of empires trace,
Till they seem founded on perfection's base;
Then (for when human things have made their way
To excellence, they hasten to decay) 560

Let me, whilst observation lends her clue,
Step after step to their decline pursue,
Enabled by a chain of facts to tell
Not only how they rose, but why they fell.
    Let me not only the distempers know
Which in all states from common causes grow,
But likewise those, which, by the will of Fate,
On each peculiar mode of empire wait;
Which in its very constitution lurk,
Too sure at last, to do its destined work :   570
Let me, forewarn'd, each sign, each system learn,
That I my people's danger may discern,
Ere 'tis too late wish'd health to re-assure,
And, if it can be found, find out a cure.
    Let me, (though great, grave brethren of the gown
Preach all faith up, and preach all reason down,
Making those jar, whom reason meant to join,
And vesting in themselves a right divine)
Let me, through reason's glass, with searching eye,
Into the depth of that religion pry   580
Which law hath sanction'd : let me find out there
What's form, what's essence; what, like vagrant air,
We well may change; and what, without a crime,
Cannot be changed to the last hour of time;
Nor let me suffer that outrageous zeal
Which, without knowledge, furious bigots feel,
Fair in pretence, though at the heart unsound,
These separate points at random to confound.
    The times have been, when priests have dared
        to tread,
Proud and insulting, on their monarch's head; 590
When, whilst they made religion a pretence,
Out of the world they banish'd common sense;

When some soft king, too open to deceit,
Easy and unsuspecting join'd the cheat,
Duped by mock piety, and gave his name
To serve the vilest purposes of shame.
Fear not, my People, where no cause of fear
Can justly rise—your king secures you here;
Your king, who scorns the haughty prelate's nod,
Nor deems the voice of priests the voice of God.
    Let me, (though lawyers may perhaps forbid
Their monarch to behold what they wish hid,
And for the purposes of knavish gain,
Would have their trade a mystery remain)
Let me, disdaining all such slavish awe,
Dive to the very bottom of the law;
Let me (the weak, dead letter left behind)
Search out the principles, the spirit find,
Till, from the parts, made master of the whole,
I see the Constitution's very soul.   610
    Let me, (though statesmen will no doubt resist,
And to my eyes present a fearful list
Of men, whose wills are opposite to mine,
Of men, great men, determined to resign)
Let me, (with firmness, which becomes a king,
Conscious from what a source my actions spring
Determined not by worlds to be withstood,
When my grand object is my country's good)
Unravel all low ministerial scenes,
Destroy their jobs, lay bare their ways and means,
And track them step by step; let me well know 621
How places, pensions, and preferments go;
Why Guilt's provided for, when Worth is not,
And why one man of merit is forgot;

---

621 Some editions have "And *trap* them step by step."

Let me in peace, in war, supreme preside,
And dare to know my way without a guide.
  Let me, (though Dignity, by nature proud,
Retires from view, and swells behind a cloud,
As if the sun shone with less powerful ray,
Less grace, less glory, shining every day;   630
Though when she comes forth into public sight,
Unbending as a ghost, she stalks upright,
With such an air as we have often seen,
And often laugh'd at in a tragic queen,
Nor, at her presence, though base myriads crook
The supple knee, vouchsafes a single look)
Let me, all vain parade, all empty pride,
All terrors of dominion laid aside,
All ornament, and needless helps of art,
All those big looks, which speak a little heart, 640
Know (which few kings, alas! have ever known)
How affability becomes a throne,
Destroys all fear, bids love with reverence live,
And gives those graces pride can never give.
Let the stern tyrant keep a distant state,
And, hating all men, fear return of hate,
Conscious of guilt, retreat behind his throne,
Secure from all upbraidings but his own:
Let all my subjects have access to me,
Be my ears open as my heart is free;   650
In full, fair tide let information flow;
That evil is half-cured, whose cause we know.
  And thou, where'er thou art, thou wretched thing,
Who art afraid to look up to a king,
Lay by thy fears—make but thy grievance plain,
And, if I not redress thee, may my reign
Close up that very moment.—To prevent,

The course of Justice, from her fair intent,
In vain my nearest, dearest friend shall plead,
In vain my mother kneel—my soul may bleed, 660
But must not change—when Justice draws the dart,
Though it is doom'd to pierce a favourite's heart,
'Tis mine to give it force, to give it aim—
I know it duty, and I feel it fame.

END OF VOL. I.